CU00864437

WOLF OF THE PAST

SPIRIT OF THE WOLF BOOK 1

A.D. MCLAIN

To my soulmate, Raymond, who proved to me
that true love does not just exist in fairy tales.

PROLOGUE

David headed back toward the door where he'd broken into the house. There was no point in staying here any longer – he wasn't going to find what he was looking for, not without a lot more time. He came up short, his breath catching in his throat when a wrinkle in the carpet held back one foot. His arms flailing for purchase, one hand hit the portrait on the wall beside him. He clung to the wall until his balance returned, the sound of his pounding heartbeat and the swinging of the portrait all he could hear. Something caught his attention, and his eyes widened to twice their normal size. Behind the portrait, the wall was different, dark and shiny instead of a dull beige. Carefully, David took the picture from the wall and set it on the floor, revealing a safe set into the wall.

He started working on it immediately, barely concealing his excitement. He'd found it. He'd actually found it! David repeated the combination, exactly as he'd heard it spoken the night before, and hastily scooped up the money, dropping it into his bag. That done, he quietly crept out through the door and left as quickly as he could.

David hurried back the way he came, forcing his way through the bushes and past trees. He kept his ears trained for the slightest sound. His eyes focused on every movement, catching only stray cats. After some time, he slowed to a normal pace. He left behind the bushes and shadows and returned to the more familiar downtown alleys. Dark stores and empty city streets greeted his return. He was a long way from the cozy little homes with their happy families that abounded in the area of town where the job took place. The moonlight lit his way, revealing the dirt and trash in the alleyway. He stepped over a stream of whiskey, which had poured from an overturned bottle. Nearby, a man dressed in filthy, ripped clothing was passed out, sprawled on a pile of newspapers and cardboard boxes saturated by snow, and probably no small amount of whiskey from the smell of things. In the distance, he could hear voices raised in argument. A woman's scream was followed by a loud crash. Home sweet home.

He crossed the street and shivered when the wind hit him. It was much colder out here in the open. He hurried to the side of the street and slid down a small embankment, taking cover beneath the bridge. Carefully securing the money in his ragged jacket, David curled up and went to sleep.

* * *

DAVID WAITED for the carriage driver to unlock the gate and return to his seat. He slipped in behind the carriage, keeping to the wall and trees, wondering again if he was doing the right thing. This wasn't like his usual jobs, but he'd been dared. Normally, he wouldn't go after anyone who hadn't done something to him or someone he knew, but this guy had a lot of money. He lived in a mansion, after all. It was the only house of its size in the area, probably in the state. Some of the other street kids jokingly called the man 'King' Richard because of how much wealth he had. He wouldn't miss a little bit. If David could pull off this job, he would gain the respect of all the kids on the street, and he would probably be set for a long time. If he didn't go through with it, they would never let him live it down. He would just be another kid on the streets. Everyone would know he didn't have the guts to do what it takes. He'd be worthless, a coward. Whatever happened, he couldn't back out now.

He moved closer to the house, still hidden by the trees and bushes. He heard the carriage come to a stop and then a couple of voices, followed by the opening and closing of a door. Footsteps came towards his position, and he fought to keep from breathing too heavily, ensuring he was completely hidden by the leaves. Slowly, the sounds died away, and he heard the large front door creak open. A swoosh of air and the clanging of metal latches accompanied its closure.. A nervous breath rushed past his lips. He was lucky they didn't keep the grounds cleared, because that had been close. Gathering up his courage, he peeked out from his hiding place and started to move. Once he'd made it to the house he started checking all the doors and windows, quietly searching for something which might have been accidentally left unlocked. If he was lucky, he'd be able to slip in and back out again without alerting anyone inside to his presence. He didn't like the thought of breaking in while people were there, but that had been the rule of the bet, and the smallest amount of noise he could make in the process, the better.

* * *

"So, how long are you going to wait?" Marcus glanced up from his paper to look at Richard.

Richard didn't look up from the book he was reading. "Until you finish that sketch. I want to see how you make me look this time. Besides, there's no hurry."

Marcus laughed. He hadn't even informed Richard he was sketching him, but he should have known Richard would have picked up on it. "Are you sure you want to wait? He's been out there for some time."

"I know, but you're almost finished anyway. There's no sense in disturbing your work."

"Okay." Marcus made quick work of the sketch, putting a few finishing touches on it before revealing it to Richard.

Richard nodded appreciatively. Marcus had captured him completely, down to the contemplative look in his downcast eyes. "One of your best yet."

"Thank you. Shall we go introduce ourselves to your young thief?"

"Of course."

DAVID CHECKED the last door and sighed. It seemed as if he was going to have to do this the hard way. He only hoped no one would hear him working the lock. Quietly, he made his way to a side door and took out his knife. Just as he lifted his hand, there was a tap on his shoulder and he jumped, spinning on the spot. His heart started racing when he realized he'd been caught. Two men stood behind him, and strangely, they both seemed amused. Okay, one point in his favor. At least they didn't look as though they wanted to kill him, but maybe they only looked amused, because they enjoyed torturing people. Even now, they could be thinking of ways to make his life miserable. What had he gotten himself into? While he watched, their grins only seemed to get wider. He gulped. Maybe he would've been better off facing the boys on the street. A lifetime of jokes and disrespect didn't seem so bad right now.

Richard gazed down at the young boy. He appeared much too young to be doing something like this. He was dressed in rags that were entirely too small and hardly suitable for the cold weather they'd been having lately. He suspected the boy probably hadn't had a decent meal or place to live in a very long time. "Don't worry. We're not going to roast you over an open fire."

"Or tie you to a post and shoot you," the second man added nonchalantly.

"Or let bloodthirsty dogs chase you and rip your body to shreds." David's eyes grew larger and larger as they continued. Vivid imaged of everything they'd said were running through his mind, but he couldn't tell if he'd thought those things before they said them, or if them saying those things made him think about them. It had to be the latter, but he could have sworn his thoughts came first. But how could they have known what was in his mind? He could feel the wheels in his head grinding to a confused halt. Much more of this and he'd never be able to think again.

Richard laughed and patted the boy on the shoulder. To his credit, the boy didn't jump. "I'm Richard."

"And I'm Marcus." The second man held out his hand, waiting for David to do the same.

David tentatively lifted his hand. It was swiftly grasped by the other man, but instead of a normal handshake, he clasped his arm. "This is how I shake hands. Remember it." The man let go of David's arm and started walking back towards the front door.

"Come in with us," Richard said. "I have something I want to talk to you about. And I'm not going to try to poison you or bury you alive in some secret dungeon in the house, so you can stop worrying." He leaned in closer, grinning conspiratorially. "I had that dungeon bricked up years ago," he whispered. The boy's face grew even paler, making it impossible for Richard not to laugh. "Come on." His hand still on the boy's shoulder, he led him into the house.

1

CONNECTICUT: PRESENT DAY

Nicole stared at the picture of the happy family they'd once been. Smiling faces stared back at her, mocking her. She experienced a stab of pain when her body was wracked by another unexpected sob, but she'd cried all her tears already. She pulled the pillow closer to her chest and sighed heavily, staring blankly at their photo. She remembered the day they'd taken it, before Billy left home. She'd been happy then, with a brother and two loving parents. They weren't her real family, but they'd seemed real enough to her.

The clock beeped, bringing her back to the present. The meeting would be starting soon and she had to go. She hadn't contributed much before, but things were different now. She owed it to them to keep their work alive, even if they couldn't.

Nicole walked toward the old brick building with determination. This was the first time she'd been back since... the accident. Some of the windows were broken and boarded up and all of them carried layers of dirt, several years old. It didn't look like much from the outside, faring only mildly better on the inside – but it was all the Smithsdale Environmental Society had for the moment.

The SES was relatively new, one of her mom and dad's pet projects before their deaths. The SES hadn't done all that much so far, but it had found a good following among the local college students. It gave them the opportunity to get involved in something meaningful.

She reached for the door handle and paused, the hairs on the back of her neck standing on end. She glanced around, but saw nothing unusual. She was probably just paranoid, but once in a while, she had the distinct impression she was being watched. Then again, everyone felt like that sometimes, so she was probably no different to anyone else. With that reassurance in mind, she shrugged it off and opened the door.

The musty smell in the interior of the building hit her instantly. She'd forgotten how bad it was. Her parents never paid much attention to keeping up the place, they were always too wrapped up in what they were doing. She needed to talk to John about airing the place out. Nicole concentrated on breathing through her mouth as she looked around. Dim light filtered in through the broken, partially covered windows. There was just enough light to see the dust motes in the air and the cobwebs which lined the windows. The room was large, with a rickety stage at the far end. Between the door and the stage were several rows of rusting, fold-up chairs and she noticed that the chairs were filling fast, with the first five rows already full. At least attendance was still up.

"Hey, Nicole! Good to see you, again," a young voice said from behind her. Nicole glanced back at the girl and recognized her as one of the regulars at the SES meetings. She nodded to the girl and turned away. "Sorry about what happened to your parents. If you need anything, just let me know," the girl announced before she walked over to the other side of the room and struck up another conversation.

Nicole's throat constricted and her head throbbed, all too common reactions in the past two months. She had to fight it, couldn't cry here, not in front of so many people. Despite her best efforts, a tear collected at the corner of each eye. She wiped them away, only to find them immediately replaced by more. She had thought she'd completely cried herself out during that week she spent in a catatonic state, curled up on the couch with only a tear-soaked pillow for company. Yet for all the tears she wiped away, she couldn't dry her eyes.

Nicole glanced around at everyone and her desire to avoid crying renewed a hundred-fold. There had been too many heartfelt condolences and sympathy. No more. She would not cry. Making a quick trip to the bathroom, Nicole splashed some cold water on her face and settled her mind on the business at hand. With her control firmly back in place, she took her seat.

Nicole sat near the back of the group and settled in to see what was going to be said – as if she couldn't guess. The topic on everyone's mind was what could be done to stop Steagel & Co. from dumping toxins into the water. The meeting began, and she listened as one person after another repeated what had been said a hundred times before. There was nothing new. Everyone wanted to do something, but no one knew what to do.

Nicole absentmindedly ran her pendant up and down the silver chain it hung on. The pendant was an old stone with a crude carving of a wolf on it. It's warmth transferred to her fingers, sending calm, peaceful feelings flowing through her skin. It was always warm to touch, but then again she did wear it right next to her skin, so that would make sense.

Her mind wandered away from the meeting. It had been two months since her parents died in the car accident. They'd been the only parents she ever known, having been adopted by them when she was young. They had been her only family and other than one son – her adoptive brother – they didn't have other relatives. No aunts or uncles. No cousins or grandparents. Other than her brother, whom she hardly ever saw, she didn't have any family to turn to. She was completely alone in the world.

A heavy weight settled on her chest, feeling like a fist was clenching her heart. She hated the thought of being alone. She was so afraid of not having anyone in her life. Few people knew how much that fear threatened to completely overwhelm her. No matter how many people she had around her, she was always afraid she would lose it all, that she would be left with no one in the end. Most of the time, it wasn't such a big deal – she could ignore it. Sometimes, she could even manage to partially convince herself it was all nonsense.

Until two months ago.

Ever since her parents died, she'd been in a fierce battle with her demons. It threatened to be too much at times. What was to keep anyone else near her? What was to keep her from losing anyone else she allowed herself to become close to? The truth was, there wasn't a single thing to keep that from happening. Perhaps she just wasn't meant to be close to anyone? Maybe she was paying the price for some bad karma. Maybe she was cursed. Maybe she was just unlucky. Those were all possibilities for why some higher force would contrive to leave her lonely, and there was nothing to interfere with the fates should they choose to sentence her to such a destiny.

She pushed the thought from her mind. There was no sense in dwelling on negative thoughts – even if it was her destiny to be alone, she didn't have to think about it. She had a lot of good things in her life. For instance, she had Meg. They'd known each other for a very long time; most of their lives, in fact. Meg knew all her secrets, and she was one of the few people Nicole had let herself get close to. But if she was honest, she sometimes found herself shutting Meg out, too. There was always a small part of herself which couldn't seem to let go.

Nicole refocused her thoughts again. Okay, so she wasn't very good with interpersonal relationships, but she had other things going for her. She had school and the SES to occupy her time. Stopping the release of toxins by Steagel & Co. was the last project her parents had worked on before their deaths. As scientists studying the local environment, they'd discovered the horrible poisoning of the local land and water. They'd founded the Smithsdale Environmental Society to deal with these problems. The SES had been important to them and now, it was her responsibility to finish their work. She owed them that much.

Nicole pushed her glasses back up on her nose and tried to draw her attention back to the meeting, which was almost over. She was restless, felt as if she should be doing something. By the grumbling around her, it was obvious everyone else was frustrated and restless, too. As she stood to leave, she noticed John walking toward her. The dim lighting made his short brown hair and blue eyes appear darker than usual and as he drew closer, she was reminded just how tall he was. She was wearing her platform boots, and he was still taller than she was. He possessed a face to match his impressive height, square and hard, but his eyes were so warm a person couldn't help liking him. His features communicated a great sens of power and charisma and Nicole thought he looked more like a CEO than the college senior he was. She could understand why her parents had given him so many responsibilities.

John Markham had done a lot of work for the SES while her parents were alive, and had taken on even more responsibilities after their deaths, and she was grateful for all his help. He'd almost been a second son to her parents, he was just a few years younger than Billy and unlike her wayward brother, John actually shared their interests. During some of those late night and weekend planning sessions, when John spent so much time over at the house, it had almost seemed like having a brother again.

She pushed aside an unwelcome pang of jealousy. It wasn't John's fault he'd fit in with them so well, where her and Billy always struggled. It was probably for the best, anyway. At least someone was able to carry on their work, as they deserved. During those first few weeks after the accident, Nicole hadn't wanted to deal with anyone or anything. Not that she would have been much help anyway – when her parents were alive, she'd come to some meetings and listened to her parents discussing their work, but Nicole didn't know the first thing about running the organization. Without John, she didn't know how the SES would have stayed operational.

John flashed a half smile. "Nicole, hey, how's it going?"

She shrugged. "Oh, it's going. And you?"

"Oh, I'm good." John shifted from foot to foot and Nicole smiled reassuringly. Despite her brave front, he'd been a little nervous lately when he spoke to her, as if he didn't want to say the wrong thing. He had tried his best over the last couple of months to make sure Nicole didn't have to worry about anything to do with the SES and seemed reluctant to bother her in the few times he had needed to ask her something. This seemed like another one of those times.

"Was there something you wanted?" she prompted.

"Yeah, um… I've been talking to some of the others. We decided we need some photos of the river and the surrounding wildlife on file, along with the soil and water samples we've been collecting, and we were wondering if you could take the photos, since you've got that really good camera.."

"Sure, I'd be happy to." Nicole smiled. At least this would be doing something constructive. "When do you need them?"

"You're sure it's no trouble?"

"Yes, I'm sure." She rested her hands on her hips in an indignant fashion. This china doll treatment was going to have to stop – sure, she was a wreck, but he didn't need to know that. "So, when do you need them?"

"There's no hurry. In the next week or so should be fine."

"No problem."

"Hey, John," a voice called from across the room and John turned to seek the source of the voice. A woman with long blonde hair and a pink flower printed skirt and matching top was waving at him.

John turned back briefly to Nicole. "I gotta go. Katie needs a ride home, her car is in the shop. I'll see you later, and thanks for doing the picture thing." John turned and started navigating his way through the crowd.

Nicole quickly went over her schedule in her head, trying to determine when she would have time to take the photos. She was meeting Meg for lunch after she left the meeting, but after that, she had the entire afternoon free.

She did have a report due tomorrow, but that would only take an hour or two to finish. She could do it after she'd taken the photos. John had said there was no hurry, but she was anxious to do something constructive. She glanced at her watch. It was almost time for lunch, so she left the SES building and headed to the diner. Maybe this day wouldn't be such a total waste, after all.

* * *

DAVID FOLLOWED Nicole for a few minutes before he turned down a different street, where tall trees surrounded the road on both sides. He hadn't been in this area in a long time, and a lot had changed since then, but he took sure steps towards his destination.

The old tree was still there. He was amazed it hadn't been cut down by now. A new, modern house stood where the old one had been. This house was built of brick, and he could see a heating and cooling unit against one side wall. He tried to remember what the old house had looked like. It had been old, even then and was practically falling apart. He could still remember the trail of smoke which drifted up from the fireplace. Instead of a heating and cooling unit, there'd been a big pile of wood. Maybe, if the house had been made of something other than wood, they would have stood a chance.

"Can I help you?"

David turned to the old man behind him. He hadn't even noticed his approach. That alone told him how much this was getting to him. "No, I was just... my family used to live on this land."

The man seemed surprised. "My family has lived here for close to two hundred years, or more."

"Do you know anything about the people who had it before that?"

The stranger looked skyward, rubbing his stubbled chin. "Hum. As a matter of fact, I do happen to know a little bit about them. If I remember correctly, they died in some kind of fire. I don't remember their name, but my father told me about it when I was young. He said it was one of the worst fires this county has ever seen. The whole place was burned to the ground in less than an hour, with the family still inside. He used to tell me the story to keep me from playing with matches. He said if it had happened once, it could happen again."

David fought to keep his emotions from becoming visible on his face and forced a smile. "So, did it work?"

"You tell me. I became a firefighter." The old man barked out a short laugh and slapped his leg.

The smile on David's face was the first genuine one in a long time. This man seemed nice enough. It was somewhat comforting to know something good had come out of this place. "Thank you for your time. I'd better be going."

Before he could take more than a couple of steps, the man called out. "Hey son! Are you related to that family?"

David felt the swelling of regret and sadness hit him again. "Yeah." This time he heard a little bit of emotion revealed by the harshness in his tone.

"Gee, I'm sorry to hear that. I hope things work out better for you than they did for them."

"Thanks." He hurried away, before the man could ask any more questions. Walking farther down the street, David forced himself not to look back.

His steps slowed once he neared the graveyard. He didn't want to go in, but he found himself walking in that direction anyway. It was crazy, he didn't even know where they were buried. He turned to leave the graveyard and stubbed his toe on a loose rock which he hadn't noticed before. He glared down at the rock angrily, it was large and had no place in a graveyard. Really, they should keep the grounds clear of hazards like this. If they had any respect for the dead, they'd take better care of the place.

He scanned the nearby area, realizing there were no other rocks like this on the ground, only neatly-mown grass. Obviously it was an isolated case, an anomaly – not the product of mass neglect and disrespect. He calmed down and bent over to pick it up, noticing the name on the tomb-stone in front of him as he straightened up.

He froze in place. It couldn't be. He read the name and dates closely and reread it again. There was no mistake. This was his father's grave. He surveyed the nearby area, quickly finding the other graves and his legs buckled, bringing him to his knees in front of them like a man awaiting judgment. But there was no judgment to be delivered; there was no redemption in this place, no forgiveness or benediction. There was nothing to assuage his guilt over failing them.

After a long while, he got to his feet. There were no answers for him here. He didn't even know why he'd come back here, to this side of town. He'd been fine on the outskirts of the city, miles away from the nearest subdivision or stores, away from everyone. The only time he ever needed to see anyone was when he did the occasional secu-rity consultation, other than that he was blissfully alone, exactly how he liked it. If it hadn't been for that damned dream about Nicole, that's exactly where he'd still be, but he owed it to Richard to ensure she was okay. She had certainly looked fine earlier. He was crazy to let a dream get to him like that – she was fine.

Still, he couldn't leave town without making sure.

2

Nicole stepped around a pile of wooden fence stakes held together with twisted wire and bent rusted nails. Sheet metal leaned up against the rotted remains of a wooden bench and picnic table. With broken down buildings and tetanus filled piles of trash overtaken by vines, rodents, and reptiles, this wasn't the area of the river most people saw.

She knelt beside the riverbank and took another photo, careful to center the image and adjust for lighting. Everyone teased her about her film camera, saying she should switch to digital, but she was always the first one they called when they needed high quality photographs. Nicole glanced around, seeking her next shot. How could anyone question the fact that something terrible was happening to the lake and the surrounding area? All the plant life around the lake's edge was wilting and dying. There had also been many cases of illness reported from people who swam downstream during the summer.

Besides those signs of pollution, an obvious warning of trouble was the orange-red coating beginning to collect on the surface of the water. That could only mean something was being leaked or dumped into the river and connecting lake. It would only get worse, unless someone did something. Maybe when the water and soil samples came back from the lab, the SES could do something. They would have already had the results, if the test facility hadn't mysteriously burned down with earlier samples inside at the time. After that it was her parents' accident, putting things on hold for quite some time. They were finally doing something again, but the new samples needed to be sent off to a test facility located several hours away, and with a long list of specimens to test before they would get to the SES samples.

Nicole leaned against the side of an old, abandoned warehouse while she took one final picture. The wind was blowing, enough to move the leaves in the trees, and making for a very nice picture, if you overlooked the signs of pollution. The breeze felt good, cooling her off a little and a welcome relief in the unseasonably warm weather.

She snapped another photograph and stiffened. She could hear low sounds coming from inside the warehouse, which sounded like voices, but why would anyone be out here? These buildings weren't used by anyone, they were practically condemned. She walked around to the other side of the building, following the noises until they were loud enough to confirm they were voices, though she couldn't make out what they were saying. She searched the immediate area and located a spot where there was a hole in the wood, an oddly-shaped opening between two planks in the wall. It wasn't large, just big enough to see through. Bracing her hands against the wall, she leaned closer and peered in through the small opening.

It was dark inside, and it took a minute for her eyes

adjust, but when they did, she was able to make out at least five people standing inside the abandoned building. Three of the men carried battery powered lanterns and moved around the back of a work truck parked near the far wall. The other two men stood in front of the light provided from the truck's headlights. Nicole recognized one of the men right away and experienced a rush of excitement. It was Rodney Steagel, the Vice President of Steagel & Company. Rodney was also the nephew of the President of the company, George Steagel. Nepotism was obviously alive and well in this particular company.

Rodney wasn't the picture of leadership his title suggested in this instance, dressed as he was in a Hawaiian shirt, black leather pants, and wearing several gold necklaces around his thick neck. They gleamed whenever they caught any stray beams of light in the abandoned building. He had long dark hair, and teeth which were just crying out for the attention of a dentist, which was surprising, considering how much money his family had.

That money hadn't stopped Rodney from leading a particularly shady life, complete with numerous run ins with authorities. Even though he'd been in regular trouble with the law, his uncle's considerable influence and money always kept Rodney out of jail. Nicole suspected if his uncle would get out of the way and let his nephew pay for his own mistakes, everyone would be better off. Steagel & Co. was a reputable business, before he he'd taken over. Rodney Steagel had no respect for anyone – least of all his family – whose good name and company he was running into the ground.

While Nicole watched, Rodney directed the other men while they loaded huge barrels into the back of a truck. The labels on the barrels read, 'Caution, Toxic Materials'.

Nicole's heart beat faster. This was her chance. Even if she couldn't prove they were dumping the toxins, she could prove the fact that Rodney Steagel and his henchmen had the toxins near the lake. Up until now, he'd been denying even that fact. This might be just the kind of evidence they needed to stop him. Nicole held the camera to the small hole and started snapping pictures. "Nancy Drew, eat your heart out," she murmured to herself.

She got several clear shots of the barrels, and some photos of the men helping Rodney. Unfortunately, Rodney was never standing where she could get a clear picture of him. If she couldn't get a photo of him with the barrels she wouldn't be able to prove he'd been there. On the other hand, if she got caught, none of the pictures could be used, and even if she didn't have a photograph of him, some of those other men could lead the police back to Rodney. Something was better than nothing. She was about to give up when he finally moved into her line of sight. She triumphantly snapped one last picture and quickly started to curse silently when her camera began to rewind the film, loudly.

"Hey, what's that noise out there?" one of them men cried.

Nicole scrambled backwards, nearly falling, stumbling over her own feet in her hurry, and ran as fast as she could back through the building toward the treeline.

She was instantly struck by how dark it had gotten. Preoccupied with getting a photograph of Rodney with the barrels, she hadn't noticed the sun setting. She noticed it now, though, barely able to see where she was going. Somehow, she made it as far as the woods. Shadows crowded in around her from every side, making each step a risk, because she had neither the light nor the time to see where her feet were landing. She only prayed she wouldn't hit a dip in the ground at a bad angle and twist an ankle, or worse.

Branches scraped her, catching and pulling on her hair and clothes. Pain emanated from multiple cuts, and her scalp was sore in several places. Still, she ran faster, the pain only feeding into her adrenaline.

She could hear them getting closer. The covering of the trees thinned enough to allow some moonlight to shine through. Nervously, she cast a quick glance over her shoulder. A gasp escaped her mouth when her toe connected with something hard. A raised tree root caught her eye when she fell forward and pain shot up through her knees and elbows. After the initial shock passed, she hurried to stand, ignoring the pain, but she froze on her hands and knees at the sound of a soft click behind her. Looking back over her shoulder, she saw a big, burly man standing about eight feet away with a gun pointed at her.

"Well, what have we got here? You're a cute one. Too bad you had to nose around, or we could have had a little fun." He chucked and the hairs on Nicole's neck stood on end. "Maybe we still could."

He leered at her, and a shiver of revulsion ran over her skin. The grin left his face when he noticed her reaction., It was replaced by a menacing glare, filled with rage. He aimed the gun at her, and slowly pressed down on the trigger. A muffled shot rang out.

Nicole dropped to the ground, the bullet barely missing her. It had been close enough that she'd felt her hair being ruffled by the movement of the bullet past her head

The man cursed under his breath and took aim to fire again. She peered up at him from the ground and swallowed heavily. This time, she had nowhere to go. Her heart pounded in her chest as he pulled the trigger again.

Out of the darkness a large, black creature appeared. It jumped from its hiding place in the forest and landed hard on the man's back. His second shot went wild, and the gun fell to the ground. Nicole scrambled to pick it up and the black creature, a wolf, backed off as she aimed the gun at the man.

"Stand up, slowly," she commanded. She managed to keep her voice steady, but it was a struggle. Out the corner of her eye she saw the wolf. She took a careful step away from the animal, but it's eyes were trained on her attacker.

"Whoa, wait a second. What do you think you're doing?" The man held his hands up, slowly getting to his feet.

In the distance, Nicole could hear the sounds of the other men searching. She didn't have long. The gunshots had been muffled by a silencer, so they couldn't betray her position, but if this man could find her, so could they. She felt panic threaten to bubble up and squashed it down. That wouldn't help her. She could break down and be afraid once this was over.

"Turn around," she said holding the gun steadily at his chest. He took a second or two before complying, muttering to himself as he turned.

She reached down and grabbed a fallen tree limb, one that looked heavy enough for her requirements and tested its weight in her free hand. Gathering her strength, she stepped up behind her would-be murderer, careful to keep her distance from the wolf, and swung the wood at the back of his head. It connected with a hollow crack which sent a shudder of revulsion through her as he fell limp at her feet. She stared at his prone form in amazement. She hadn't really thought she had the strength to knock someone out in a single hit, but the proof was lying right in front of her. The noises in the woods around her began to get louder, drawing her attention from the man lying at her feet. They were clearly getting closer, but she didn't know what to do. Should she just start running again, trying desperately to feel her way through the dark patches of the forest where moonlight failed to reach?

The wolf startled her from her thoughts and gripped the corner of her jacket in his teeth, pulling her to one side. She yelped and stared down at the wolf with fear. She contemplated using the gun or the wood against the animal, but he let go of her clothes and took a step back from her. His muzzle lowered deferentially. A wave of calm came over her. She experienced a strange certainty that the animal was trying to lead her away from the approaching danger, but could she even consider following a wild animal through the night?

Nicole mentally shook herself. *Yeah, right, a strange wolf was just going to show up and rescue her, showing her exactly which way to go. That would be the day.* Nicole cast a quick look over her shoulder, in the direction of the sounds. She didn't have much time. Turning in the opposite direction from the one the wolf was pulling her towards, Nicole began to run. She ran for several minutes, before admitting to herself that she was completely lost. The trees were too thick in most spots for her to see even a hint of the stars overhead, and she had to admit to herself that she'd lost all sense of direction. For all she knew, she could be headed back toward the water or in a completely different direction. Taking a moment to catch her breath in one of the rarely lit areas, an oasis in the darkness, she collapsed on the ground, resting her head in her hands.

A warm muzzle pushed closer to her, moving her hands

out of the way until she was looking directly in the wolf's eyes. Beautifully clear eyes stared back at her. For a moment, she forgot these were the eyes of an animal – they seemed so coherent, staring directly into her soul. And in that instant, she knew. There was something different about this animal. She could trust this wolf. She didn't know how she knew, but with this realization came such a sense of rightness, she didn't doubt the truth of her decision. If she was going to survive the night, she had to follow the wolf. Inhaling sharply, she stood and followed her unlikely ally.

The wolf led her through the woods for several minutes, before he came to a stop in front of a thick section of bushes. Nicole looked questioningly from the bushes to the wolf and he angled his head towards them.

"Okay, so what's behind bush number one?" she mumbled to herself. Leaning forward, Nicole pushed the bushes to one side and found herself staring down the beginning of a long tunnel. The wolf leapt in past the bushes and waited for her to follow.

"Why not?" she muttered to herself. It was better than the alternative of running blindly through a dark forest. She activated the safety catch on the gun, tucking it into the back of her pants. There wasn't much room to maneuver in the tunnel, and she didn't want to chance it accidentally firing. Grasping at her necklace she drew on its warmth for comfort and tentatively entered the tunnel entrance.

Nicole winced when her knees and arms rubbed up against the tunnel wall. She suspected she'd suffered some pretty good scrapes during her earlier fall. There was no time to worry about that now, so she ignored the pain and pushed on.

The wolf led her through what seemed like miles of tunnel. She crawled through them silently, one hand resting on the wall of the tunnel, and the other on the back of the wolf. It was much colder in the tunnel than it had been outside, and the longer she crawled, the colder it got. Her hands began to shake where she touched the tunnel wall and she suspected she would easily see her breath if there'd been enough light to allow it. She wished she'd worn a thicker coat. Nevertheless, she pushed the cold from her mind and continued to crawl. Instead, she concentrated on the sound of her camera hitting her chest as it swung back and forth in front of her. She was lucky she'd used the strap today, or she would have lost the camera ages ago, in her mad dash from the warehouse.

She slowly became aware of a light up ahead. Minute by minute, she found she was able to see the tunnel walls and the mysterious wolf beside her. Everything was bathed in a mixture of light and shadows filtering in from between the branches of wild bushes.

Nicole climbed out of the tunnel, the bushes snapping back into place covering the tunnel opening behind her, and stared at her surroundings in shock. She found herself standing a hundred feet away from her own apartment building. "How did you..." she began, but when she looked behind her, the wolf was gone. She turned back to the building, her necklace clutched between her fingers, and then turned back to where the wolf had been. "Thank you," she whispered into the darkness.

Hurrying upstairs, she picked up the phone, dialing the numbers swiftly.

"Hello."

"Hey John, it's Nicole. You know how you wanted those photos?"

* * *

ARTEMIS DISAPPEARED BACK into the shadows. So, this was where Nicole lived now. It had to be her, she was wearing the amulet, and he could see a distinct resemblance to Richard and Caroline. David Coverton had done a good job of hiding her all these years. Who would have thought that pitiful excuse for a man would have so many connections, willing to help him in this town? It must have been through his association with Richard.

Artemis spat on the ground in disgust, the spit congealing in the dirt. He trudged on, dispersing the gathered pieces of muddy earth in short order.

In the days after the crash, David had managed to hide all traces of Nicole, and no one he'd approached would say a word about her whereabouts. But no matter. Now, David had led Artemis right to her. Following David had been a long shot, but it had finally paid off, and what a payoff it would be. Now, that he'd located Nicole, he could finally put his plans into action.

The events of tonight had been an interesting development. It looked as if she'd managed to get herself into quite a bit of trouble. Maybe he could use this threat against her to further his own plans.

He felt a shiver run down his spine when a particularly cold breeze blew past, but he knew this was no natural wind. In fact, he knew it all too well. The darkness gathered around him, and fog began rolling in, obstructing any ability to see beyond a few feet. What felt like immense pressure pressed down all around him in the air. The fog swirled around, a figure slowly taking shape in the darkness. "I see you've finally found her," a deep, resonating voice said.

"Yes." Artemis ignored the stubborn desire to defend

himself against the implication that his search had taken too long and forced the word past his lips.

"Good. Have you found out anything useful?"

"She has apparently made some enemy. She was attacked a short while ago, down near the river."

The voice was quiet for a moment. "Yes, that is good information to know. Keep watching her and tell me anything you discover."

"Of course."

Quickly, the fog and unnatural darkness disappeared. Artemis took a moment to get his bearings, then continued on his way. If he was going to be staying in town for a while, he needed to find a place to stay. Maybe that old inn would still be open for business and he could go for a drink in the bar. He grinned and changed directions. He'd quite enjoyed the old inn the last time he was in town. Now, it probably didn't offer the same...services it had offered back then, but he might still find himself a little entertainment for the night. It was usually easy enough to find, for the right price. Artemis grinned and licked his lips in anticipation.

3

David unlocked and opened the large gate. It creaked noisily as the hinges protested many years of disuse. He'd hoped he wouldn't have to come back here, and for years, that wish had been granted. Ever since those first couple of months after the plane crash, he'd stayed away.

He walked up to the front doors of the house and paused, remembering the first time he saw them. They'd seemed even larger to the young boy he'd been back then and this place had intimidated him. He was a lot older now, but he was surprised to realize it still intimidated him. So much was expected of him here. He couldn't hide from his potential. He couldn't hide from other people. After a while, he hadn't minded so much, but all that changed when Richard died. David had fallen into the same old patterns, leaving everything he knew, again. He'd stayed away from everyone and everything. It was a lonely but safe existence.

Now, he was out of hiding and had to face the world again. Damn Richard. Even from beyond the grave, he was forcing David to face his demons. What if he didn't want to face them? What if he liked them just fine where they were – hidden? Unfortunately, it looked as if it didn't matter what he wanted, he wasn't going to get it. He might as well get things over with.

David pushed open the large door with a sigh. The creaking sound it made echoed through the empty rooms. Dim, early morning light shone through the curtains and the open door, illuminating the otherwise darkened room. There was dust everywhere, even though he'd hired people to come in and clean the place a couple of times each year. It was nothing like it had been, Richard and Caroline had kept the place spotless most of the time. What would Richard think if he could see it now?

David quickly pushed that thought back and focused on more practical matters. He needed to call someone to take care of the place if he was going to be staying here. It was much too big for one person to manage alone. He braced himself and walked through the many rooms, stubbornly refusing to let the long-forgotten memories overwhelm him. He had a job to do and after that, he could leave again. But for now, first things first – he needed to get this place suitable to live in. Pulling out his cell phone, David started making calls.

NICOLE PUSHED BACK the covers and swung her legs around, giving up on the prospect of going back to sleep. She was too anxious to be rid of the film. She started when her bare feet touched the cold floor, and quickly pulled on some socks before she traversed the floor. Careful to avoid her bruises and sore muscles, she threw on the first shirt and pair of jeans she found, from her 'only worn once so still mostly clean' pile of dirty laundry and decided on a walk before class.

It was still quiet on the streets. Most sane people were still asleep, but she liked the quiet. It was the easiest time to think at this hour of day. The sun was just rising, causing all kinds of colors to play across the sky. There was no sign of the wolf, not even by the tunnel, mostly hidden unless you knew precisely where to look.

She walked the few blocks to school, not really knowing where else to go. The campus was even quieter than the rest of the city. A few office lights were on here and there, and she found herself wondering what had other people up at this early hour. Were they working on some important research which just had to be completed right away? Maybe they loved their jobs so much, they couldn't wait to get started, or they hated being at home so much, the office was a better alternative. Maybe they were just grading a few last papers before classes started.

Nicole smiled at an early morning jogger, and he smiled back when he passed her on the sidewalk. Whatever brought those other people out, she felt oddly comforted by them being there, even knowing most weren't even aware she was here.

Nicole tested the chapel door, and it opened with a creak. Surprisingly enough, there was one other person already inside. A young girl sitting in the front row turned her tear-stained face to Nicole when she entered.

Nicole smiled comfortingly, and the girl offered a weak half-smile back before retreating into her thoughts once again. Nicole sighed. It seemed she wasn't the only one with problems.

Nicole settled down in a nearby pew and stared at the cross in the front of the church. She tried to remember the last time she'd attended church, acknowledging that it had been a long time. The last time she'd come close had been her parents' funeral. She didn't really know why she was here now. She didn't have any questions or favors to ask, she just felt unsettled. No matter what she did lately, she was restless, as if there was something else she needed to be doing. She wasn't accomplishing anything. She wasn't going anywhere. Nothing ever changed. Where was the excitement which was supposed to follow just being alive? She was only in college, and she was already locked into a pattern. These were supposed to be the exciting years in her life, but there was never any real excitement. There was never any spontaneity. Everything was planned. She went to class. She went to SES meetings. She ate lunch with Meg at the diner. She went home, watched TV, did homework, and went to bed.

Occasionally, if she was lucky, she would have a new errand to run or some shopping to do. She'd known it was bad when she thought back on almost getting shot last night as a refreshing change of pace.

Nicole tilted her head from side to side, stretching out a crick in her neck and looked at her watch. It was still early, but she might as well go wait in the classroom. There was no point in walking all the way back to her apartment, and she could read until class started. She glanced once more at the girl in the front pew before slipping silently out of the chapel.

* * *

NICOLE WATCHED over the top of her book as one person after another entered the classroom. John only came in just as class was about to start and Nicole scowled at him for being so late, but she experienced a wave of relief. She would be glad to rid herself of the burden of the incriminating film.

"What happened to you?" A crease formed on John's forehead as he scanned her, his eyes settling on her face.

"Huh?" she asked in confusion. She hadn't slept well, but she didn't think she looked that bad.

"You've got a nasty scrape on your chin."

"Oh." She'd forgotten all about most of the scrapes she received last night, and hadn't even noticed the one on her chin. It was the bruises on her knees and arms which really hurt and her palms didn't feel too good either. "I fell in the woods last night."

"Are you okay?"

"Yeah, I'm fine." She shrugged it off. "It's just a few scrapes and scratches... a couple of bruises... maybe a splinter or two... oh, and I don't recommend running so far or fast when you haven't had time to properly stretch first. But otherwise, I'm no worse for wear. Don't worry about it. Here's the roll of film." She purposely left out any reference to the wolf. He would think she was crazy if she started talking about a wild animal knowing exactly where she lives. Or worse, he'd call animal control to check out the wolf sighting and possibly get the animal killed in the process.

John didn't look convinced that she was okay, but he took the film without further comment about her physical state. "This will definitely do some good. I'll give it to Susan today." He pocketed the film and leaned on a nearby desk.

"Susan? You don't mean Susan Anderson, do you?"

Susan Anderson was the Junior Attorney working on the case against Steagel & Co. Nicole had heard the name mentioned at SES meetings many times before, but never by first name alone.

"Yeah," he said nonchalantly. "I went to school with her younger sister. We were all pretty close."

Nicole laughed. "Have you got any other influential people stashed away I should know about?"

John just smiled. The teacher walked in, and the other students started settling into their seats. "I'll talk to you later, let you know how everything goes."

"You'd better. Oh, hey, walk with me to my apartment after class. I have something else Susan may want, but I couldn't bring it here."

"Sure thing."

An hour later, Nicole handed over the gun to John. She explained a few more details of her forest escape, still leaving out the wolf, and they both headed out – Nicole to class and John to see Susan. Several of the wrinkles on her forehead smooth out now that she had one less thing to worry about. Now, all she had to worry about was school.

Her classes crawled by, as usual and Nicole fought to stay awake during her lectures. A couple of times, she actually jerked awake when her chin dipped towards her chest. When the last class finished, she headed to the diner to have a late lunch with Meg.

Nicole reached for the door handle of the diner and paused when a reflection in the glass door caught her eye. There was a man standing across the street, and he appeared to be staring right at her, through the reflection. The man wore sunglasses and a dark trench coat which moved hypnotically in the wind. She couldn't seem to look away, not even to search the street behind her where he must surely be standing. The reflection of a large truck driving by temporarily blocked her view, breaking the spell. She turned to look for him, but when the truck had passed, he was gone. She surveyed up and down the street, but there were no obvious places he could have disappeared so quickly.

Nicole shook her head to clear the confusion filling her mind. She'd probably imagined the whole thing. That's what happened when you didn't get enough sleep, especially after the night she'd had. Obviously, her imagination was working overtime. That was the only explanation. Pushing the strange incident out of her mind, she opened the door and entered the diner.

Nicole sat down at her usual table and ordered a cup of coffee to drink while she waited for Meg. She didn't have to wait long. Meg came in with her usual enormous load of books and tossed them all on the seat along with herself. Typical Meghan over-dramatics. She pulled her long, curly, red-brown hair back into a clip, making her heart-shaped face and perfect tan even more noticeable.

"Hey, Meg. Hard day?"

"Oh, no more than usual," Meg said with a sigh. "Oh, course, my usual would stress out the President."

"Yeah, he only has to deal with nuclear take-overs and global annihilation. You have Physics with Ms. Fortenberry. No contest."

"Fun-ny." Meg kicked out at Nicole, making them both laugh. "So, what happened?" Meg asked, after she'd managed to stop laughing.

"What do you mean?"

"Nicole, this is me you're talking to. I know you too well. You're drinking coffee, and you only do that when you've got something on your mind. Besides, I count a least three scrapes, and you're not that clumsy." Nicole stared down at her coffee cup. She'd known the scrapes would probably give her away, but she hadn't even thought about the coffee. Meg was right, though, drinking coffee when she was preoccupied was a habit she'd picked up in Middle School. She'd started drinking it initially to stay awake after she'd had... the nightmare. The habit seemed to reemerge nowadays whenever something worried or intrigued her. Today, it was a little of both. "Yeah, you're right. Something happened yesterday when I went to take the photos down by the river."

"What happened?" Meg leaned across the table, interest visible in her pretty features.

Nicole took a breath and started talking, spewing out a stream of words. "I stumbled across Steagel trying to get rid of some toxins by the lake, so I took some photos, but I got caught. I got the scrapes when I was running away from Steagel and his cronies, because they'd heard my camera rewinding the film. I tripped over a tree root and fell and one guy caught up with me and he had a gun. Just when I was about to get shot, a wolf jumped out of the woods and knocked over the guy with the gun. I got lost again, and the wolf helped me find my way home. But that's all over now. I gave the film to John, and he's going to take care of things from here."

Meg leaned back in the seat and whistled. "Wow! No wonder you're drinking coffee."

With a brief grin, Nicole leaned in, tapping her fingers against the side of her coffee cup. "I've been thinking about that black wolf. Don't you think it's weird; I'm about to become a statistic, when he just shows up out of nowhere?" She shook her head.

"Are you sure it was a wolf?" Meg asked and Nicole shot her a frustrated look. "Never mind, you're the wolf expert."

She sighed and thought for a second. "Someone was definitely looking out for you. Hey, maybe the wolf was your spirit guide or something! You've always been obsessed with all things wolf related. It would make sense that a spirit guide would take a form that has meaning for you."

"I did get a strange feeling when I looked in his eyes. It seemed as if I could completely trust him, like I knew him. And then he led me home, away from the other men who were chasing me. Do you really think he could be a spirit guide?"

Meg shrugged. "Anything's possible. I mean, whatever way you want to look at it, you were being protected. I don't know if it's a spirit guide or even an angel, but someone was definitely watching over you."

Nicole shuddered when a thought occurred to her. "If someone or something, supernatural or not, is looking out for me, I hope they keep doing it. If that guy got a good look at me…"

Meg reached across the table and took Nicole's hands in her own, careful not to touch her scrapes. "Look, whether he did or not, you'll end up on your feet. I've always said you have nine lives, and you're nowhere near using them all up."

"Meg," she groaned, "you know I don't like that cat analogy. It's not even accurate."

"Sure it is. You're the luckiest person I know."

"I don't know if lucky is how I'd characterize it."

"Nicole, remember the time a wrong number woke you up, just in time to make you aware of that gas leak you and Billy were sleeping through? And what about the time we accidentally got locked in that freezer when you wanted to go exploring?"

"Hey, it wasn't just me," Nicole replied defensively.

"True," Meg conceded, "but we were in there for what

had to be an hour when the door suddenly opened, with no sign of anyone releasing the catch. Now, you're getting shot at and saved by a wolf. Sounds like par for the course to me. Anyway, let's eat, I'm starved."

Nicole laughed. Deep down, she was still worried about everything, but there was nothing she could do to change the situation, so she decided to concentrate on other things for now.

They ate lunch without broaching any serious subjects and Meg kept her entertained with a running commentary regarding students on campus. Nicole always found herself amazed by how much gossip Meg knew. How did she hear so much? No matter what the source, she always felt better after talking to Meg. She was a reminder that Nicole had a friend who would listen to her ramblings, and not judge her for trusting a strange wolf, and be concerned about her well being but respectful enough of Nicole not to be overbearing with well-meaning advice.

Nicole chuckled when Meg finished a story about the psych major who'd shown up to her drama class wearing fishnet stockings, diving flippers and goggles along with a feathered boa. No reason. Just because he wanted to. "Tell me you got pictures."

"No," Meg shook her head regretfully. "But someone else in class took pics with her phone, and she said she'd download the pictures and send them to everyone."

"That's great. They'll make the perfect addition to your wall of shame." Both girls grinned in agreement. Meg's wall of shame had started out simply enough as just a few pictures taped to the wall beside her bed. It had since evolved into almost an entire wall full of pictures of them and their friends – and a few strangers – caught in a range of funny and memorable poses. Everything worth photographing which had happened in the last five years, since Nicole first got her camera, had been added to Meg's wall. Nicole was responsible for about two thirds of the pictures on the wall, but once word spread to their friends and acquaintances, several pictures had been donated to the wall. There was even one picture of some guy neither of them had met, wearing nothing but a roll of yellow police tape. Pretty soon, Meg was going to have to move on to another wall... or buy a scrap book.

They lapsed into a comfortable silence while they waited for their bills, Nicole absentmindedly tapping her fork on the side of her plate and Meg glancing at her 'to do' list in her planner. Nicole was halfway through tapping out the latest car insurance jingle before she realized the song was stuck in her head again. Great. Just when she got the song out of her head, now she would be singing it all day. She rolled her eyes and forced herself to stop tapping. Just then, she noticed Meg tapping out the same beat with her fingers. "How long have you been thinking that jingle?" Nicole asked, suspiciously.

Meg looked up, momentarily confused until she realized what Nicole was referring to. "Oh, I don't know. Pretty much all day, I guess. It got stuck in my head this morning, and I haven't been able to get rid of it." Nicole groaned. "Can't you think of any better songs? Now you've got it stuck in my head, too." Meg put her hands up defensively, but the gesture was belied by the teasing grin. "Hey, can I help it if you always seem to tap into my brain when I'm thinking of annoying songs? You should tune in when I get musicals going through my mind."

Nicole gave her the, 'and you're telling me this because?' look. "Okay, I'll think of another song." Meg was quiet for a moment, her teeth nibbling on her bottom lip. Then, a big grin broke out on her face. Instantly, Nicole could hear the chorus of "I need a Hero" going through her head. She sighed and rested heavily on her bent arms on the table. "What? I thought it would be appropriate," Meg said with an innocent look on her face. Looking very proud of herself, Meg proceeded to tap out the new tune on the table.

In spite of herself, Nicole was humming along by the time the waitress walked up with their checks. The waitress picked up the rest of their dishes and left behind their bills. "I've got it," Nicole said, picking up both bills.

"What? No, I've got mine covered," Meg argued, digging around in her bag for her purse. "Besides, I know with all the expenses you've had lately, you can't afford to keep doing things like this."

Nicole sobered at the reminder of the funeral and the other expenses which the life insurance hadn't quite covered. "I can afford what I want to afford. Besides this is my treat for you listening to all my crap. And I won't take 'no' for an answer."

"If you insist." Meg's lips curved in a mischievous grin. "But I just remembered I still owe you for the movie we went to last week, so here you go," she said, passing Nicole a ten-dollar bill. Nicole rolled her eyes and gave an exaggerated sigh, but took the money.

They both stood to leave and headed for the exit. "So," Meg slapped a hand down on Nicole's shoulder. "These guys who are after you; you want I should beat any of them up for you?" she asked with a wicked grin and a twinkle in her eyes.

Nicole smiled back. "Sure, but only if I can help."

Meg's grin broke into a full-blown smile. "Oh, I do love it when you get all violent." Her eyes sparkled brightly as she put emphasis on the last word.

"Just paying homage to the master," Nicole said, indicating Meg with the gesture of her hand. Meg simply gave a little half bow and opened the door for them both.

With a higher spring in her step than before, Nicole headed home.

4

Nicole walked the couple of blocks back from the diner quickly. It was turning out to be a pretty good day, the sun was high in the sky, and there wasn't a cloud to be seen. She sat down on the steps of the apartment building and forced herself to relax. She found that she wasn't quite ready to go inside yet, it was a beautiful day, and she might as well enjoy it. She pulled a piece of candy from her bag and leaned over the rail to toss the wrapper in the alley trashcan. The lid was open, broken pieces of plumbing pipe sticking out the top. She smiled. Hopefully that meant the leak in her neighbor's apartment was finally fixed, so she wouldn't need to keep coming over to Nicole's apartment to shower after step class on Thursdays.

Sitting back down, Nicole chewed on the candy and closed her eyes. A light breeze blew and tugged some strands of hair from her braid. She ignored them brushing across her face and listened to the birds singing in the trees. Their melodic voices filled the air, creating a peaceful atmosphere.

Approaching footsteps caught her attention, distracting her from the birdsong. Surveying the sidewalk she saw two men heading in her direction and mental alarms went off. One was dressed completely in leather, he had dark hair and a scar on his left cheek. The second man wore worn out blue jeans and a greasy, torn up shirt. He had sandy colored hair and a beard.

Nicole went to stand up, but the one in leather put on a sudden burst of speed and reached her before she could get into the building. Grabbing her wrist, he yanked her away from the steps and pushed her into the alley. The way the steps curled around, she knew she was virtually invisible to anyone passing by the building. The other man stood watch by the street.

Before she could make sense of what was happening, he had her braced up against the wall so she couldn't move or defend herself. The smell of sweat and cheap cologne, mingled with cigarette smoke, filled her nostrils. She gagged against the oppressive smell, even as her pounding heartbeat started echoing in her ears. For a long moment, all that existed was the stench, the sound of her heart, and the pain.

Nicole flinched when he pushed her wrists against the wall behind her. The brick rubbed hard against her damaged skin, and his fingernails dug painfully into her arm.

The man revealed a knife, holding it up in front of her chest. "You've got to learn to mind your own business." His hot, moist breath raised the hairs on the back of her neck and bile rose in her throat. All she could think about was the knife which was about to be plunged into her heart.

She watched as the knife stopped on its downward descent toward her chest, no more than an inch from her heart. She held her breath, her eyes focused on the deadly metal for a moment before she lifted her gaze.

Her attacker's eyes had widened as he stared at the hand which was currently holding his arm. He strained against the grip, apparently unable to budge. He wasn't the only one who seemed surprised.

Nicole stared up at the man who was now, literally, holding her life in his hand. She hadn't seen or heard him approach, but here he was. "You've got to learn how to treat a lady," the new man said in a low, intense voice. The timbre of his voice caused an entirely different type of shiver to run down her spine.

He was dressed in black, and didn't seem to be that much older than herself. For a moment, Nicole found herself unable to take her eyes off him. She watched him as he bent back 'leather man's' wrist until she heard a satisfying crack, and then he pulled the man's arm behind his back in a very awkward position. The man screamed. Her mystery defender then pushed the perp into the trash bin.

Nicole pried her gaze away from the two men and turned her attention to the second perp, who was hurrying toward her. She glanced around for a way to defend herself and saw a piece of discarded pipe. Grabbing it, she hit the second perp in the stomach and then over his head. He collapsed to the ground for a moment or two before he scrambled to his feet, stumbling after the first attacker, who was limping, a knife protruding from his leg.

Nicole let the pipe slip from her hand onto the ground, and rubbed her wrists as she watched them escape. Her wrists were extremely sore after she'd been gripped with no small amount of force. Old and new cuts alike were covered in a mixture of blood, dirt and sweat.

"Are you okay?" the man in black asked. She turned

toward him to respond, when she saw a nasty gash on his arm.

"You're hurt!" she cried.

"It's nothing." He shrugged off the injury, his dark, disheveled hair falling across his face at the movement, but the pained expression in his blue-green eyes gave him away. Blood was dripping from his torn sleeve.

"Nothing? I'd hardly call that nothing. Why don't you come with me, and I'll clean up the wound and bandage it?" Reluctantly, he agreed, letting her lead him upstairs.

Nicole called the police while she rinsed off the worst of the blood and dirt from her hands. She decided she should clean the man's injury first and filled a bowl with hot water, bringing it across to where he stood by the front door. "Sit down and roll up that sleeve." She motioned to a chair and went to find the first aid kit and some clean rags.

"I don't think rolling up my sleeve is going to work."

He'd spoken from right behind, and her heart began to race. Once she was confident she could talk without her voice sounding shaky, she responded. "Oh?" Nicole looked closely at the sleeve and decided he was right. It probably wouldn't make it past the middle of his forearm.

The coppery smell of blood filled her with a renewed sense of urgency and his sleeve was already slick with it. "Do you think you can take off the shirt without it hurting too badly, or do I need to cut the sleeve off?"

He smiled softly, seeming warmed by her concern over him feeling too much pain. "Don't worry about it hurting, but are you sure you need me to do that?"

"If I'm going to clean it properly, yes."

"Alright. But I might need a hand."

"No problem." She set down the first aid kit and rags and helped him remove his shirt. Slowly, she pulled the sleeve down over his injured arm, careful not to touch the gash. "There," she announced triumphantly when she was done. She took the shirt and draped it over the sink, then picking up her materials, she led him back to the chair she'd motioned to earlier. "Now, let me look at that cut."

Nicole leaned forward and studied the gash. It actually seemed a little better than it had when she'd first seen it outside. Maybe it was just the indoor lighting. It didn't look as if it would need stitches, but it had certainly bled a lot.

She snatched up one of the rags, and it almost fell out of her hand when she first touched his arm. Just that small touch sent shivers rippling down her spine. The hairs on her arms stood on end, and goose bumps covered her flesh. She managed, just barely, to keep her composure and continued to clean his wound. *She needed to concentrate on the task at hand,* she reminded herself. After all, he'd gotten injured while helping her.

Despite the warning she'd given herself, she kept finding herself glancing at his broad, bare chest, just inches away. How easy it would be, to reach over and touch it!

Very gently, she washed away the blood from the injury. There was a lot of it. To break the silence and take her mind off her close proximity to her mysterious rescuer, she started talking. "Thank, you, for what you did." She laughed lightly looking up into his eyes. "I don't even know your name."

She dropped her gaze back to the injury. With most of the blood cleaned away, it looked even better. Still, the cut was pretty deep. He'd need to take good care of it to ensure it didn't get infected.

He smiled. "My name is David Coverton."

She looked at that smile and the man who was wearing it. He had deeply set, blue-green eyes and midnight black hair. Every intake of breath brought her eyes back to his muscular chest. There was no denying he was alluring. She suddenly realized she was staring and quickly began to get bandages out of the first aid box.

"David," she repeated thoughtfully.

David took a deep breath. For some reason, his name sounded so much better the way she said it.

She spoke again, drawing him back to the conversation. "My name is Nicole Cameron. Here, put your arm up a little." She started bandaging his arm, and he noticed she focused on the way his muscles flexed as he moved his arm. "So, what do you do Mr. Coverton? When you're not rescuing people, that is?"

"You can call me David," he responded, wanting to hear her say his name again, "and I keep myself busy. This and that." He glanced around the room, searching for a way to distract himself from Nicole. What he saw surprised him even more than the way he was reacting to her.

At first glance, there wasn't anything out of the ordinary in the small apartment. Beside him was a large bookcase, full of books, and at the back of the apartment there were glass doors opening onto a balcony. To the right of the front door was a roomy kitchenette with a sizable counter. She even had a potted tree sitting in one corner. But what really caught his eye was the abundance of wolves. There were pictures, statues, a clock, and a calendar, all depicting a variety of wolves. A glance at her bookshelf revealed several books were about wolves. It was amazing. She couldn't know, yet something in her must have some sort of inkling. Maybe it wasn't that strange that she'd focused so heavily on wolves – maybe it was a natural part of her. "You have a nice place here. Tell me, what is it that you do?"

She smiled at his obvious evasion and the way he turned the attention back to her but let it slide. After all, he had just saved her life. "Right now, I'm attending Smithsdale University." She leaned in conspiratorially. "I'm hoping to have selected a major by senior year." She winked and smiled.

He smiled back, and Nicole's heart skipped a beat. She quickly finished bandaging David's arm and gently slapped his good arm when she stood up. She didn't want to delve too deeply into what that smile was doing to her.

A knock sounded at the door, and Nicole let the police officer in. He introduced himself as Officer Stevenson and questioned what had happened. Nicole did most of the talking, with David occasionally adding a small detail. The officer took down a note of their phone numbers, and promised to have a patrol car drive by a few times that night as a precaution. It might take some time to identify the men, since neither of them knew her attackers.

Once the door closed, David turned to Nicole. "Will you be all right here tonight?" he asked.

She smiled reassuringly. "Yeah. Thanks... for everything."

She helped him pull on his shirt and walked him to the door. Before he left, he gazed deeply into her eyes for a long moment. "If you need anything – anything at all – just call and I'll come." He turned and left before she could say other word. She looked at the end table and saw a simple black business card with his name and number. Putting the card on the counter by her phone, Nicole set about the task of cleaning up.

DAVID WALKED down the steps and turned into the alley. He could hardly remember a single word he'd spoken while he'd been inside Nicole's apartment. He hadn't been able to concentrate on anything but Nicole herself. Fortunately, she didn't seem to have noticed.

He'd experienced an uncontrollable urge to watch Nicole constantly, and since she'd mostly been focused on cleaning and bandaging his arm, he'd had ample time to indulge the urge. And he'd studied every inch of her. Although her hair was pulled back in a braid, he could tell it was long and held a slight wave. It was a dark, deep brown, just like Caroline's hair had been. And her eyes! Nicole had the bluest eyes he'd ever seen. Not even her glasses detracted from their beauty. He'd noticed a constant sparkle in them, but looking closely he'd seen a little sadness beneath the surface.

He smiled when he thought about the one crooked tooth, which was only revealed when she smiled. Even her imperfections seemed to enchant him. She wasn't the most beautiful woman he'd ever seen, but she was definitely intriguing, and there was no denying he was strongly attracted to her. He couldn't remember ever being this attracted to anyone before. The question was, what was he going to do about it?

"David... David."

The whisper came from out of the shadows, before Officer Stevenson stepped forward, the low rays of the mid-afternoon sun highlighting his dark hair and hazel eyes.

"Mark," David said. "It's good to see you again." He released the startled breath he'd been holding on hearing his name and offered Mark Stevenson a short smile In truth he was a little angry with himself for letting anyone sneak up on him. He was getting much too complacent.

"It's been a while," Mark said. He still wasn't quite over his surprise at seeing David in Nicole Cameron's apartment. David wasn't even supposed to be in town, hadn't been back in years. He made it clear to everyone he wanted to be alone. Something pretty big must have happened to bring him back to the world of the living. Whatever caused him to come out of his long hiatus, Mark was glad to see him. "So, how bad is that cut, really?"

David flexed his arm a little. There was hardly any pain in the wound. "It's not too bad. It's already started to heal, and Nicole did a good job of cleaning and bandaging it."

Mark nodded. "Speaking of Nicole, does she know anything?"

"No." David shifted his focus to the shadows and contemplated his next move. He hadn't intended to have any contact with Nicole, but the situation had changed now. Things weren't so clear anymore, especially after seeing the multitude of wolves decorating her apartment. Maybe she *should* know. "I suppose I should tell her, but she has a lot on her mind right now. I only found out recently that her adoptive parents had died."

"Yes, they did. David, you should know – there was some question about their deaths. They died in a car accident and to all intents and purposes, it did appear to be an accident. But when we investigated, there were a few things that didn't add up. We could never prove anything, but considering what happened today, I think it's fair to say Nicole might be in danger. Will you be keeping an eye on her?"

David pushed down the pleasure which blossomed at the prospect of watching over Nicole and reminded himself of the gravity of the situation. He was here to make sure nothing happened to her – nothing more. He needed to get past this intense attraction; he didn't need anything clouding his judgment. Besides, he was too old for her. "Yeah, I'll be on the job. She needs someone to watch over her," he told Mark. He didn't intend to let her out of his sight.

Mark narrowed his eyes, but kept his thoughts to himself. "I'll ask some of the other guys who patrol this area to keep an eye out, too."

"I appreciate it."

"Hey, no problem." Mark glanced at his watch. "I need to be getting back to the station. Call me if you need anything."

"I will."

The two men clasped arms and David experienced a moment of nostalgia. It had been a long time since Mark had first clasped his arm in that manner, forever changing the course of his life with a simple gesture of friendship.

Casually tapping in to his train of thought, Mark said, "You were very young then."

"I don't know what I would have done without you and Richard."

Mark grinned. "You know, it was his idea to take you in. I suggested we just scare the living daylights out of you."

"I'd say you did both."

Mark laughed lightly. "I need to go and file this report. You know where to reach me."

With that, he released David's arm and strode away.

5

She couldn't sleep and the nightmare was taunting her again. Giving up her vain attempt at rest, Nicole got up and went into the living room. Her eyes peered into the dark room, looking for something to do. They barely paused on the bookshelf, that idea disregarded almost immediately. She wasn't really in the mood to read. She wouldn't be able to concentrate on it enough. Her eyes moved on to the kitchen and the coffee that was just waiting to be brewed. The smell was almost real, as she imagined the warm liquid flowing down her throat, but that idea was also disregarded quickly. Sleep had not begun its pull on her yet. It was possible she could stay up for quite some time on her own. She should hold off on the coffee until she was really tired. Then it would be the most beneficial.

Sure fingers reached for the light switch but withdrew before turning the light on. Let it be dark, it suited her mood better. Besides, it wasn't as if she needed the light to get around, she knew the apartment like the back of her hand.

Maybe some fresh air and watching the stars would make her feel better. She gripped the cold metal door handle and turned, a gasp escaping her mouth. A black wolf stared up at her, a wolf with beautiful blue-green eyes. He appeared to be exactly like the one that saved her the night before. It had to be him. He'd led her home, and wolves didn't just wander around Connecticut cities every day.

Following instincts rather than reason, she knelt beside the wolf and laid a hand on its fur. "How did you get up here?" she questioned. She looked around, and her gaze fell on the fire escape stairs. "I guess you must have come up there." The wolf leaned into her stroking touch. He emitted a low growl of contentment, sending warm breath across her skin.

She wondered if Meg was right. He wasn't acting like a wild animal. Wild wolves didn't stand vigil on an exposed balcony when they could be safe in a den with their pack. Could he be a spirit animal or a protector? The wind blew through the rails, and she felt the goosebumps raise on his flesh. He was no spirit. He was out here in the cold for her, watching over her. Why?

She felt a stab of guilt and wondered if she should invite him inside. He was still an animal, but for some crazy reason she couldn't figure out, she trusted him. Maybe, it didn't matter. What if he preferred to be outside? *Do you want to come inside?* she thought. The wolf was on his feet and inside without needing any further coaxing. "I guess that's a yes." Nicole stared in surprise. Maybe he was a spirit, after all. How else could he respond to her thoughts? Still confused, she got to her feet, following the wolf inside.

She tried to stay awake, not wanting to revisit the nightmare, but even with drinking her habitual cup of coffee, sleep eventually reclaimed her.

The sound of birdsong greeted Nicole when she awoke. It took a moment to figure out what she was doing on the couch, but when the wolf moved beside her, she quickly remembered everything. She sat up, aware of a crick in her neck and pain throughout her back, and stretched her arms above her head. "Str... e... ee... tch," she groaned, ending with a yawn. The wolf bounded off the couch, much too energetic for her liking. How could anyone have so much energy this early in the morning? True, she had taken that long walk yesterday, but that was different. She hadn't wanted to be awake and out and about. She'd just had too many things on her mind.

She poured a bowl of water for the wolf and went to change her clothes, running on autopilot most of the way. When she came back, the wolf was curled up on the couch. She scratched affectionately behind his ear and sat down beside him. "Maybe you should come over more often. I actually got some sleep last night, albeit on the couch, but sleep is sleep, right?" Still running her hand across his fur, Nicole leaned back and stared off into space. "I just wish I could do something about these nightmares. I thought I was over them, but this makes two nights in the same week. Why now, after all these years?" She sighed, beginning to feel slightly trapped in the small apartment, as if the walls were closing in and she had no way to get out. It seemed she couldn't escape the nightmare anywhere. "I need some fresh air," she said to herself.

Nicole stood up and walked swiftly to the balcony. The sharp cold air sent renewed energy coursing through her sluggish veins and with her eyes closed, she tilted her head back and took in a deep breath. The wind took control of her hair, blowing it in whatever direction it chose. Standing with her hands on the rail, she felt the wolf rub against her legs, and drew herself back to the present. Inhaling one more deep breath, Nicole opened her eyes and lowered herself onto her knees, beside the wolf. She rubbed her fingers across the back of his neck and his fur presses into her hand and arm. It was so comforting she was reluctant to let it end, but she had things to do.

"I have to go to class now, but something tells me this isn't the last time we'll see each other," she mused. Pushing off her legs with her hands, Nicole got to her feet and watched the wolf turn and leave down the fire escape. She remained on the balcony until she could no longer hear his paws on the metal, then reentered her apartment, closing the balcony doors behind her. Her life was getting interesting.

"WHY DOES every teacher assign papers and schedule tests at the same time?" Nicole muttered to herself. Between the SES and her growing mountain of homework, she'd never get the chance to read the book on Stonehenge she'd checked out, much less the one on psychics. She dropped her pencil and leaned back with a sigh. "Do they get together and plan it?"

"Probably," a voice announced behind her.

Startled, Nicole turned around and saw John heading in her direction. *She must be tired,* she thought, *if he could walk up without her hearing him.* Hardly anyone could manage to catch her off guard normally. "Hey, John."

"Hey, what's this I heard about you getting attacked last night?" John asked, avoiding pointless pleasantries and getting straight to the point.

"Word travels fast." Nicole closed her book and put the discarded pencil away. She wouldn't be getting any more work done for now. "Look, it was nothing. A couple of thugs tried to rough me up a bit, but I'm fine."

John shook his head in exasperation. "Yeah, only because some stranger happened upon you. Who was he, anyway?" he asked, settling onto the chair by her side.

The campus gossips must be working overtime. How could he have heard all of that, especially so soon? It had to be his friend, that attorney, Anderson. "His name's David Coverton."

"Coverton? Never heard of him. Anyway," he said, frowning, "you've got to be more careful. You're not exactly on everyone's 'A' list right now. You—"

"Hey guys. What's going on?" Meg asked with her typical cheerfulness as she approached the table.

"Nicole almost got herself killed again is what," John announced.

Nicole groaned.

Meg sat down across from Nicole, glancing back and forth between the two. "What happened this time?" she asked.

"She was attacked right outside her apartment building."

"Are you okay?" she asked Nicole, her voice filled with concern.

"Yes, I'm fine." Nicole rolled her eyes. "A guy named David Coverton showed up and helped me."

"Did I hear my name?"

Nicole turned in her chair to see David standing behind her. Just seeing him was enough to take her breath away. A shiver ran up her spine being near him again. Nicole looked up into his blue-green eyes, noticing the green was more prevalent today. Such a deep, beautiful green, full and pure with small specks of blue mixed through for effect, creating the most amazing eyes she'd ever had the pleasure of gazing into. It took a few seconds before she regained her presence of mind.

She surveyed her now-crowded study area and decided humor was the best defense against well-meaning friends. "What is this, Grand Central Station?" She tried to keep her voice steady but failed, wavering when she glanced back at David. "What are you doing here?"

David looked at Nicole, wondering again what had made him enter the library. He certainly hadn't planned on doing it. He'd only planned to keep an eye on her, make sure no one else tried anything. But then he'd found himself walking through the library doors and heading straight towards her. It seemed where she was concerned, his mind just didn't get a vote. Now he had no idea what to say or do next. Through much self-control he managed not to fidget. "I was driving by and saw you come in here. Thought I'd check if you were still okay?"

Nicole rolled her eyes again. "Why does everyone keep asking me that? I'm fine."

David took a breath and glanced back at the library door. This had been a mistake. "I'm sorry. I didn't mean to bother you."

A twinge of guilt knotted in Nicole's chest when he turned to leave. "I'm sorry. That was rude of me, especially considering what you did yesterday." She waited for David to turn back and meet her gaze. "Thank you."

She was rewarded by a soft smile when David turned back to the group.

After glancing around the table at the other two people sitting there, his entire focus was fixed on Nicole. He heard the other young girl speaking and managed, with a good deal of difficulty, to shift his attention away from Nicole long enough to catch her say, "So, you're the one who saved Nicole." She stood up and offered him her hand. "My name's Meghan Freeman. It's a pleasure to meet you."

David took the proffered hand and brushed a light kiss across the back of it. "The pleasure is mine."

Meg was momentarily at a loss, a rarity for her. "You're very chivalrous." She finally managed.

"I try," he said, smiling. Who would ever have thought, during his misspent youth, that he would ever have been described as chivalrous? His father would have never believed he was the same person who left all those years ago. Then again, maybe he wasn't. David quickly pushed back an unexpected pang of sadness. This was neither the time nor the place to delve into those feelings.

"My name is John Markham." For a reason John couldn't explain, he knew immediately that he liked this guy. Regardless of what he'd done to help Nicole, David Coverton, seemed to exude an aura of trust. Being one to follow his instincts, John stood and shook David's hand firmly. "I want to thank you for what you did for Nicole."

David grinned. "I'm sure she could have taken care of herself. She seems very resourceful." The way she'd handled herself with those attackers had been impressive. Few people would have been able to adapt to a dangerous situation so well, but she had. Her parents would have been proud of her.

David stared deep into Nicole's eyes as he talked, and a shiver ran through her limbs. She needed to get out of here, it was too much to handle right now. "Okay, if everyone is through talking about me in the third person, I should be getting home."

"You shouldn't be walking home by yourself." Meg frowned. "It isn't safe."

"I'll be fine." Nicole tapped her foot absentmindedly. Once she was alone, she imagined that she could figure out what was going on with her, but right now, she needed to get away.

"No, your friend is right," David replied softly. Whether she liked it or not, she was in danger. Nicole needed to realize precautions had to be taken. Then he looked a little closer at Nicole's face and wished he hadn't spoken. He saw panic in her eyes, a very real need to be away from this place... these people... everything, in fact. He tried to think of a way to help. He didn't know what was bothering her, but he couldn't ignore it. He couldn't believe he'd missed it in the first place.

Making a conscious effort to release the tension in his chest, he spoke again. "I'll walk you home," he announced without thinking. As soon as the words had left his lips, he wondered at them. He had no idea where that thought had come from. He shouldn't be spending more time alone with her. He should just help her find an excuse to leave, then follow her from a distance. Then again maybe he wouldn't have to come up with any excuse, maybe she would reject his offer and decide to go home on her own. That would be for the best – for them both. He tried to ignore the tension in his chest.

Just what she needed, more time alone with him. She didn't know whether to be upset, or happy at the prospect. She stood and opted for upset. "Arrghh, this is ridiculous." She ran her hands through her hair with an exasperated motion.

"No, it's not," he responded calmly, though he felt anything but. He couldn't believe he was doing this, trying to talk her into doing what just a moment ago he'd hoped she would turn down, but it was too late to back out now.

Nicole inhaled sharply. David was standing right beside her now. Another inch, and they'd be touching. His voice was low and gentle, like a caress. It quickly calmed her, dissipating the caged feeling she was suffering.

"Someone's already tried to harm you twice. Let me walk you home. You'll have some company, at least, and you'll take a little of the worry away from your friends. What harm can it do?"

Nicole lifted an eyebrow. Who could argue with logic like that, especially when it came in that smooth, calm voice? "Okay, you can walk me home." She said it as if she thought she had a choice in the matter, even knowing she didn't. She knew, with an odd certainty, David would end up accompanying her one way or another. She picked up her books and waved to John and Meg before heading for the exit. She wasn't even surprised when David held the door for her. Giving him a wry smile, Nicole paused in the doorway and looked directly at David. "One question, Coverton. How did you know it had been twice?"

David cringed inwardly. He'd hoped she wouldn't catch that slip up. He needed to be more careful about what he said around her. "Let's just say I keep informed."

She stared at him for a second, then shook her head and walked out the door. He was an enigma all right – but she liked a challenge. She suspected she should be more alarmed by his strange reply, but for some unknown reason, she wasn't. After these past two months, it was refreshing to have something to wrap her mind around.

A few minutes passed by in silence, before David spoke. "Is my company really that bad?"

"What? No." Nicole shook her head. "I just wish everyone would stop worrying about me."

"Your friends care about you." David thought it felt strange to be on this side of the argument.

"I know, but they can be smothering sometimes. Meg isn't so bad. We've known each other a lot of years. I've only known John a short time. He's a good friend, but he always treats me like I'm going to break."

"How did you and Meg meet?"

"That is a very long story, one only a few people know." She narrowed her eyes at him. "Maybe someday, if you're still around, I'll tell you about it." She turned away as the second the words left her mouth. What was wrong with her? She'd only just met the guy, and she was already making insinuations he would be sticking around. She wasn't even sure if she wanted him to stick around yet, and even if she did, any girl worth her salt knew you didn't put that kind of pressure on a guy you'd only just met... not that she wanted him to stick around, anyway. Luckily, he seemed not to notice her complete and utter faux pas. Either that, or he was too polite to bring attention to it.

She put the comment behind her and concentrated on trying to enjoy the walk. It was a nice day, and the company was pleasant, too. She'd successfully begun to relax by the time they reached her building, but when Nicole reflexively stole a glance down the alley beside the building, felt herself she shuddered.

"Are you all right?" David asked.

She nodded. "It's funny how memories can hit you harder than the actual event." She stared off into the distance, not really seeing anything.

He thought against a desire to pull her into his arms and hold her until she forgot the previous night. "The actual event only takes a short time. Memories can last forever.

They're filled with what if's, and other unanswerable questions."

The tone of his voice penetrated her thoughts. Her eyes cleared, and she turned her attention back to him. "Sounds like you know that from experience."

"Hey, don't we all?" He offered her a weak grin and shrugged.

"I guess." For a moment, she'd felt inexplicably close to him, but then again, he had saved her life, so maybe it wasn't so strange. "How's your arm?"

He shrugged. "It's fine."

"Fine? It was a deep gash."

"I'm very resilient."

There was that spark of amusement in his eye again, a spark which went well with his mischievous smile. Her eyes were drawn to a small dimple at the corner of his mouth. "Thanks for walking me home." She suspected her eyes needed a leash.

"No problem. Just promise me you'll be careful, that you won't take any stupid risks."

"What kind of risks would you like me to take?" She smiled.

"Nicole..." Her name rumbled in his throat, sounding almost like a growl.

She laughed, oddly aroused by the way his voice growled in his throat. "Okay, okay, I promise. There's no need to worry, I've gotten good at taking care of myself." There was a wistful note in her voice that she couldn't quite conceal.

Their eyes locked. A few strands of Nicole's hair blew across her face, and David quelled the absurd urge to reach out and tuck them behind her ear. What was he thinking? He needed to put some distance between them. He forced his eyes away and broke the spell their interlocked gaze had been weaving.

Nicole forced herself to breathe again. "Well then, Coverton, guess I'll see you later." She turned and walked up the steps hurriedly, throwing a casual "Bye," over her shoulder and entered the building.

He watched her toss her hair over her shoulder just before the door closed. He stood silently for a couple of minutes, his gaze on the building. "Bye" he whispered once before he turned, walking away.

Nicole paused outside her apartment door and shook her head. For a moment, she was certain she'd heard David whisper 'Bye'.

It was probably just stress she was under. There was no way she could have heard him from in here. Unlocking the door, she went inside tossing her books on the couch, and started working on dinner.

* * *

DAVID SWIRLED the scotch in the glass, listening to the way the ice clinked against the sides. A car door closed outside, and he listened as footsteps approached the house. He sighed and stood up, heading for the door. It opened with a loud creak. "I've got to remember to oil that thing," he muttered to himself. "Mark, what are you doing here?"

"I thought you'd be here. I wanted to check in on you and see how you were doing."

"Never better," he answered sarcastically. "Want a drink?"

"No, thanks."

David shrugged and headed back into the study, Mark following behind.

Mark studied David carefully. His hair was wild and unkempt, his clothes wrinkled, and judging from the dark circles under his eyes, David hadn't had a good night's sleep in some time. He looked as if he needed to seriously de-stress. Mark watched him swallow the contents of the whiskey glass in a single swallow and sighed. "What made you come back?"

"Hmm?"

"You haven't been back here in years, and then you show up all the sudden, right when Nicole is in trouble. That's excellent timing. I'm just wondering what made you decide to come back."

David looked to the wall at the picture of Richard. "I just remembered something."

"What?"

David turned to his friend. "I had a dream. It was regarding something Richard said before he died. He asked me to make sure Nicole was okay, if anything ever happened to him. I tried to shrug it off, but I couldn't stop thinking about it, so I figured I'd come check things out. I thought I could be in and out in a couple of days, tops. I never imag-ined she'd actually be in danger."

Mark studied David closely. "Are you still planning on leaving, once all this is over?"

"Yeah, I mean, why wouldn't I?"

"Because you've been living like a hermit for sixteen years. You're a wreck right now. I know Richard's death hit you hard but…"

"It's not just that. It's part of it, but it's not all of it."

"So, what is it that's bothering you so much?"

David exhaled heavily. He might as well tell him, maybe another point of view could prove useful. At least it would be better than only listening to the voice in his head. "I... uh... I've been thinking a lot about Nicole."

"You mean, worrying about her?"

"More than that. This is crazy." He pushed his fingers through his hair, turning his back on Mark before he spoke quietly. "I've been thinking about the way she looks, the sound of her voice, random things she says."

There was a brief silence followed by a burst of laughter. David turned back to stare at Mark, who had a big smile on his face.

"You're attracted to her?"

"Yeah, I'm attracted to her. What's so funny?"

"You. You're attracted to a woman, and you're squirming like a child confessing they stole a cookie. There's nothing wrong with how you feel. It's not like you've just found out you've got the plague."

David fought the urge to squirm. "But it's Nicole."

"So, what? She's not a child, and I don't think Richard would think any less of you for it. Hell, he'd probably be happy about the idea. You know you were like a son to him."

"I didn't say I was going to marry her. I just said I was attracted to her," David responded defensively.

Mark softened his tone a little, conscious of how irritable David was getting. "Look, you want my advice? Don't think too much about it. Just explore the concept a little. You've been closed off for so long and you think too much. You need to live in the moment. Everything else will come."

"You think so?" For the first time in a while, David was hopeful.

"Yeah, I do. Have I ever led you wrong?" Mark grinned and winked at David, drawing a smile. Confident he'd done all he could for the time being, he glanced at his watch and confirmed the time. "Look, I have to go. Are you going to be okay?"

"Yeah, I'll be fine. Thanks."

"No problem. If you need to talk, call me. Better yet, come by. I've got some new sketches I'd like to show you."

"I'll keep that in mind." David walked him to the door, clasping arms with Mark before closing the door and heading back to the study. He eyed the bottle of scotch for a second or two, before putting it away and grabbing his jacket.

6

———

Rodney tossed back another beer and slapped the shoulder of the man standing beside him. "So, they're coming after me. I mean, what have I to them did... done... they did... I ain't done nut'in. They just got too much free time that they gotta mess with me."

The other man cringed away from Rodney's foul breath and endless tirade. Quickly paying for his own drink, he moved away to find a better seat elsewhere in the bar.

Rodney shrugged, already forgetting about the stranger, and pushed his glass toward the bartender. "I'll have 'nother one."

The bartender looked him over. Rodney reeked of alcohol, and his clothes were a disheveled mess. His shirt was stained with dirt, sweat, and drink in several places. His pants were worn through at the knees and had dark stains all over them. He could barely stay upright without leaning on the bar, and even that perch seemed precarious at times. "Don't you think you've had enough?" he asked, already knowing what Rodney's answer would be as he filled the glass. Beer foamed up and spilled over the rim or the glass, forming a ring-shaped puddle on the bar.

"There's no such thing as too much," Rodney slurred. He waved his new drink around, the contents splashing out in all directions as he spoke to the bartender and anyone else within earshot. Raising his voice, he continued where he'd left off with the other man a minute before. "I used to really be something, ya know. Before all these people started nosing around in my business, everything was jus' fine. But I'll show 'em. I'm gonna have all the power. I'm gonna be a millionaire someday, and I'm gonna have a big fancy house with an indoor heated pool, lots of expensive cars, and women... lots of women. I'm gonna be able to get any woman I want. People are gonna to be sucking up to me, doing anything just to get a little piece of the pie." Rodney downed the rest of his beer and slammed the glass down. "Give me 'nother one."

"Sorry, I can't do that." The bartender took the glass and wiped down the bar with a rag. "You're at your limit. That's all the drinks you're getting here tonight." He was starting to scare away the other customers, and that wasn't good for business.

"What? That's stupid. I don't need your damn drinks anyway. I'll just go somewhere else." Rodney stumbled across the crowded bar, people gladly making a path for his departure. "You just wait," he said, almost falling when he turned back around at the door. "Someday, I'm gonna run this whole damn town, and you'll all have to answer to me."

The door slammed behind him, the sound lost in the hum of a car passing by. Rodney stumbled down the street, mumbling to himself. It was exceptionally dark outside, making it difficult to see ahead of him. It must be later than he thought. It meant he wouldn't be able to go just anywhere to get another drink, not many places would be open this late at night. He tried to figure out how long he'd been at the bar, but his mind wouldn't count past three hours before he completely lost his train of thought and remembered he needed a new place to drink. Currently, that question took precedence over everything else. He'd probably end up having to buy beer at the store and take it home with him, if he could find a store that was open.

This was just great. He had to go to all this trouble just because some bartender thought he'd had too much to drink. Who the hell was he to tell him how much he could drink? Rodney would show him, along with the rest of this town. They'd all be sorry they hadn't been nicer to him. They'd be sorry when he was in charge, when he had all the power. They'd be sorry. "You just wait," he yelled into the night, shaking his fist in the air.

"Wait for what?" A voice, barely audible, spoke from behind him.

Rodney swung around, nearly losing his balance, but there was no one there. He squinted into the darkness, scanning his surroundings and realized he didn't recognize where he was. Nothing on the street seemed familiar. Even the street name was unfamiliar. He must have taken a wrong turn. It was all that stupid bartender's fault, if he hadn't gotten him so worked up, making him go look for beer somewhere else, he wouldn't be in this mess. Now he'd have to backtrack to find his way.

A cold wind blew past Rodney on his right, and it seemed a lot darker all of a sudden. Now he could only see a couple of feet in front of his face.

"What are you going to do, pass out on me?"

The voice sounded as if it was right beside his left ear

this time. He even felt someone's breath on his skin, but there was nobody to be seen.

"Who are you?" His eyes darted around, the hairs on the back of his neck standing on end.

"I'm the one who is going to help you achieve your goals – you know, the power, the money, the women. I can help you get all of that."

Rodney turned in a circle, but the voice stayed behind him, and there was no sign of who was speaking. "Where are you? How are you doing that?" He didn't like this, didn't like it one bit.

"Don't worry about that. Just worry about what I can do for you. I can make your dreams come true."

"How are you going to do that?" Despite the strangeness of this entire situation, he was starting to get interested. What if this guy really could help him?

"Guidance. You listen to me, and we both get what we want." A low fog started rolling in, covering the ground and making his feet disappear from sight.

"And what do you want?" There had to be some trick here.

"Nicole Cameron. I want her dead." A figure appeared in the shadows to his right. In the blink of an eye, the figure was at his left. No matter how hard Rodney tried, he couldn't make out any details. The figure was barely visible, blending in and out of the darkness. He found himself questioning if the figure was really there.

"Yeah, well, I already tried that once. What else am I supposed to do?"

"You have to get a little creative. Think of some way to attack when she's not expecting it. Wait until she feels safe, then strike." The fog thickened, completely enveloping the shadowy figure. "Whatever you do, you must kill Nicole

Cameron." The words came from every direction at once, echoing into the night. The fog rolled out as swiftly as it had arrived, and the darkness lifted some. There still wasn't a lot of light, but it wasn't quite as dark as it had been a moment ago.

As Rodney stumbled away, his mind cleared, and he thought over several options, trying to decide on the best way to kill Nicole Cameron.

* * *

ARTEMIS PULLED on his pants and stepped outside. The cold night air hit his bare chest, but he barely noticed. He surveyed the buildings around him. They were all empty and dark, testament to the sleeping town. In the street, pieces of trash, newspaper, plastic bags and all other manner of discarded refuse blew in the wind. A stray cat scrambled about in the shadows, one of the forgotten in the night. Artemis was momentarily distracted from his perusal of the sleeping city by the sounds of the night's entertainment, moving about in the room behind him. A low moan was followed by the movement of sheets and slow footsteps. Soft arms wrapped around his waist, and he could feel a face resting against his back. With little effort, he picked up the girl's thoughts. They were practically screaming at him. The foolish girl was actually indulging in small fantasies about them as a couple. Damn. It looked as if he was going to have to cut this little arrangement short. He couldn't have her imagining that they had something together. Why did women always have to make more of things than there was? Why couldn't they just be happy with what was given to them and stop throwing themselves on any man who showed them the least little bit of attention? They couldn't just enjoy a nice little physical arrangement. No, they had to dream of a future, and once that happened, they became much too needy. It was a shame. She'd been pretty good – not the best, but he would gladly indulge in a little recreation with her again – if it wasn't for her romantic little ideas. Oh, well, no sense in putting it off. He turned around and opened his mouth to speak, but she quickly pressed her little body against his larger frame and leaned in for a kiss. Lust ran through his veins. Maybe he'd indulge once more. After all, it had been a long time.

He took her to the bed and began to assuage his body's needs one last time. His expert hands quickly brought her to the precipice as well. He partook of her bountiful offering, taking her breasts and lips with his mouth and burying himself deeply within her body, until his own body cried out in relief. She shuddered beneath him and collapsed, falling quickly into a satisfied sleep.

QUIETLY, he donned his clothes again and slipped outside. Artemis started walking across town heading towards the room he'd procured for the duration of his stay. It was a good distance away, so he had quite a walk ahead of him. It was always wise to seek entertainment as far away from one's base as possible, that way, there was less chance of awkward encounters later. As it was, there was a very little chance he'd run into her again.

He walked confidently down the dark streets, exuding an aura of power and strength. Only a fool would risk bothering him. He laughed when a black cat crossed in front of him – bad luck, indeed.

A breeze cold enough to make him shiver blew past and he stopped laughing. That had been no normal wind. The shadows thickened, and a form took shape before him. "Have you discovered anything new?" the voice asked, sounding almost amused.

"Uh, actually, no, not much. I haven't been able to do much without letting everyone know I'm here."

"Really? So, what exactly *have* you been doing?"

Artemis ignored the suggestive tone in the voice. There was no telling what he'd meant by his comment, so Artemis would be better off just trying to answer the question. "I've found out what name she's going by. It's Nicole Cameron." It had taken Artemis a while to discover that piece of information. Hopefully it would be enough to appease.

"Wonderful. What else have you learned?"

What more did he want? It wasn't as easy to find out information as he thought. Who did he think Artemis was? "Actually, seeing as her records were hidden, I had to start by finding out the names of everyone who lived in the building and narrowed it down to likely names. Then I had to look up each one separately to figure out if it was her. I haven't actually been able to find out anything else, yet, but I will," he added hastily. "It should go a lot quicker now."

"That won't be necessary." Artemis jumped when a large manila envelope landed on the ground at his feet. "There's all the information you will be needing."

Artemis picked up the envelope carefully. "How did you..."

"Maybe if you'd kept your mind on the job at hand, instead of fraternizing with the locals, you wouldn't need me to do your work for you." There was no misinterpreting his meaning this time. "I'm not going to just hand it to you. My help only goes so far. If you want the power and respect you deserve, you must do some of the work yourself. Now, do you think you can handle the rest of this job on your own?"

Artemis visibly cringed. "Yes. I can convince her to trust me, to join us. I'll just need some time. It won't be easy to get near her in the first place, and I'll have to be careful with her initially, but I can do this."

"Good. You'd better be right, if you ever want to assume what is rightfully yours. You need her on your side if you're going to succeed. No one would dare stand against her."

"I know what's at stake." He bit the words out. He'd heard this same speech hundreds of times over the past century or so. He understood exactly what he needed to do if he was going to take the place of honor and power Richard had held for so long. The very fact that they all conspired to keep her away from him was the biggest slap on the face. He wouldn't endure any more insults, it was time he received the respect he so rightfully deserved. "I will win her over, and she'll gladly do anything I ask of her when this is over."

"See that you're right." The words faded and the shadows retreated to their normal condition, leaving Artemis alone again. He hurried back to his room to get some sleep before the dawn. He would need the rest if he was going to put his plans into action. He had a lot of work to do.

7

Nicole finished the last of the week's assigned readings for class and put away her school things, finally getting an opportunity to look at her library books. Skimming over the stories of Bigfoot and Nessie from the books she checked out the week before, she began reading about Stonehenge. It was one subject she didn't know much about. The book drew her in quickly, and she put it down with an aggravated sigh when she heard a knock at the door.

Confusion briefly replaced frustration. Who would be knocking on her door at this time of night, anyway? Hardly anyone ever stopped by much past early evening. She briefly considered pretending to be asleep but thought better of it. She should see who it was, it might be important.

Nicole opened the door and discovered David standing in the hallway. He was half turned away from the door, as if he intended to leave. "What are you doing here? It's pretty late." She cringed. That was her reaction to his visit? Smooth – real smooth. Now he was going to think he wasn't welcome. She focused on his shirt, unable to meet his eyes. Irrational fear gripped her at the prospect of him feeling unwelcome, but for the life of her, she couldn't figure out why it bothered her so much.

Nicole forced her eyes up to his face, knowing she owed him that much, even if she didn't know why.

David was fidgeting, and looked a little uncertain. "I'm sorry. I didn't even think about the time. I'll just go." He turned and stepped away.

"Wait." She reached out and touched his arm, sending shock waves rippling up her own. How could that simple touch create such a reaction? "Don't worry about the time, I was only reading. I usually stay up late. What brought you by?"

David shifted his weight and cleared his throat. He couldn't decide if he wanted her to move her hand or not. It would make thinking a little easier, but then, he would probably miss her touch. Why couldn't he decide what he wanted? "Actually, I was taking a walk and I thought I might come check on you, make sure you didn't have any more trouble tonight." *Good, that sounds plausible. I mean, it is plausible. I mean that's why I came here... sort of.*

She narrowed her eyes and grinned broadly. "Are you a stalker?" she asked with mock seriousness.

He grinned back. "Nope." *I'm just a guy trying to keep a promise to your long-dead father by keeping you safe. Oh, and I have the hots for you, too, by the way.* "I just don't know many people here. And you seem like you could use the company, too. I can go if I'm bothering you."

"No, It's not you. I'm kind of difficult to everyone right now. I'm just not much fun lately. I guess it's hard to believe anyone would want to be around me."

"You're the only one I want to be around."

Nicole smiled slightly uncomfortably and lowered her gaze.

"But then," he added, grinning, "as I said before, I don't know too many people around here..." His voice trailed off and he lifted his eyes towards the ceiling.

She laughed. "That's very kind of you," she said, the words dripping with sarcasm. "Why don't you come in?"

She closed the door behind him and hastily smoothed out her hair while his back was turned. "Can I get you anything?" She was already wishing for another excuse to touch him.

"Nah, I'm fine." He looked around the room, hoping something to say would pop into his head. He really should have thought this plan through a little better. "Uh, have you heard anything about the guys who attacked you?"

"No, but I'm not expecting to hear anything. I know they were probably sent by Rodney Steagel."

"Steagel?" David's ears perked up on hearing the name of the man who could be behind the attacks on Nicole. He wished he could get the guy alone for ten minutes. David was surprised when he realized his hands were clenched into fists. He deliberately forced himself to relax, careful not to let Nicole notice that little betrayal of how strong his feelings toward her were becoming.

"Yeah, I took some pictures which could tie Rodney Steagel of Steagel & Co. to some illegal activities. I'm pretty sure he sent those guys to get rid of me." She finished with a half-smile, proud that she'd managed to say all that without letting her voice crack.

He shook his head. How could someone so young get involved in so much trouble? Then again... "How did you get involved in something like that?"

Nicole plopped down on the couch with a sigh. "If you

really want to know..." He nodded for her to continue. "It was basically because of my parents." She took a moment to swallow down the lump in her throat and continued. "They started a group to fight environmental injustices, specifically from this one company, run by Steagel. He's been polluting the river, so I was taking pictures of the damage when I stumbled across him and his men dumping toxic waste. He probably didn't figure anyone would be near the river at this time of year," she mused. "I just can't understand how anyone could so willfully destroy the environment like that. We should be taking care of the world, not polluting it. Everyone just keeps destroying the world, and then they're surprised when it starts to show. They wonder why people get sick, why it's harder to breath nowadays and why the water isn't safe to drink. No one takes responsibility for their own actions.

And most so-called environmentalists aren't much better. They're only worried about the world at the exclusion of the people in it. They use environmentalism to control and manipulate people, instead of trying to make food safe to eat. They claim to cherish nature while ignoring the cycle of life and death that exists in it. Change happens. Destruction happens. It's unavoidable. Life moves on. But there's no reason we should haphazardly poison ourselves in the meantime. Everyone is all or nothing, one way or the other, without applying any logic to their arguments. I'm as worried about the birds and fish as the next person, but call me crazy, I'm a little more worried about the people."

"You seem to feel pretty strongly about that the issue," David said, sitting down beside her on the couch. He was impressed by her passion, and wanted to hear more, much more. He never wanted her to stop talking. She was intriguing, and so passionate. He hadn't heard anyone else talk like this in a very long time. He hadn't even known it was possible for someone to feel so strongly about anything anymore.

She was a little stunned. All those years of listening to her parents saying things like that, she'd never realized how passionately she believed in what they'd been doing. It was comforting to realize that maybe she'd been closer to them, to their dreams, than she'd thought. It was almost like having them back with her again. She smiled. "I do," she said with complete honesty. "I'd like to do something to make a difference. But then, who wouldn't?"

"A lot of people. To care so deeply is a very special trait. You're a special person."

Nicole shrugged uncomfortably beneath the unexpected praise. The comforting feeling remained for a second or two, before it was replaced by guilt. Her parents – they were the special ones, not her. She should have realized how she felt sooner, should have reached out to her parents, helped them with their work. She looked around the room, her critical eye noticing all the picture frames which were turned away or lying flat and had been since her parents' death. She reached over to the picture frame lying face down on the end table and stood it up. Slowly blinking away tears, she stared at a snapshot Meg had taken of Nicole and her parents last summer. She smiled wistfully. They'd finished moving Nicole's stuff into her apartment when the photo was taken. Tired, covered in dirt and sweat, the three of them posed in front of a stack of boxes. Blinking harder, Nicole carefully stood the frame upright on the end table and put on a brave smile, only to find David staring at the picture, understanding in his expression. It was the understanding which undid her. She squeezed her eyes closed and clapped her hand over her mouth to keep from crying aloud. Several deep breaths later, she was able to remove her hand. "I'm sorry," she said, eyes still closed.

"You never have to apologize for how you feel."

She smiled gratefully. "Thank you." She opened her eyes, staring down at her clasped hands. "I... my parents died in a car accident recently. Things are getting easier, but sometimes... I still have trouble looking at photographs of them." She gestured to the overturned picture frames scattered throughout the room.

David noticed the picture frames for the first time. They blended in so well with their surroundings. Several had ornaments, or other picture frames standing in front of them. Looking back at Nicole, he was pleased to see she'd almost regained her composure. She fell right in when he changed the subject to a more mundane topic.

David listened to her talking, contributing to the conversation from time to time, for what seemed like hours. The chiming of a clock marked the passing of an hour and David reluctantly admitted to himself it was too late to continue their conversation, as much as he loved the sound of Nicole's voice. It would be selfishness on his part to keep her up any later. "I should be going. I should let you get some sleep." He stood up and walked to the door.

"Um, okay. I appreciate you coming by." Quickly, she followed him to the door, subduing the urge to touch him. Her breath caught in her throat. If only she didn't have to let him go. Just having him near was such a comfort. "Good night."

David smiled and took her hand, kissing her fingers. "Good night." He had to admit to some satisfaction when she sucked in a breath as his lips touched her fingers. He'd have to remember to thank Mark for teaching him that little move. It was one of his only charming traits, and women loved it. Most importantly, *this* woman loved it.

Nicole watched as he disappeared down the hall, before closing and locking her door. One little late-night visit from her neighborhood rescuer, and she was putty. How did he make her react so strongly in so short a time? Unable to come up with any real answers to the question, she made her way back to the couch and plopped down on the cushions with a sigh. Whatever this was, it was definitely exciting.

Nicole stayed up a little longer, reading the books from the library, a couple of magazines, and anything else she could find, anything to put off going to sleep. She even allowed herself to think about David some more, but she still couldn't come to any conclusions about him. Eventually, despite her efforts, sleep found her.

SHE WAS SURROUNDED by an inky blackness which draped over her like a heavy cloak. Sensations washed over her, but she couldn't see a thing.

She felt weightless one second and heavy the next. It seemed to be a terrifying roller coaster, one she couldn't get off. Stray bursts of light appeared, providing brief moments of illumination where she could see her surrounding slightly. She was in a seat, with identical seats to her left side and in front of her. Thunder shook the walls and vibrated through her body. A jagged bolt of lightning cut through thick storm clouds, outside the window to her right.

The sound and the light abruptly came together, drowning out everything else. A steady drumming sound, which made her think of some heavy object hitting metal, surrounded her and she crouched down on the floor between the seats, covering her ears and squeezing her eyes shut to avoid the crescendo.

There were people there, in the darkness. She could hear one of them, a woman, offering soothing words of comfort between deafening blasts of thunder. The woman's voice was close. She was on the floor, too. In the distance, she could hear people arguing, but it was t too loud to make out what they were saying.

A sensation of weightlessness overwhelmed her again. The floor dropped away from under her. She clung to the arm of her chair and pulled herself back into her original seat. Then, the world shifted again, and her body slammed into the metal frame around the cushion. Her body jerked once more, nearly slipping back to the floor, before the shifting stopped, and she was able to relax. There was another flash of light, brighter than before, followed by a large booming sound. Her body tumbled forward, her head hitting the back of the seat in front of her, before she landed on the floor. She gripped the metal base of a chair as everything shook and screeched around her. Her body continued to shake long after everything else was still.

Determining her orientation in relation to her surroundings was nearly impossible. She'd lost her grip on the chair during the chaos. There was no lightning from the window. The thunder was far away. The voices were quiet. With dizziness overwhelming her senses, she closed her eyes and gave in to the darkness.

NICOLE GRABBED the arm of the couch with one hand and the back of the couch with the other. The book she'd fallen asleep reading fell from her lap to the floor. She picked it up, trying without much success to straighten the bent pages, and placed it on the end table. She noticed her hands were shaking, and she was covered in a cold sweat. Her breathing was erratic, her thoughts still jumbled.

She took a couple of deep breaths and checked the clock. It was almost the same time she'd woken up last night, give or take a half hour. It never failed, once the dreams started coming, they began almost like clockwork. They always seemed to come in the darkest hour of the night, too. She always woke up, cold, sweaty, frightened, and alone in the darkness.

Last night had been different though; she'd had the wolf to keep her company and help her get back to sleep. For once, she hadn't been alone.

His presence had been a comfort, and having him there helped distract her. She hadn't felt so alone, which was a welcome change. Even if he was just a wolf, he'd made her feel better.

If only he was with her now, she could hold him, listen to his breathing. She wouldn't have to be alone with the nightmare. Maybe he would be there again, asleep on the balcony, waiting for her to let him in. She tried to dismiss the thought but found herself going to the balcony doors anyway.

She pulled open the doors and was greeted with an empty balcony and a dark night. He wasn't there. She leaned against the railing and released an exhausted sigh. She'd just have to deal with the nightmares on her own.

She turned to go inside but stopped when she heard a sound coming from the fire escape. It sounded like claws clicking against the metal steps and her heart skipped a beat. She turned to the fire escape and saw the wolf climbing the last couple of steps onto her balcony. Forgetting her resolution to deal with the nightmares on her own, she ran over to the wolf and threw her arms around him. "You came back!"

He nuzzled her neck and it almost seemed as if he hugged her back.

"Would you mind coming inside with me for a little while? I could really use the company." Her voice sounded unsteady to her own ears.

To her relief, he padded inside as quickly as he had the night before. She closed the balcony doors and turned back to the wolf to find him sitting at her feet, looking up at her. She sat down on the floor beside him and hugged him close, threading her fingers through his fur. The wolf quickly warmed her after the cold outside. She rested her cheek on his side and finally relaxed.

How long they stayed like that, she didn't know. She could feel the wolf's even breathing and his heartbeat pulsed through her, until she wasn't sure which beat was hers and which belonged to him. His fur was soft against her skin. There was something about holding another living creature close that made the world seem better, not so overwhelming and her fears dissipated and somehow, she could accept the comfort easier from this wolf than from anyone else. He wouldn't think any less of her for her weaknesses. He offered comfort without asking her to divulge her fears and problems. He was just what she needed right now. "Oh, Wolf, I don't know what I'd do without you."

She stiffened the second the words left her lips. Even if she'd been thinking it, she wished she hadn't put it into words. Thinking about him as a comfort, and thinking she needed him were two different matters. He was nice to have around, but she didn't need the wolf, and she would manage just fine even if he never showed up again.

She ignored the momentary ache in her chest and shook

her head. "I need some sleep." She got to her feet and walked into the bedroom, determined to face her fears. She couldn't let them control her.

Fear tightened its grip as she entered the darkened room and she stopped. What if she immediately started having the nightmare again? As long as she was awake, she didn't have to worry about it, but the second she closed her eyes and slept, her control over the situation was over. She would be completely at the mercy of her nightmares.

Rubbing her tired eyes, she realized she didn't really have a choice in the matter. She needed to sleep. Even now, the desire to close her eyes and rest was pulling at her. Her fear was great, but the need for sleep was stronger.

Accepting that she couldn't control what would happen, , she took a deep breath and slipped under the covers, closing her eyes. She almost shrieked when a warm weight settled against her feet and a range of irrational fears related to the nightmare raced through her head before she could stop them. Gathering the reins of her imagination and shoring up her courage, she snuck a peek at the bottom of the bed.

The wolf lifted his head, looking completely innocent and suddenly opened his jaws in a big yawn, before he lay his head down on his front paws and shut his eyes.

Nicole released a nervous laugh. It was only the wolf, not some manifestation of her fears come to haunt her while she was awake. More convinced than ever that her fears had no grounds in reality, she spent a minute trying to decide whether she should let the wolf stay on the bed. The decision came swiftly. He was so adorable all curled up at her feet and there was no harm in letting him stay there. Besides, she didn't have the heart to disturb him She yawned and closed her eyes, drifting off to sleep.

* * *

DAVID THREW another rock at the lake. It skipped three times before sinking beneath the water. "I don't know what I'm going to do. I can't stop thinking about her."

Mark had never seen David like this before. It had been years since David let anything get under his skin. Mark sighed, he didn't want to see his friend get hurt, but he didn't know what he could do for him. "Before you do anything, maybe you should tell her the truth." Mark flicked a rock over the water, and it skipped five times before sinking.

"I know I probably should, but she hardly knows me. If I tell her the black wolf and I are one in the same, she's liable to call the guys in white coats to take me away." Two skips.

"Maybe not. You said she's reacted well to the wolf." Four skips.

"You know as well as I do, a human friendly with our wolf form doesn't always translate to easily accepting we're shape changing werewolves." Mark nodded his acceptance of that truth. Eric sighed. "Even if she can accept that without freaking out, I've been in her apartment, at night, while she's sleeping. When she finds out that was me, she could feel betrayed and lied to."

One skip.

"She probably will." Mark laughed at the frustrated look David shot him. "I think you should let her get to know you, grow more comfortable in your company Why don't you take her out, maybe go to the fair in Starview? Fairs are always a good place to relax and get to know someone without the pressure of it seeming as if it's a date." Six skips.

"Maybe." David considered his friend's advice for a moment or two and decided it just might be a good idea. He smiled. "I'll ask her." Eight skips.

* * *

Nicole glanced up from her papers and listened to ensure she really had heard a knock at the door. A second knock confirmed it. Putting aside her books, she stood and stretched before going to answer the knock. She yanked open the door to find David standing on the other side, that beautiful smile of his lighting up his entire face. "Hey, I thought I'd stop by to see how you were doing."

Her lips curled into a big smile and she realized it was the first time she'd smiled all evening. "I'm doing okay, except for this paper I'm working on."

"Can I help?" he asked eagerly.

The offer caught her off guard. Was he serious? No one had ever volunteered to help her with a paper before. "Um... yeah, I guess," she responded hesitantly, "if you really want to."

David's smile broadened and he stepped through the doorway. Nicole was about to close the door when she noticed him stepping into the room awkwardly, and she could have sworn he was trying to keep her from seeing something. Before she could question his odd behavior, he spoke.

"I have something for you." He pulled a stuffed animal, a wolf, from behind his back. "I noticed you seem to have an affinity for wolves." He motioned to the decor. "I thought he could watch over you when I'm not around."

Nicole took the wolf, holding it close to her chest and blinked away a tear. She threw her other arm around David's neck and squeezed tightly. David wrapped his arms around her and he tightened his hold as he hugged her back. The air seemed to vibrate all around them, as if she and David were surrounded by a sphere of warmth and energy.

After a moment, they moved apart, both breathing deeply and Nicole's skin flushed. The look in David's eyes was enough to let her know he'd experienced the exact same thing and she felt closer to him than she'd ever done to anyone in her life. "Thank you. This is one of the kindest gifts anyone has ever given me." Her voice broke on the last word. She found she couldn't completely hide her response to his intense gaze and the strong emotions running through her body.

"I'm glad you like it." David had noticed the catch in Nicole's voice, and he forced a lightness into his words and eyes. If she felt half of what he was struggling with right now, he could hardly blame her for being a little over-whelmed. The least he could do was to back off a little bit and give her some breathing room. In all honesty, he needed the breathing room as much as she did.

Nicole breathed a little easier when David offered her a playful grin. "I love it."

He smiled broadly. "Okay, so you said you were working on a paper?"

"Yeah." She wiped a tear from the corner of her eye and walked across to where piles of papers and books were spread out over the floor. Sitting down in front of the pile, she started sorting through some of the papers, still clutching the toy wolf. She found she didn't want to let go of it. "I'm still trying to get a clear focus for my paper. I'm thinking about something about how to find your purpose in the world and help people without giving away all your worldly possessions and meditating in the wilderness for years or putting yourself in immanent danger of death, or something like that."

"Immanent danger of death?" he quirked an eyebrow. "You mean like trying to expose pollution and nearly getting killed?"

"What? No. Maybe. Not really. I was thinking people who travel to countries at war and do relief work, or doctors and nurses who take care of sick people in epidemics. How do you reconcile wanting to be a good person and help those in need with the desire to have indoor plumbing and central air conditioning, and not eat bugs in a jungle or get beheaded by some militant crazy person in another country?"

"You're trying to do things to help clean up your environment. That has to count for something, right?"

"I know cleaning up our river and lake will be a good thing, and it will definitely help the people who swim in the water and get sick, but there are places in the world where the water doesn't just give you a rash. Children die from drinking water that isn't clean. Families are persecuted for their religious beliefs. People are dying of curable illnesses. Can we fulfill our purpose and become the best version of ourselves if we don't do something to ease the suffering of all the people in the world who face injustice and adversity on a daily basis?"

David rubbed his chin thoughtfully. "You can't help everyone, and that's okay. Humanity is like a big family. People always wonder how big families work. How does one mom and dad take care of ten kids with all the laundry, dishes, cleaning, cooking, etc.? They do it by sharing the load. Everyone in the family does something. Everyone helps out in some little way. It may not look like much on the surface, but if everyone does a little, the work gets done."

"Okay," she mulled over his words, "but how am I

helping do my little part if I'm in my apartment eating ice cream and playing video games while other people are rescuing children from sex traffickers or relocating refugees from religious persecution and genocide? It feels like I'm just hiding from the world and all it's problems."

Her words struck a spear at his conscience. Here she was worried she wasn't doing enough to be a good person, and he had been actively hiding for decades, without ever once thinking about how he could help anyone else. It was a sobering thought. "We can all probably do more than what we do, but that doesn't mean small gestures are meaningless. If everyone ran off to fight the good fight across the world, there would be no one to grow food, develop medicines or life saving technology, fund relief efforts, or provide homes for refugees and orphans once they're saved. Everyone has a part of play, but it isn't the same part."

"What was that about 'small gestures?'" Nicole scrambled to sort through her books and notes. "Small gestures," she repeated. "Small gestures have meaning, Oh, where is it?" she blew out a frustrated sigh. "I know I read something like that somewhere. Here it is!" she held up a small blue book with the face of a nun on the cover. "There was this saint who taught about living a holy life in little ways. She folded laundry and stuff like that, like what you said about the 'humanity as a big family' thing." Nicole pulled out a pencil and notepad and began writing down notes.

An hour later, she had a thesis and a good idea of where the rest of the paper was going. With a satisfied smile, she gathered her work and added everything to the stack of books on the end table. "Would you like me to top off your drink?" she asked, clambering to her feet.

"Sure."

She took their cups into the kitchen area. "Why don't you see if you can find anything on the television?"

"Okay. Any preference?"

"Oh, I don't care." Nicole finished refilling their drinks and lit a couple of aromatherapy candles, before sitting down beside David on the floor. "Find anything good?"

He looked deeply into her eyes when he took his glass. "Yes... oh, you mean on TV." He turned back to the television. "How about this?"

Nicole's cheeks warmed. She turned her attention to the screen, grateful for a diversion. "Oh, Labyrinth is on! I love that movie."

"You do?" David sounded surprised.

"Yeah, it's one of my favorite movies."

He smiled. "Why do you like it so much?"

"Oh, I don't know." She thought about the question for a moment. He seemed legitimately interested, so she should give him an honest answer. "I guess because it's so much fun. It's got magic and suspense. It reveals a world where normal rules don't apply. For instance, there can be thirteen hours on a clock face. Walls can appear out of nowhere. Doorknockers can talk back to the person who wants to get inside. It's everything the real world isn't."

"But everything she saw, she already had, before she went in the labyrinth. It was with her all along, in the real world," David pointed out.

Nicole couldn't hide her surprise. "You know the movie?"

"Yeah, I've watched it a few times. I like it because of the challenges she needs to face. She has to use her mind to solve the riddle with the card guys. She's got to trust her instincts with all the creatures she meets, but she also needs to realize things aren't always going to be what they appear.

And she needed to learn not to expect everything to be fair. It's one of my favorite movies".

"You're kidding."

"No." He looked sheepish. "I can quote just about every line."

"Oh, really?" She challenged and leaned forward. "Prove it."

He smiled back. "'I have sworn with my life's blood, none shall pass this way without my permission!'"

Nicole leaned forward and grinned mischievously. "'May we have your permission?'" David noted her tone had a sultry edge to it, in far contrast to the way the line was actually delivered in the movie.

"'Well I, uh,'" He nearly forgot he was supposed to be quoting a movie and stumbled with bated breath. "'Yes?'"

Nicole laughed and kissed his cheek. "Don't worry. I won't tell the goblin king about the kiss. We wouldn't want you being sent to the land of stench."

David laughed. "At least I'd be a prince."

The both laughed and settled in for the show. As the credits ran across the screen, she looked at David and smiled. "I can't remember the last time I've had this much fun."

"Me either." David lapsed into silence for a moment or two before he spoke again, the words coming out in a rush. "Would you like to go to the fair in Starview tomorrow night?" There – he'd done it – he'd asked her to go out.

Nicole thought for a second or two. It had been a long time since she'd been to a fair, and she didn't have any plans. Why not? "Sure, I'd love to."

David smiled broadly. "Great." He turned back to her and his breath caught in his throat. When had her face gotten so close to his? He could feel her warm breath against his own lips and his heart started to thump.

Nicole found herself staring into David's beautiful eyes and frightened of the rush of emotions she experienced she started to panic. As much as she wanted to kiss him, it was too soon for her. She cleared her throat and turned her head. Snatching up their cups, she got up and hurried over to the sink. "What time would you want to leave for the fair tomorrow?" she asked over the sound of running water.

"How about seven?" David said softly in her ear. She was startled by his proximity, she hadn't heard him approaching.

He placed his hands on her shoulders and turned her around to face him but he saw the apprehension in her eyes, the apprehension that was always there. For a few hours, it had dissipated, but now it was back. If only he could find a way to make it go away for more than a couple of hours at a time. "I should go."

"Are you sure?" Suddenly, Nicole found she didn't want him to leave.

"Yes." He smiled and cupped his hand against the side of her face. "You have the wolf to keep you company, after all."

She wondered briefly how he could know about the black wolf, before she realized he meant the stuffed wolf he'd given her earlier. She smiled. "Yeah, I do. Thank you again."

"No problem." He let his hand drop and stepped back. "I'll see you tomorrow."

She walked him to the door. He gently took her hand and kissed her fingers and her heart skipped another beat when he looked up at her over her fingers. "Until tomorrow." His breath caressed her fingers before he let go of her hand and left.

Nicole put away her books and checked the clock. It was

late, so she checked the balcony, and sure enough, the wolf was waiting there. This time, when she went to sleep, one hand was on the black wolf, and the other was holding the stuffed wolf David had given her. She didn't have any bad dreams.

8

"What are you doing?"

Artemis jumped at the abruptness of the question and the sharp tone. Taking a deep breath to calm his racing heartbeat, he turned in the direction the voice had come from. As usual, he was playing games with Artemis, blurring his form in mist and shadows. It was a successful intimidation tool. Even after all this time, it could still affect Artemis far more than he was comfortable with. "What does it look like I'm doing? I'm watching the girl."

The shadowy form solidified, inches from Artemis' face. "I would recommend a more civil tone in my presence. I'm in a good mood today, but you might not be so lucky next time."

Artemis visibly gulped and a slow smile crept over his face just before he faded back into the shadows. "Now, as I was saying, why are you just watching her? Don't you think it's about time you approach her? After all, she's just a girl, a child; defenseless in her ignorance."

"She is rarely alone," Artemis said defensively. "That one is always watching her." He pointed to the shadow of a man, crouched low in the far away trees. As Nicole moved, the man moved to follow her. "David follows during the day and the wolf is with her at night."

"Very well. Since you feel incapable of taking on that whelp, I will see to it they are separated. But I warn you, be ready to take advantage of the situation." With that, he was gone.

Artemis turned his attention back to Nicole in disgust. "Watch your tone," he muttered. "I'd like to tell him just what *he* can watch."

He watched as Nicole paused to tie her shoelace. Her foot propped up on a bench, she took a thermos from her bag and drank some of its contents.

Artemis experienced a momentary burst of nostalgia. She looked so much like her father when she turned just the right way. She reminded him of the way Richard had looked the night he'd come back from the war.

"Richard's home!" Artemis had cringed when those two words were yelled throughout the house. The excitement level rising throughout the house had been tangible. The Council members he'd been speaking to only moments before, left mid-sentence to greet Richard on his triumphant return from the war and beseech him once again to join their hallowed ranks. Artemis crumpled a napkin in his hand and threw it into the fireplace. The cloth ignited with a snap and burned swiftly.

Artemis walked through the main hall, coming to a halt at the edge of the entry hall, tucked in behind the crowd of well-wishers gathered to talk to Richard. Unnoticed, he watched Richard smile and hug everyone, even the servants. Honestly, the man had no sense of decorum.

"Come on in," Richard called into the darkness beyond the front door.

A woman slowly entered. Artemis stared at her familiar face for a moment, trying to place it. Other than a small shock of white hair at one temple, she was a picture of youth and beauty. "Mara!" his mother cried, gathering the woman into a hug.

Mara smiled weakly and gracefully removed herself from the embrace. "You didn't tell me so many people would be here," she whispered to Richard. He shrugged as he was pulled into another conversation by the acting head of the Council, Vardum.

Artemis tried to listen in on Richard's conversation, but his mother had pulled Mara to the side, closer to Artemis and started talking her ear off, questioning her on what she had been doing, where she'd met up with Richard and a million other inconsequential questions. All he could hear was their voices.

As they spoke, he finally realized where he knew Mara from. She was the woman his father had been such good friends with, when Artemis and Richard were still children. For some reason he didn't understand, his father and mother had always loved Mara, always tried to make her feel welcome. But for some reason, years ago, she'd stopped coming by.

Artemis hadn't heard anyone mention her name in a very long time.

"That must have been horrible," his mother announced, responding to something Mara had said regarding an explosion and some children.

"I'm just grateful Richard and Marcus were the one who found me and tended my wounds."

"And the children?" his mother asked cautiously.

"All but one of them lived. Luckily, I was able to get them out in time." Mara took his mother's hand in hers and looked down at her sympathetically. "I was very sad to hear about Ari's death."

His mother swallowed hard and blinked away tears at the

mention of his father. "Thank you. But I know he is at peace. He died helping others, fighting for a cause he believed in. And I'm sure he would be very pleased to know you found your way back to us. He always hated how things ended the way they did."

"As did I."

His mother shook their joined hands emphatically and smiled broadly. "But you're here now. It's fate, that's what it is. Now, let's go and see about getting you something to eat. You must be famished after your long journey."

Mara smiled at her exuberance and let herself be led toward the kitchen.

With them gone, Artemis inched toward Richard. Many of the people gathered had congregated into groups around the room and others had stared to retire for the night, leaving more room to move around.

"Are you sure you won't reconsider?" he heard Vardum ask Richard.

Richard sighed and leaned against the wall. "I'm sure. Maybe someday, but right now, don't feel ready to take a place on the Council. My father was a wise man. I can't even begin to fill his place. You should find someone more deserving. I am honored, honestly, but I don't feel worthy of such great responsibility. I have done nothing to warrant your trust and I don't want to obtain this position because of who my father was. I want to join the Council when the position is offered to me based on my own merits, when I believe I deserve it."

Vardum laid a hand on his shoulder and smiled wistfully. "The fact that you would refuse the position based on that reasoning proves how worthy you are of it, but I will honor your wishes and back off for the time being. Remember, if you ever change your mind, there will always be a place on the Council for you."

Artemis clenched his fists and hurriedly left the room. This *was ridiculous! He was eldest born. He should be the one asked to fill his father's place! Not Richard! That ungrateful little brat didn't even want the position, and here they were, all fawning over him, trying to make him take it. It was pathetic and wrong.*

He paused at the servants' quarters when he heard his name mentioned. Listening closely, he fought the urge to rip out all their throats.

"Would you believe, Master Artie was actually expecting the position to be offered to him!" One of the servant's laughed, crudely using the vulgar shortening of his name which Richard was so fond of using.

"What do you expect?" another servant responded. "He never has been the brightest of fellows."

Others laughed and threw in their own additions to that statement.

"Or strongest."

"Or bravest."

"He didn't even go off to the war to reclaim his father's body," the first voice announced. "What kind of coward does something like that? He stays at home while his father and little brother are risking their lives at war, doing the honorable thing?"

Artemis backed away before he could do something he was fairly certain he wouldn't regret, and continued on his way to the library. Closing the door behind him, Artemis slumped down in a chair by the fire and started to read.

"It was utterly disgraceful, the way they were talking about you back there."

Artemis spun about to discover a man sitting in a chair in the corner of the room, bathed in shadows created by the burning fire. He hadn't been there before, and a glance confirmed the door was still closed, as he'd left it. So how had this man gotten into the library without Artemis' knowledge?

"I could help you if you want," the man continued.

"Help me with what?" Artemis narrowed his eyes, hoping to get a better look at the man, but all he could see was vague outlines in the shadows.

"I could help you gain the respect you deserve, the power you seek."

"And how are you going to do that?" Artemis opened his book again and leaned back in the chair. He'd been trying to get respect his entire life, and for nothing. Not even the servants respected him. He might as well leap off a high bridge and be done with it.

"But what would that accomplish?" the man asked.

Artemis turned to stare at the man. "What?"

"If you kill yourself, they'll still laugh at you, only louder and without restraint. With my help, you will win their respect, at last. No more, 'Richard the hero'. No more, 'Artemis the coward'." The man watched Artemis pointedly, convincing him he was referring to the comments the servants had made.

A shiver rippled down Artemis' spine. "Who are you, and why would you help me?"

The man in the shadows shrugged. "Merely someone who thinks we could be mutually beneficial to one another. I have the power to grant you something you want, and you have the power to get something I want."

Artemis' eyes glazed over and his head was filled with images – images of himself walking into a room where the entire household had gathered to greet him. Visions of Vardum, begging him to join the Council while Richard stood off to the side, the dutiful little brother. A slow smile curled his lips. "Where do we start?"

Artemis shook his head to clear the memory and followed Nicole to her next class. He'd come too far to back out now. Soon, his hard work would finally pay off.

* * *

MARA CLOSED the balcony door and suppressed a shudder. Something was out there. She could sense it, but she couldn't make sense of what it might be. Why couldn't she get a clear impression of it? Nothing had ever withstood her probing before. Whatever it was, it was incredibly strong, because she could sense it without even trying. An icy chill crept over her again, even though the balcony doors were closed. She needed to get to the bottom of this. Evil seemed to permeate the air and she needed to find its source before something horrible happened.

She sat on the carpeted floor with her legs crossed, letting the fragrance of the incense focus her senses and help clear her mind. She worked through her breathing exercises slowly, focusing on her breathing and the smell of the incense. She took herself deeper, opening to whatever she might perceive, careful to keep her thoughts to a minimum. She could pinpoint the darkness very clearly now. Carefully, she studied it, trying to learn more about it. A sensation of pressure built up around her, and she quickly backed off. She'd have to find another way. Before she'd gotten very far though, the pressure increased again, this time far stronger. Mara blinked and waited for her vision to clear, realizing that she was staring up at the ceiling, with the floor beneath her back. Slowly, she sat up and surveyed her surroundings. The incense had already burned out and she decided to fix some tea and rest some before trying again. With that plan in mind, she headed to the kitchen, pausing at a small wall mirror on the way.

She studied herself closely. The streak of white still stood out against her otherwise black hair. It was the only sign which revealed her age. Her face was still smooth and young, but perhaps if someone looked closely enough into her eyes, they'd see some of the many demons harbored there – but no one ever looked that close. She laughed. Most people thought she purposefully added the white streak to her hair for the effect. After all, no one else of their kind had lived long enough to develop any such signs of aging. Why should they assume any different of her? She shook her head at the young reflection staring back at her. Why indeed? She took a deep breath and went to make the tea. She had a lot of work to do.

RODNEY PUT down the phone and leaned his elbows on the desk, resting his face in his hands. He sighed in frustration. He had to find a way to get rid of Nicole Cameron and the evidence against him, but so far, nothing was working out. The girl always had people around her! He couldn't get anyone near her place, not since the cops had started sending patrol cars around there all the time. He either had to risk snatching her in public, or risk the cops seeing him at her place. Neither option was particularly appealing.

"Giving up so soon?"

Rodney jumped and hurriedly surveyed the room for the source of the voice. A figure stood in one corner, hidden by the shadows.

"Who's there?" How could someone get into his office without him knowing it?

"How soon they forget."

Abruptly, Rodney realized this was the same voice he'd heard in the street that night, on the way back from the bar. He'd almost convinced himself he'd imagined the whole thing, but now he wasn't so sure.

"I am very much real," the voice said, sending chills up Rodney's spine. "Now, about Miss Cameron. As I said before, you need to get a little creative. Surely you remember how you dealt with her parents? Draw from that experience."

Rodney's eyes widened. "How could you know about that? No one knew." If this guy had found out what he'd done, that meant others could. If that happened, he would be completely ruined.

The only response was a low laugh, and the figure disappeared into the shadows. Rodney gathered up his nerve and walked over to that corner where the figure had stood, but there was nothing there, leaving Rodney to wonder once again if he'd imagined it all.

Those haunting words echoed in his head. *I am very much real.* Rodney shivered and retreated back to his desk to figure out some way to get rid of Nicole Cameron. Maybe then, whoever the shadowy voice was would leave him alone.

* * *

HE SLIPPED THROUGH THE SHADOWS, unseen. Lightly touching a stop sign, he turned it to face in the opposite direction. A short time later, the sound of squealing tires and honking horns caught his ear. Unfortunately, the cars didn't seem to have hit each other though. What a pity. Oh well – the night was still young. He chuckled.

He heard some small animals running off, rushing to escape him, and he grinned at the terror they were experiencing. Animals were the only ones he couldn't completely hide his presence from – except for her. Her gentle mind probed again, and he pushed her away, wondering how many times he would have to do it before she would give up. That last attempt had been significant. He was impressed she'd kept at it this long. Still, she would stop when she learned her attempts were futile. He wasn't about to let her discover his identity, not until he was ready. By then, he would finally have what was rightfully his, and she wouldn't have a chance against him.

He gazed up at Nicole Cameron's window and a smile spread on his face. These long years of waiting would finally be over.

He took a folder from his robe and looked at the single file he'd withheld from Artemis, absentmindedly pushing away another mind probe, in the manner one would swat at an insect. He opened the file and studied the picture. Meghan Freeman didn't look a thing like her father, which was fortunate for her. It had been quite the stroke of luck, finding that information regarding Nicole's one good friend. It was certainly interesting how things had a way of turning out. He didn't know exactly how he'd present this information, and he didn't really think it would assist with his plans, but he could still have some fun with it. He chuckled softly. It was so much fun manipulating people, because they were so easily led. He tucked the folder back beneath his robe and walked away. He had to admit, he was really beginning to enjoy himself.

* * *

THE CLOCK on the wall ticked loudly, echoing through the otherwise silent room. The light above Mark flickered and made a popping noise before finally giving out. "Wonderful," he muttered. At least the sun was coming up, so he could see well enough. The sunlight made the room appear much different to how it had been under the artificial light. The blinds on the window were cast their shadows across the room. He glanced outside and saw the many colors swirling in the sky as the sun passed the horizon and began its inexorable march toward the sky. Some things never changed, no matter how long one lived. The sun always rose in the morning and it always set at night. Mark turned his attention away from the sunrise and got back to the matter at hand.

He sorted through his papers, making sure he'd finished everything. Satisfied he was done, he put the papers aside and pulled out an unmarked file folder from his personal investigations. 'Nicole Cameron' was written clearly on the first page. He stared at Nicole's picture and thought briefly about Richard. The resemblance between them was easily apparent.

The artist in him was itching to do a sketch of Nicole's pretty features. Maybe he'd get the chance sometime. He scanned the words below the picture. If only he could prove Steagel had something to do with her adoptive parent's death, then he could remove that threat. Perhaps they should have told her the truth from the beginning, then she would have been able to take better care of herself.

No, David was right. If they hadn't hidden her away as they did, she would have been at greater risk for years. They would have needed to watch her a lot more closely, taking away most of her freedom. At least this way, she'd been allowed to have a normal childhood.

But now she was no longer a child. It was time she knew where she came from. She should know about her real parents. At least David had agreed with him on that point.

He heard footsteps, followed by the door opening, and Tony entered. Tony was a young cop with all the enthusiasm which went along with youth. He was always excited to take on a new assignment, but this was only his first couple of weeks on the job. Before long, he'd be just as cynical as everyone else. It was too bad, because Mark kind of liked the kid. He reminded him a lot of himself, before his wide-eyed enthusiasm had been snuffed out by years of witnessing death and suffering.

"Hey," Tony said in surprise. "I thought I'd be the only one crazy enough to be here this early. How long you been here?"

Mark glanced back down at the file. "A while."

"Weren't you wearing the same thing yesterday?" Tony squinted in the dim light. "You haven't been here all night, have you?"

"I had a lot of paperwork to do."

"Have you at least gotten some sleep?"

"I'm not all that tired."

Tony shook his head and whistled in amazement. "Man, even I'm not that energetic. Do you do this a lot?"

"Sometimes." Mark shrugged, still reading over the file and only half paying attention to the conversation.

Tony just shook his head and settled at his own desk, starting on his own stack of paperwork.

MEGHAN TRUDGED up the last couple of steps to her apartment and unlocked the door, trying twice before she realized she was turning the key in the wrong direction. She let her bag slip down to the floor and turned the television on, unable to stand the silence. She flipped through a few channels before picking one and going to heat up some leftovers. Pouring a glass of water, she jumped up on the counter and let her legs swing back and forth as she contemplated what to do for the evening. Her options were TV, sleeping, eating, sleeping, a shower, sleeping, homework, and sleeping. She thought about the homework, deciding she didn't absolutely have to do it tonight. She could goof off and eat large quantities of chocolate instead.

The microwave dinged, and she jumped down from the counter and grabbed the food. Deciding to flip through the channels once more before settling on a movie, she plopped down onto the couch and started eating. She paused in her channel surfing a few times, momentarily captivated by a program on the history of sex, one about celebrity homes, and an infomercial regarding some new workout machine.

Finally, she got up and started going through her movies. A piece of white paper lying near the door caught her eye, and she picked it up. It seemed as if it had been slid under the door, because she didn't recognize the paper.

She unfolded it slowly and read the note.

The paper fell from her hands, a chill rippling over her skin. Taking a deep breath, she knelt down and picked up the paper again. Reread the words carefully, there was no mistake.

The past never really dies.
—Tammy Knight

Carefully, she refolded the paper and clutched it in her hand. She needed to talk to someone about this. How could anyone know? Maybe whoever had slipped this paper under her door was still in the hall. After all, she had no idea when it was left. She went to the door and peered up and down the hall, but nobody was there. So much for that idea.

She studied the paper for another minute and decided to call Nicole. She was the only one Meg could possibly talk to about this.

She dialed Nicole's number and waited impatiently as the phone rang several times with no answer. That was strange, Nicole was usually always home at this time of day. Maybe she was doing research at the library.

Meghan reluctantly set down the phone and thought about what she should do. She didn't know who'd left this here, so she couldn't question them about it. She couldn't talk to Nicole, and there was no one else who would understand. It seemed her only option was to wait and see what happened. She hated the idea, but in this case, she had no other choice.

She was suddenly very cold. Absentmindedly, she turned up the heater and grabbed a sweater. She decided to do some of that homework, after all.

* * *

"Aaaaaaaaaaaaaaahhhhh!" Nicole yelled, the wind rushing up to meet her and blow her hair back. Her stomach seemed as if it was back where her head had been, but it felt great. She laughed giddily and looked over at David. His much shorter hair was standing straight in the air, and he was laughing, too.

A sudden jolt stopped their downward descent and her hair tumbled down, covering her face and momentarily blocking her vision. The hum of the ride grew softer, and her stomach started to settle back into its correct position as the ride ended.

The shoulder harness was lifted and David took hold of her hand, helping her stand. She stumbled anyway and fell up against him, laughing. He held her tightly, and she allowed herself to stay there, in his arms, enjoying the sensation. She looked up at him with what she knew was a goofy grin and found him grinning back. There was some emotion in his eyes, too, but she didn't allow herself to think about that too much. Tonight, no thinking was allowed.

She nodded when he asked her if she could stand and managed not to cry out in protest when his arms loosened from around her. Instead, she put her own arm around his waist and leaned up against him, as he led her to the next ride.

* * *

DAVID GLANCED over at Nicole as they walked up the steps to her apartment. The fair had been great and Nicole had really begun to relax by the end of the night. And she'd laughed – a lot. He loved spending time with her and after tonight, it seemed she felt the same way. After all, she'd agreed to go back with him the following night to see a concert at the fairgrounds. David reluctantly removed his arm from her shoulders when she unlocked the door. She pushed the door open and turned back to David. "I had a great time"

"Me too." A second later, her arms were wrapped around him. He recovered quickly from his surprise and hugged her back. After a minute, Nicole pulled away. "I'll see you tomorrow."

"Goodnight."

"Goodnight."

She closed the door and sighed. David wasn't the only

one she had surprised with that impetuous hug. She didn't generally go around hugging people, but she was glad she'd hugged him. It felt right. It felt so absolutely right to be in his arms. She relived every moment of the evening as she fell asleep, her two wolves nearby. She found herself still smiling the following morning.

9

Billy dropped the stack of books on his desk, creating a loud thud and unsettling a lot of dust. His hand closed on empty air when he attempted to catch a falling picture, and it hit the floor with a shattering sound. Carefully, he picked up the picture frame and gathered the broken pieces of glass. At least the picture hadn't been damaged. He stared at the smiling faces of him, Nicole, and his parents. It was the last photo they'd taken together, so long ago, yet it was the most recent picture he had of them. Dad had never liked professional photos that much. It had taken a long time to convince him to have one taken. Now, his parents were both gone.

He wondered how Nicole was doing with all of this. He hadn't spoken to her since before the funeral. He should never have left that to her to deal with, she deserved better than that. He should call her, but what good would that do? A few minutes on the phone to assuage his guilty conscience is all it would be. It wouldn't make up for anything.

He looked from the photo to his desk and sighed. Maybe

there *was* something he could do. With a new sense of purpose, Billy pulled out the phone book and started dialing.

* * *

NICOLE WAS ROUSED from the book she was reading by a knock at the door. She reluctantly set the book down and went to find out who it was. Before she'd even reached the door, she heard soft music starting to filter through her mind through her near telepathic connection with her best friend.. She smiled. They never shared thoughts with each other, but somehow Nicole was always able to hear whatever music or song Meg was thinking about when they were in close proximity..As soon as she opened the door, Nicole was greeted by Meg's cheerful face.

"Hello, Megnificent."

Meghan's face brightened considerably. "You haven't called me that in forever."

Nicole shrugged. "Well, it seems like a Megnificent kind of day."

Meg smiled. "Cool. So, are you busy?"

"No. Why?" Nicole asked suspiciously.

"I was wondering if you'd help me pick out a dress for that committee thing I'm going to on Friday. I don't have anything except formals and sundresses, and I'm going to be busy all week, so today is the only day I can shop for one." Meg plopped down on the couch, catching sight of the book Nicole had been reading. "So what's this one about? Bigfoot or the Bermuda Triangle?"

Nicole closed the door and joined Meg on the couch. "Actually, this one's about vampires, werewolves, and other paranormal creatures. So far, all it's done is come up with a hundred scientific reasons why none of them really exist. My parents could have written it."

Meg scrutinized Nicole. "What are you really looking for in all these books? Do you just want someone to agree with you, or do you want someone to convince you that your parents were wrong, and you're justified in thinking the way you do?"

"What are you talking about?" Nicole twirled a piece of the fringing on the couch around her finger and fought back the usual nauseated reaction to discussing her parents. Refusing to dwell on the bad thoughts, she concentrated only on the current conversation.

"Nicole, I saw how you were around your parents. Whenever they talked about paranormal studies being a waste of time, you started to doubt yourself. You could never bring yourself to argue with them, because you were too afraid they might be right."

Nicole squirmed uncomfortably. "So, what about getting you a dress?"

Meg sighed, conceding the topic for the moment and returning to her reason for coming over. "I figured we could hit Cleo's, but I've got to hurry, because I still have to find another source for my paper today."

"Okay, I'll get my purse."

They traveled in Meg's car to Cleo's Clothing Hunters, where there was always a large selection of dresses ranging from replica medieval gowns to simple sundresses. Meg and Nicole headed for one of the dress racks which held more formal attire and started searching.

A wisp of black material on a nearby rack caught Meg's eye. She ran her hand across the slinky material. It was like nothing she'd touched before. Pulling out the dress, she saw it had a plunging neckline and she suspected it revealed a lot more than it covered. It was exactly the type of dress a femme fatale in the movies might wear. A quick glance confirmed it was her size.

"I thought you were looking for a professional dress?" Nicole said from over Meg's shoulder.

"I am, but just look at it. Better yet, touch this material."

Nicole reached for the dress and ran her fingers over the material. It had to be the softest fabric she'd ever felt. And smooth... it was incredibly smooth and lightweight.. "Wow."

"I know. I've got to try it on, at least." Meg turned back to the other rack of dresses her purpose for being there, the black dress draped over her arm. "Oh, by the way – where were you yesterday evening? I tried to call." She suppressed the shudder which tried to escape at the thought of the note. She'd already convinced herself it was silly to get so worked up about it. She'd just gotten carried away. It had probably come from some whack job who happened across an old newspaper article about what happened and decided it would be a kick to mess around with her head. Still, she could feel goose bumps erupting over her arms.

"Oh, David took me to that fair in Starview. He's taking me again tonight. There's going to be a concert."

"Oooooh, he's taking you to a concert. This is getting serious."

"What's getting serious?" Nicole asked innocently from the other side of the clothes rack.

Meg shot her an incredulous look. "You and David, that's what."

"There is no me and David. Coverton is just being nice. That's just the kind of guy he is. He's nice, and considerate, and..."

"And sooooo cute," Meg finished for her.

Nicole chose her words carefully. "Yeah, I suppose he is a little attractive," she conceded.

"A little attractive?" Meg scoffed. "He's drop dead gorgeous."

"You think everyone is drop dead gorgeous."

"Maybe, but even you've got to admit I'm right this time."

Nicole wasn't about to let Meg know she completely agreed with her assessment of David's appearance. Admitting to her ever-growing attraction would mean she had to do something about it, and she wasn't ready for that just yet. Still, she couldn't help thinking about him.

"Hey, Nicole, are you listening?"

Nicole almost responded that she had been, but she knew Meg would only make her prove it. "I'm sorry, I guess I drifted off somewhere else."

"I'll say. Care to say where?"

"No. What were you saying?"

Meg shrugged. "What do you think of this one?" She held up a yellow dress which had an overcoat, making it the ideal dress for a professional look, yet easily switching to more casual event.

"It's perfect."

Meg took both dresses and tried them on, saving the black dress for last. It fit her like a second skin. "What do you think?"

Nicole studied her briefly before responding. "And you're planning on breaking how many laws?"

"Perfect." Meg twirled around a couple of times, admiring herself in the mirror.

The sound of a bell caught their attention. A woman walked through the beaded curtain separating the main store from the changing rooms out back. She had long, black wavy hair with a streak of white at the temple, and she wore a flowing dress in rich, dark purple. She had a presence about her which drew everyone's attention. Her eyes sparkled in the light and she had an ethereal look about her. She was the lady who owned the store, and Nicole had seen her many times before. Each time, Nicole was entranced by those eyes. It often seemed as if the woman was watching her, but then again, Nicole always felt as if she was being watched. Still, the woman's presence was unsettling.

The woman strode up to them and smiled at Meghan. "That dress does look lovely on you, my dear."

Meghan suddenly seemed more self-conscious. She ran her hands along the side of the dress, smoothing out imagined wrinkles and shifted her balance from one foot to the other. "Th— thank you."

"Are you going to buy it?" Nicole asked, trying to shake off her own apprehension.

Meg checked the price tag. "I don't know. I wasn't really planning on spending that much today."

"If you really love it, I could knock off twenty percent," the woman interjected.

"Really?" Hope sparked in Meg's eyes.

"Yes. It's been here a while, and it does look wonderful on you."

"Thank you!" Meg went back into the dressing room to change, leaving Nicole standing with the strange woman.

Nicole couldn't really pinpoint what made her so uncomfortable, the woman only appeared to be a couple of years older than she and Meg, but for some reason Nicole suspected the woman was much older, with knowledge to go along with her age.

"Sometimes it's good to trust one's instincts."

Nicole started at the woman's words. "Excuse me?"

The woman smiled briefly, then turned towards the

dressing room. "The dress. Your friend's instincts about that dress were good. Sometimes instincts can be stronger and more trustworthy than reason." She glanced back at Nicole. "Don't you agree?"

"I guess," Nicole responded cautiously. She had an odd certainty that they weren't just talking about the dress, but Meg came out before she could figure out what the woman really meant.

Nicole waited while Meg paid for her purchases, then followed her to the car. By the time Meg had balanced the bags against the car and dug out her keys, Nicole's mind had already turned to other things. Namely, David. Not even the strange shop owner could distract her for long from that subject. Then again, considering how her thoughts had been focused on such traumatic events not too long ago, a little obsession with a cute guy couldn't be such a bad thing.

"Hey, guys." John's voice boomed from further down the sidewalk. "What's up?"

"Just shopping. You?" Meg replied, just managing to catch her purse before it fell from the roof of the car.

"Actually, I was looking for Nicole. Here." Ignoring her confused expression, John handed her a cell phone. "This is from the SES. Don't worry," he added, "it's just a basic flip phone. I know you aren't into phones with all the bells and whistles."

"What?" She eyed the phone speculatively. "Why would the SES give me a cell phone?"

He glanced away, avoiding eye contact. "We were talking at the meeting last night about everything that's happened to you since you took those photos, and we all agreed you'd be safer with a cell phone on you."

"Whoa, what? Since when did *we* have a meeting last night?" Nicole demanded.

"It was a last-minute thing." He shrugged and his efforts to avoid her eye were even more noticeable.

"I can't take this." Nicole held the phone out to him, but he pushed her hand away. "The SES doesn't have money to spend on something like this," she argued.

John shook his head. "It was a unanimous vote. We want you to have it."

"A vote? You guys voted – on me! Is that why I didn't know about the meeting? Because it was about me?" This was too much. It wasn't enough for everyone to give her a hard time and worry over her while she was around. Now they were going out of their way to worry when she *wasn't* around. How did she go from the quiet girl who went about her life without drawing attention to herself, to someone who had people trying to kill her, other people holding meetings to discuss her and an amazing amount of attention from a cute guy and a wolf?

John looked uncomfortable. "We're just worried about you. After what happened to your par—" He stopped short, but the unfinished word hung in the air between them.

And suddenly, she understood. It wasn't about her at all. It never had been. This was about her parents. She was being pursued because of her parents, because she'd taken up their work with the SES. John and everyone else who missed them were being overprotective – not because of her so much as because they were still feeling raw after the accident. This was their way of coping.

After a moment, Nicole sighed and pushed back her aggravation. "I'm not my parents. I'm going to be fine." All the same, she tucked the cell phone into her purse and offered John a weak smile. She couldn't stay mad at him, after all, it was a very sweet– if misguided – gesture. With a small sense of satisfaction, she noticed John seemed relieved now that she'd taken the phone. At least she'd made one of them feel better.

"Before I forget," John said, changing the subject, "Meg, what are you doing tonight?"

"Why?" Meg hedged.

"I was wondering if you wanted to go to that club on 5th Street with me and some friends."

"Why, John Markham – are you asking me out?" Meg teased.

"I... no... I mean, I kinda... well, there's someone else I kind of was hoping that maybe we'd... start something. You know?"

"Really? Who?" Nicole smiled. John was a sweet guy, despite the aggravation he caused her. He deserved to meet someone nice who liked him back.

"Just... well... Susan.".

"Susan?" Nicole repeated, and she grinned.

"Yeah," He offered her a sheepish grin and shoved his hands into his pockets.

"Wait," Meg scrunched her face in thought, "is she the attorney you guys are always talking about?"

"Yeah," John grinned.

Meg offered him a triumphant smile. "Cool."

Nicole had to agree. The few times she'd spoken to Susan, she'd seemed really nice, and she appeared to like John well enough.

Meg held a hand to her hip. "Why are you asking me to go out with you and your friends, if you're interested in this Susan?"

"Yeah, and why aren't I invited?" Nicole teased. "Are you planning an orgy without me?" She put her hand to her chest. "Humph. I'm hurt. Really." She batted her eyelashes a couple of times for effect and threw a wink over to Meg.

Sure enough, Meg was smiling proudly at Nicole's very Meg-like response.

John shot Nicole a look but chose not to respond to the sarcasm. "I didn't invite you, because you always complain about how loud clubs. As for you," he turned back to Meg, "Susan knows this guy she wants to set you up with. He's a cop, his name is Mark."

Meg turned her attention back to John and started counting off fingers. "One, why would Susan want to set me up when we haven't even met? Two, what makes her think this guy is my type?"

John flushed. "I guess it's because I talk about you guys all the time. She said Mark is great, but he never goes out or seems to do anything outside of work. He's really devoted to helping people, which makes him an awesome guy, but he doesn't really take the time to take care of himself. I told her how you are tough, smart, loyal, always seizing the day, and she figured someone with a strong personality like yours would be able to get through to him."

"Oh." It was Meg's turn to have heated cheeks. "Well, the answer is, no."

"Why not?" John's brow crinkled in confusion.

"Got too much work to do. I'm working on about ten projects at once right now. Maybe another time."

John shrugged. "Okay. If you change your mind, we'll be there from eight 'til about ten."

"Okay, I'll keep it in mind."

John said his goodbyes and headed off to his own car and Nicole settled into the passenger seat of Meg's car. Now all the madness with John was over, her mind went straight back to daydreaming about a certain Mr. Coverton.

"Nicole," Meg's voice broke through her thoughts. "You know you can talk to me about anything, don't you?"

"I know."

"Do you want to talk about what's on your mind?"

"Not right now."

Meg indicated to turn a corner. "Is this about that David guy?"

Nicole swallowed heavily before she responded. "Yeah, it is, but I don't want talk about him right now. I mean, I do think about him a lot, but I don't really have everything figured out in my head yet. I need some more time to think about what I'm feeling before I talk about it. Do you understand?"

"Yeah, but you know, sometimes talking helps to figure things out." Meg cringed, knowing she should really learn to take her own advice.

"I do know, but I still need to work this out on my own first. Okay?"

"Okay." Meg pulled over in front of the apartment building and parked, leaning over to give Nicole a hug. "Call me if you need me."

"I will."

10

Nicole dropped the cell phone onto the couch and kicked off her shoes. "Okay," she muttered, "so what if they mean well, and they're just reacting to some underlying fear that I'll follow my parents to an early grave? What am I supposed to do with a cell phone?" Her parents were gone, so she didn't have anyone to keep track of her comings and goings. No one noticed if she didn't text when she arrived at school or came home for the night. Hers was a small town, and she knew it well, so GPS was unnecessary. She had her own professional camera, so she never saw the need to get an expensive phone to take pictures. She and Meg preferred hanging out in person to talking on a phone. Being on the phone for too long always gave Nicole a headache. Her ears were sensitive to loud sounds, and no matter how low she turned the volume on phones, they always bothered her eventually. And they cost money. She could put the money for a cell phone toward groceries or school books. She sat down, propping her feet up on the coffee table and started to fiddle with the cell phone's antenna.

She stared at the blank phone display and grimaced. Okay, she was probably being too hard on everyone but she couldn't seem to help herself, she was too used to being left alone. This center of attention thing was getting really old, real fast. She snapped the antenna back down and set the phone down on the end table. At least she didn't have to worry about being coddled tonight. John was out with friends, and Meg was busy with homework, so she was unlikely to be disturbed. A smile crept over her face. A night alone – this was exactly what she needed. No phone calls. No worrying friends. No pressure. Maybe, she could relax with a hot bath and watch a little TV 'til she fell asleep. Now there was a plan.

* * *

NICOLE TOOK one look at Meg on the other side of the doorway and said, "No."

"No, what?" Meg asked in confusion.

"You're here because you and John both have it in your heads that I need some type of bodyguard or something."

Meg rolled her eyes. "No, smart ass. I'm here because I thought you might like the company, and oh … I don't know, maybe because we're best friends, and I thought you might like to help me procrastinate with some ice cream and video games? But if you're not interested in Phish Food ice cream…." Meg waved the delectable ice cream pint through the crack in the door.

Nicole stared longingly at the treat and found herself salivating.

Meg smiled triumphantly. "That's what I thought."

"What game did you have in mind?" Nicole smiled in spite of herself and opened the door all the way.

"Nalagata Strike." Meg pulled out the fighter game Nicole had given her for her last birthday. They'd played it a lot the first couple of weeks, but then the accident happened, and Nicole hadn't been in a video game mood. "I am so going to kick your butt as Yoyamanae, the Elven Samurai." Meg's eyes twinkled.

"As long as I can play Groztu. I love that little imp."

Setting the game down, the two girls walked into the kitchen to serve the ice cream. Nicole started pulling out the various toppings they'd need, while Meg grabbed the bowls and spoons. "Hey, do you have any more of the Fudge Brownie ice cream left?" Meg asked.

"Do camels live in the desert?"

Meg chuckled. "That's my girl." Taking the toppings, Meg spooned generous servings of both flavors of ice creams into their bowls and covered the already rich treat with walnuts, chocolate syrup and whipped cream.

"Ahh... you do make the best sundaes ever." Nicole sighed appreciatively.

"I can't take all the credit. The ice cream does a lot of the work for me. You know, I heard somewhere once that ice cream is actually a temporary fix for being sad, or depression, or something."

"Really? But then, I suppose any girl over fifteen already knew that."

"Yeah," Meg grinned in agreement. "It temporarily raises the serotonin levels in the brain, I think."

"I don't really care what's in it or what it does, as long as it keeps on doing it." Nicole dripped some chocolate syrup onto her tongue and licked the bottom of her overfilled spoon. They both laughed as they headed back into the living room.

The girls watched some TV while they ate, not wanting

to get the game controllers sticky with the ice cream. When they were both done, Nicole gathered the bowls and headed back into the kitchen, leaving Meg watching some weird commercial with a football player dancing in a tutu, selling shampoo. "That's just weird," she mumbled to herself while she ran water into the dishes and dried her hands on a dishrag.

"Here he comes to save the day," Meg started to sing, and it was so loud, Nicole thought Meg had come into the kitchen with her.

She turned to comment on Meg's awful song choice, but to her surprise, Meg was still sitting in the living room. Nicole shook her head and turned off the kitchen light. It was so strange, Meg had sounded as if she was right behind her. She sighed and sat down beside her friend. Must be the unusually strong hearing everyone always accused her of having. "Why on Earth were you singing the theme song to Mighty Mouse?" she asked with a wry smile.

Meg looked momentarily taken back and shook her head. "Get out of my mind, Cameron."

Nicole blinked. "Wait... you mean I did it again?"

Meg nodded. Wow, they must really be on the same wave length lately. She'd never picked up this much from Meg before. "So, why were you thinking the theme song to Mighty Mouse?" she questioned.

Meg smiled. "Don't know. You know me, I'm a veritable jukebox of mismatched music."

Five hours later, they were still sitting on the couch, playing the video game. "So, why didn't you go out with John tonight?" Nicole asked as she barely got her fighter out of the corner before Meg's special hit her.

"I just had a lot of work to do tonight." Meg shrugged and grabbed the imp with a Class Seven grapple hold.

"Hence the five hour 'Video Game and Ice Creamathon'."Nicole gritted her teeth and finally broke the grapple, managing a nice combo in the process.

MEG'S only response was a special combo that had the screen lighting up with all the points she was racking up, leaving Nicole's fighter obliterated in the assault. "I win again," she announced triumphantly. That means you get to order the pizza."

"Pizza? It's II o'clock at night!"

"So? I skipped lunch." Meg shrugged.

"Meg, what's really going on?"

Meg sighed and put down her controller. "What do you mean?" She looked over at Nicole's pointed stare and leaned back on the couch. "I was worried about you. I was flipping through the channels on TV, and I saw some 'Cars Attacking People' or 'Spectacular Wrecks', or some show like that, and I got a bad feeling about you. Promise me you'll be extra careful."

"I promise," Nicole said sincerely, not even thinking of making light of her friend's comments.

A lot of the tension drained out of Meg with Nicole's words. "Good."

"You know, you could have just told me this over the phone. Then you could have gone out and met that guy John was talking about."

Meg shrugged. "You know I usually avoid bars anyway... unless a really cute guy is involved."

Nicole snorted. "I don't know why. It's not like you ever go out with any of them."

"What's that supposed to mean?"

"You love to flirt, but as soon as a guy starts to put off the

'I'm serious' vibes, you get so cold and closed off, it's like watching an ice wall literally go up in front of you. You were so cold to that last guy, I thought his face would shatter."

"Well, maybe not his face..." Meg trailed off meaningfully.

They both started laughing. "That's horrible!" Nicole announced between giggles.

"I know."

Meg smiled, but there was something besides the humor in her eyes, something sad. "Meg, what's really going on? Is something bothering you?" Nicole questioned.

"I'm just... restless. I was feeling a little claustrophobic in my apartment, so I needed to get out for a while. But you're right, it's late. I should be going." She got up to unplug the controller but Nicole stopped her with a hand on her arm.

People generally thought Meg was cheerful, and usually she was. Other times it was a facade. Meg's childhood left invisible scars. Nicole was the only one who Meg let near her when the burden became too heavy and the mask fell. She went to great lengths to keep everyone else out. Once, she went so far as to fake chickenpox just to be left alone for a couple of weeks. But that was years ago. "It brought back memories... my attack... didn't it?"

"No! Well... maybe. Maybe a little, but I don't want you beating yourself up over this. I'm fine, really. Just a little restless. But honestly, I'm fine, now. I should get going." She stood to go, but Nicole stopped her a second time.

"Okay, I'll order the pizza," she said with mock resignation, "but only if we can have extra cheese."

Meg smiled slowly and sat back down. "Alright, you've twisted my arm. You order, and I'll see what's on TV."

"You got it. I'll be right back." She headed to the kitchen, but paused by the balcony doors, hearing a sound. Peeking through the blinds, she saw the wolf and smiled, letting him in. "Hey," she laughed, rubbing behind his ear.

"Holy Hallucinations!" Meg jumped off the couch. "Is that a wolf?"

Nicole chuckled. "He's the one that saved me in the woods. He's been showing up here at night."

Meg cautiously approached. The wolf lowered his head calmly. With a trembling hand, she touched his fur. "He's not a spirit guide." Her voice was barely audible.

"Nope, he's definitely real. I probably should have warned you, but honestly I wanted to see your reaction." Meg shot her an aggravated look.

"Okay, so this is cool, weird, but cool. But are you sure it's safe?" The wolf padded over to the couch and found a spot on the floor to lie down. Settling in, he closed his eyes.

"I've been sleeping in the same room with him ever since what happened. I know it's crazy, but it feels like he's here to watch over me. It's been comforting to have him here." Meg quietly resumed her seat, keeping a skeptical eye on the wolf, but he didn't acknowledge her movement. Nicole smiled and resumed her task of ordering food. Two hours later, she was stuffed and holding the stitch in her side from all the laughing she'd done at some late-night comedy sketches.

Meg flipped off the TV as the national anthem portended the end of broadcasting for the night. "I should go. I probably need a little sleep, after all."

"Stay here," Nicole said, straightening up. "It's late, you're tired and you shouldn't be driving."

"I would, but you snore," Meg said, completely straight faced.

"Hey!" Nicole cried out indignantly.

"Just calling it like I hear it." The corners of Meg's lips

curled up. She released a short laugh when Nicole pelted her with a pillow from the couch. Still grinning, she helped Nicole finish cleaning up. The two exchanged a tight hug before said their good nights.

"I don't snore," Nicole muttered after the front door had closed.

"Yes, you do," Meg called from the hall. Smiling, Nicole cast a mock evil glare at the door and went to bed.

NICOLE LISTENED to the message on her machine a second time. There was no mistake, it was Billy and he'd announced that he would be arriving on a ten-thirty flight that night.

She tried to restrain her excitement. His visit was coming out of the blue, and she had a lot to do before his flight got in. She definitely needed to clean up a little bit. Briefly she considered what food she had in stock. There was bread, some peanut butter and sandwich meat, assorted breakfast cereals and plenty of snacks. That should be good for now, she decided, so she wouldn't need to go shopping. She did need to get some gas for her car, but she could do that on the way to the airport. What should she wear? She hadn't seen Billy in so long. Would he be proud of her, happy about the way she was living her life? Would he still see her as the responsible, intelligent individual he always had? A million questions ran through her head, not the least of which being the reason for his visit, but she couldn't wait to see him again.

They'd grown up together as brother and sister, close despite the eight-year age gap. He'd always acted the part of an overprotective older brother, but that was before he left home when he was eighteen. He'd left to make a life for himself as a world-famous fiction writer. Their parents, both so scientifically minded, believed there wasn't any point in wasting his time on such a frivolous dream and had wanted him to do something more realistic. Determined to follow his dreams, Billy had left, but he'd kept in touch through post cards and occasional letters.

After their parents died, Billy had claimed he couldn't make the funeral, because he was too swamped with work. Nicole had told him she understood, and she really had. He was the head professor of Historical Literature at a local university. It was a subject he'd discovered and instantly loved while he studied to become a writer and he'd decided to focus on that and write on the side. He loved what he did, and he was very dedicated.

Still, Nicole wasn't sure if it was truly his busy schedule which had kept him from the funeral, or if it was his guilt over how he'd left things with their parents. In reality, she suspected it was probably a little of both.

Nicole heard her watch beep. David would be there any minute. She started tidying up a little and getting ready. It was a good thing the concert was early, it meant she could go to the concert with David and still have enough time to pick up Billy from the airport. She could hardly wait to see either of them.

This was turning out to be a pretty good day.

11

———

Nicole and David walked along the lines of games and rides. A few times she noticed stray shadows and unfriendly faces in the crowd that pulled her mind to thoughts of attack and survival, but David's calm presence by her side was enough to silence most of the unease in her chest. The feel of his arm under her hand reminded her she was protected. She wasn't alone. She could relax and enjoy the night and the company.

Nicole munched on her cotton candy and studied the pictures she'd won at the darts and balloons booth. It had always been her favorite fairground game, and she was pretty good at it, as revealed by the three pictures she'd won. They were beautiful, each one portraying some magical scene. She could hardly wait to put them up on the wall beside her bed.

Since they'd spent their previous visit enjoying the rides, they decided to try the sideshow games tonight, and David was holding an armful of assorted stuffed animals they'd won. She took another bite of the cotton candy and peered through the mound of animals, to David's barely visible face. "You sure you don't want me to carry some of those?" she asked.

"Nah, I've got it covered."

"Never one to complain." She smiled. He was too strong and too stubborn to complain she suspected. In fact, that strength was what kept her going some days. Even though she acted as if it bothered her when he kept showing up and following her around, the truth was she found herself looking forward to his visits. It had been especially true after the past few days. With the trial approaching, her mind repeatedly turned to thoughts of worry and fear. "You know, you've been a Godsend to me. Tell me, Coverton, how is it that you always seem to show up just when I need you around?" The words slipped out before she could stop them.

David almost stumbled. He turned toward her and caught the expression on her face. She was obviously wishing she could take back those words.

He could understand why. It obviously wasn't easy for Nicole to rely on anyone else, something they had in common. He knew that an admission like she'd just made, however unintentional, couldn't have come easy, and it warmed him to think she felt close enough to him to let her defenses down enough for that kind of slip. "Did you need me around tonight?"

Nicole pushed aside the uneasiness growing in her stomach. While part of her wanted to deal with her feelings on her own, another part wanted to tell him everything, and it was that part which was taking control now. She was beginning to feel like two people. One was doing all the thinking, while the other one did the talking, and neither one seemed to care what the other one wanted. She heard herself start to speak again, not really certain what she was going to say. "John called right before you showed up," she said. "He talked to Susan, an attorney on the case. The trial has been set for a week from Tuesday. Susan said she's going to do her best to keep me out of it, but she might need me to testify, but Steagel already knows I took the photos, so I don't know what good it would do to try to keep me out of it anyway." The words poured out.

David somehow managed to shift the stuffed animals into one arm and wrapped his other arm protectively around Nicole. She wrapped her own arm around his waist and sighed. This felt safe and good. She didn't want him to ever let her go. "You know what your problem is?" David said. "It's the same as mine. You think too much. You just need to take things one day at a time. Hasn't everything worked out so far?"

"I have been pretty lucky, I guess. Whenever someone tries to kill me, I always get rescued. First by the wolf, and then you."

"Wolf?" he asked.

"In the woods. You know, the first time I was almost harmed – the one that you just happened to know about."

She pinned David with a pointed stare, but he ignored the stare and the implied question. "Were you afraid?" he asked.

"Of almost getting shot?"

"Of the wolf."

"Why would I be afraid of the wolf? It was the guy with the gun who had me wishing for a stunt double. No, the wolf didn't scare me." She wrinkled her nose. "I suppose I should have been more afraid, but I wasn't. Wolves have always been my favorite animals, as you probably guessed from my apartment decor." She smiled. "I even did a report on them once. They're magnificent and graceful. No, I'm not afraid of wolves."

Nicole settled in closer against his shoulder. She could just make out his heartbeat up against her arm. He hugged her tightly and steered them toward the area where the concert would be taking place. They hadn't been over to this side of the fair yet, and they passed food and drink vendors, more games of chance, and some kiddie rides.

Nicole hesitated when they passed a unique attraction. It was a tent which appeared to have candlelight glowing inside it. Nicole could also detect the faint aroma of lavender incense burning. Shadows played against the tent, forming impossible shapes. A large shadow rose tall, then disappeared as the front of the tent flap was opened, revealing a woman with long white hair and dressed in traditional fortune teller garb. Her long, flowing skirt blew in the light breeze, as did her many scarves, and her jewelry reflected some of the candlelight. Her bracelets jangled as she walked toward them.

"Hello," she said, "my name is Madame Francisca VaMoore." She spoke with an accent Nicole couldn't quite place, but it sounded foreign, perhaps a mixture of many accents. "Would you like I should tell your fortunes?"

"I don't think so," Nicole said, and she turned to go. She didn't fancy listening to the fanciful predictions of some self-proclaimed psychic. Most of these carnival psychics were just frauds anyway and they made it more difficult to believe in legitimate psychics. Of course, if Billy were here, he'd jump at the chance to hear from a fortune teller. Like Nicole, he'd tried to justify his actions and beliefs, by searching for truth in anything unscientific. Unlike Nicole, he hadn't developed a strong skepticism regarding such things. Nicole could believe in them theoretically, but she was too afraid to believe in them when they were right in front of her, when there was the possibility they could be disproven.

Thinking about him, her thoughts dwelled on Billy. She was worried about him. His voice had sounded strained on the answering machine, as if something was bothering him. Of course, something was always bothering Billy. But this seemed different, somehow.

"He will be fine, eventually."

Nicole was brought to a stop by the woman's words. "Who?" she asked.

"The one you think of now. He is your brother, but he is not your blood. He will find the peace you wish for him, but it will take time. It will get worse before it gets better, but things will work themselves out."

"How do you know about Billy?" Nicole demanded.

"I told you. I am a fortune teller, a psychic – whatever you want to call it."

"I don't believe you."

The woman laughed. "Have it your way. Your eyes will soon be opened." With that, Madame VaMoore went back into her tent.

Nicole heard David chuckling and glared at him. "Are you laughing at me?"

"Yeah." He grinned.

"I suppose you believe in psychics."

"You suppose right. I have a friend who's psychic."

She sent a glance heavenward. "Why am I not surprised?"

David laughed. "I told you why I believe in psychics. You want to tell me why you don't?"

"Not particularly."

"Oh, come on."

Nicole smiled. "No, I think I'll pay you back for all of my questions you haven't answered."

"Point taken." He glanced down dejectedly, then looked up again with a mischievous smile. "Now, will you tell me?"

Nicole laughed. "No. It's not important anyway."

"Oh, come on."

"It's stupid. It doesn't make sense even to me."

"Try me."

Nicole looked up at his big, pleading eyes and gave in. "Okay. I guess you could say that I don't believe because I've spent too long trying to believe."

"You want to run that by me again?"

"I told you. It doesn't make any sense." She sighed. "You see, my parents were both very scientifically minded. They didn't believe in anything paranormal. I spent years searching for proof that could successfully change their minds, but I never found anything. After years of searching, one begins to wonder if the other person really is right. Does that make any sense? Maybe I couldn't find anything, because there was nothing to find. I don't know. What's the point in psychics anyway, even if they do exist? It's not as if anyone can change what happens."

"So you think we're locked into a predestined path?"

"Not exactly. I believe in fate, and I believe God has a plan for us, but I think each person has a certain amount of influence over their path."

"But doesn't that mean people can change things?"

"I guess." Her forehead wrinkled. "But not by knowing the future."

"So you believe psychics could exist, but doubt their usefulness?"

"Yeah... no... I don't know."

"Okay, I'll let you off the hook. Tell me about this brother of yours."

Nicole offered him a grateful smile. "Billy is my adoptive brother. He's flying in tonight.

"How long will he be in town?"

"I don't know. I haven't seen him in years. When my parents died in the car accident two months ago, he didn't even show up for the funeral. He made some excuse about business, but I think it was more than that. He didn't exactly end things well with them."

"Losing family is always difficult, especially when there was tension beforehand. It leaves a lot of guilt for those left alive." Maybe he should talk to this Billy, it sounded as if they had a lot in common. David pulled himself up short. What was he thinking? He wasn't going to be in town long enough to build a friendship with this person, and he wasn't about open himself up to a complete stranger, no matter what they had in common.

Nicole gazed up at David. He looked distant, as if he was caught up in something in another time and place. She wondered what he was thinking. She was all too aware of how little she knew about him, yet here she was, telling him about her and her family. "You know, I don't usually say much about my family to other people, especially people I've only known for a couple of weeks. I don't like the sympathy I get when people find out I'm adopted. They tend to walk on eggshells around me. Nobody knows what to say, and it's even worse when people find out my parents have died. It's a scene I prefer to avoid."

"So why open up to me?" He'd wondered about it before, but he'd chalked it up to her personality. Now, he knew that wasn't the case. Could it be she felt the same way about him as he did for her?

"I can't explain it, but I know I don't have to worry about it with you. Maybe it's because you seem to know everything about me already. You seem to already know how I feel."

David's spirits sank. It wasn't that she felt the same, she was only picking up on his familiarity with her background. He pushed back the turmoil and led them to a couple of seats near the back of the crowd. He carefully placed the stuffed animals down beside his seat as they sat down for the concert then put his arm back around Nicole, relishing the way it felt to hold her.

Nicole automatically laid her head on his shoulder. She breathed in his scent and sighed. She settled in even closer and placed a hand on his chest, feeling his heart beat beneath her fingers. The sensation soothed her, and she began to really relax. She felt so close to him right now and wondered if he felt the same way. He probably didn't, but she could hope he did. Maybe he could feel the same energy between them. Maybe he was thinking how good it felt to be this close to each other. "I've been thinking more and more about my real parents since the accident," she said softly, her voice sounding tired.

"Do you remember anything about them?" His voice was gentle, and he lightly stroked her hair.

"Feelings, more than anything else. They're like shadows. Sometimes I have a nightmare which I think has something to do with them, but I can never remember enough details to be sure. It's as if something keeps me from remembering. It's annoying," she explained.

"I can imagine it would get on your nerves after a while."

"I'm used to it. I've been having the same nightmare, off and on for as long as I can remember. I had it a lot more when I was younger, but I've just started having it again recently.

"Is it always the same?" David asked curiously.

"For the most part. Sometimes I'll see or hear something I hadn't seen before, but I can tell there's a lot more I need to see before I fully understand it."

Before they could finish their conversation, the music started, and Nicole pushed the thought of the nightmare to the back of her mind.

* * *

DAVID MANEUVERED the car down the dark country road with ease. In fact, he did everything with ease, Nicole thought. She stared out of the window at the dark landscape, deep in thought.

The concert had been great. In fact, the whole evening had been great. David was so easy to talk to.

She hadn't told anyone else half of what she'd told David, and the few times when she had mention her nightmares and fears to anyone, she'd always played them down. She didn't want people worrying about her when there was nothing anyone could do. David was different from anyone she'd ever met. It occurred to Nicole that David knew more about her than anyone else she'd ever met, but she still didn't know much about him. She suspected he was keeping something from her, she'd thought that almost from the start. She just didn't know what that something was.

"Penny for your thoughts," David asked.

She turned her head to look at him. "I was just thinking about how little I know about you." She smiled. "I know more about my mailman than I know about you. And I was thinking I would try to get some answers tonight."

"There's not much to know."

"I don't believe that for a minute."

"I want my penny back."

"No refunds allowed. Start talking."

David sighed. It didn't look as if he was going to be able to dissuade her this time. There was nowhere to go, and he couldn't think of any way to change the subject. Besides, Nicole deserved some answers. He had no right to ask her to tell him everything about herself if he wasn't willing to do a little of the same. "I...." he blinked, bright light suddenly filling his vision.

It took him a second to realize it was someone's headlights, reflected in the rear view mirror. Where had they come from? There hadn't been anyone behind him a moment ago. He moved his arm to block the light, but he was still partially blinded, so he honked his horn a couple of times in an effort to communicate with the offending driver.

Nicole glanced over her shoulder, but couldn't see anything but bright light. "What's his problem?" she questioned.

"I don't know, but I've got a bad feeling about this."

David breathed a sigh of relief when the light abruptly disappeared from his mirror, but the relief was short lived. The other car had pulled up alongside them, staying with them even as David slowed the car. Without warning, the other car swerved, bumping into them. David felt the jolt and heard Nicole gasp, but he didn't have time to check on her. He needed to get away from whoever was driving the other car.

He sped up, watching as the other car match his speed and started to swerve a second. This time, David was prepared. He swerved at the same time, and sped up, successfully pulling in front of the other vehicle again.

Nicole clutched the sides of the seat, afraid to breathe. In the distance she heard a train whistle. She glanced out of the corner of her eye and saw the train coming towards them. She could barely make out railroad tracks ahead, crossing the road they were driving along. She didn't know how they would be able to make it in time and suspected that the train would slam into them as they tried to cross the tracks. David accelerated hard, and the pressure on the increased speed pinned her back against the seat. In the side mirror, she noticed the other car dropping behind.

She squeezed her eyes shut and abruptly her body got tossed up against the seat belt and then she hit the seat again. The car bounced several times, tossing her around.

The train whistle screeched behind them, and she jumped. She could just make out the sound of screeching tires as the whistle stopped. She peered again into the mirror and saw the train passing by, the other vehicle just visible between the train cars.

They'd made it. They'd actually made it, and judging by how far they'd traveled from the tracks, she could tell it must have been close. Another couple of seconds either way, and they'd have collided with the train.

David and Nicole rode in silence for a while, and Nicole's heartbeat slowly began to return to normal.

They passed the city limits sign and the darkness began to lighten up as city lights came into view. Only then did David realize how fast he'd been driving. He lifted his foot off the gas and brought the car down to a more reasonable speed. He suspected they should be safe now they were back in town. Still, he kept a sharp eye on all the mirrors.

"At least each time they try to kill me, they do it in a new and interesting way," Nicole said, trying to break the tension.

At first, she didn't think David was going to respond, but he finally smiled. "At least you won't get bored."

They both laughed, but it was a hollow sound in the car. "What time is your brother's flight arriving?"

Nicole glanced at her watch. "About an hour."

David nodded. "Good, I'll drive you to the airport."

She shook her head. "That isn't necessary."

"I'm not taking 'no' for an answer. I don't want anyone to hurt you."

Nicole couldn't think of any response. "All right." As he turned the car in the direction of the airport, she let herself wonder why he cared so much about what happened to her.

12

Things had gone relatively well, Nicole mused. Billy and David had hit it off, in fact, they got along so well, she wondered if there really was something to the introspective tone she'd noticed David take during their conversation at the fair. It was something Billy and he had in common because Billy never talked to her either. They were both so frustrating, and they were both overprotective, too. Billy had understandably been worried when he learned what had happened since she took the pictures, and David only left the apartment after Billy promised he would keep an eye on her.

Just what she needed; someone else keeping an eye on her.

She sighed and stared out at the stars through the balcony doors.

"You're having the nightmares again, aren't you?" Billy questioned. He was sitting on the arm of the couch, rummaging through his bag.

She studied his reflection in the glass doors. "You always could tell when I was having them."

He shrugged. "I'm your brother."

She glanced over at him and raised an eyebrow. "Mom and Dad never knew." She could remember sneaking into Billy's room when she'd been woken by the nightmare. She'd stopped sneaking in there as she'd gotten older, better able to deal with them on her own, but he'd always been able to tell when she'd suffered through one.

"Mom and Dad weren't as observant as I was."

Nicole smiled weakly. "You always told me what an observant lot writers are."

He grinned. "Yeah, that's true." His eyes grew serious before he spoke again. "Do you want to talk about it?"

"There's nothing to talk about. It's the same nightmare as always." She turned back to the glass doors, clutching the pendant between her fingers. "I thought they were over. I hadn't had one in years and then they suddenly started up again for no apparent reason, just as intense as ever. I get the feeling there's something I'm supposed to be seeing, something I'm missing. It's right there, on the edges of my mind, and then it's gone. I think the only way the nightmares are ever going to stop now is if I can figure it out."

Billy put a comforting hand on her shoulder. "Don't worry, you'll figure it out. You're good at that." He smiled. "Remember when you figured out what was happening to everyone's lunches?"

Nicole thought back with a smile. She'd been in third grade when kids in the neighborhood started losing their school lunches. No one had known what was happening to them, they'd just disappear from the playground. It was Nicole who discovered a local dog had been stealing and burying them. "It's only because I noticed the smell."

"And modest too." Billy yawned loudly. "I think we could

both use some sleep. Can we talk about this more tomorrow?"

"Okay, I'll grab you a pillow and blanket for the couch, since you're determined you're staying here tonight." She laughed and jabbed Billy in the side.

"You bet I'm staying here tonight." Billy smiled. "Besides, you can't fool me, you're glad I said I'm staying. You just don't want to admit it."

Nicole tilted her chin defiantly. "I was doing just fine without you, Billy. Besides, I have a wolf to protect me."

Billy's eyebrows rose. "What wolf?"

"Oh, there's a wolf that's been hanging around. He's been coming up onto my balcony each night."

"Have you called animal control?"

"Nicole laughed.,"No, I let him in."

"Inside the apartment? A wild animal?"

"Billy, he saved my life. When I took the pictures, he kept me from getting hurt and led me home. This isn't some ordinary animal." Nicole sat down beside him. "Besides, I've been letting him in every night. He stays through the night and leaves every morning. I don't have anything to fear from him."

"What about me? He doesn't know me from Adam. What if he thinks I don't belong here?"

"I don't think there will be a problem. You're so likable." She pinched both his cheeks and chuckled. "Don't worry. It only causes wrinkles."

Billy watched Nicole thoughtfully. "You've changed," he said at last.

"Have I?" she asked. She thought for a moment, realizing that she *did* feel different. "Maybe I'm becoming who I was supposed to be all along."

"See? That's what I'm talking about. Your entire life, it's

been as if you were searching for the answer to some mysterious question. Now, it seems like you've found it."

Nicole considered Billy's words. "No, I haven't found it yet. But I think I'm closer than I've ever been before." She smiled and laughed. "At least, now I almost know what the question is." She got to her feet. "Good night," she said.

"Good night."

Right before she drifted off to sleep, it occurred to her that David had managed to avoid her questions tonight, again.

* * *

NICOLE PUSHED *a branch out of her way as she ran through the forest. She could see the wolf running up ahead. When it glanced over its shoulder, she saw its blue-green eyes shining brightly in the darkness. The wolf wasn't very far ahead of her now – or was he?*

Just when she thought she was about to catch up to him, she saw him again, even farther in front of her than he'd been only a moment before. Then she lost sight of him and she stumbled to a halt. Hearing his howl, she started running again, although she couldn't see past five feet in front of her.

Guided by the howl of the wolf she ran between the trees, ducking one way, then the other.

The howling stopped abruptly again. Not knowing which way to go, she came to a stop again.

A twig snapped behind her and she turned quickly. Standing directly behind her was David, his blue-green eyes seemingly glowing with an inner light.

. . .

THE SHRILL BEEPING of the alarm clock roused Nicole. She slowly dug her way out from under the pillows and sheets. When she forced her eyes open, she discovered Billy leaning over her alarm clock, trying to shut the noise off. He finally succeeded.

"Your alarm clock went off," he said, stating the obvious.

She collapsed back onto the mound of pillows. "I must have accidentally turned it on when I put my glasses up last night."

The bed sunk under Billy's weight when he sat down beside her. "So, this is the time you usually get up?" he asked.

"Unlike you, who never sleeps."

"Hey, I have a lot of work to do," he replied defensively. "What about you? Have you decided what career you're interested in?"

"I don't know. I'd like to do something with the SES, but I don't know about a long-term career. Maybe... I don't know. Look, I refuse to answer any questions until that clock is showing double digits."

Billy held up his hands. "Okay, okay, I can take a hint. If I can't get back to sleep, I'll raid the fridge." He walked over to the door, then turned back to Nicole. "You know," he said, "I was thinking—"

"Don't strain yourself."

Billy ignored her and continued. "You'd make a good writer."

"Yeah, there's a shortage of good doorstops in the world," she muttered.

"No, really. All you'd have to do is write about your life. Of course, you'd have to sell it as fiction. No one would believe it was true."

"Yeah, whatever. Talk to me when I've got more than one eye open."

Billy closed the door and walked back over to the couch. He smiled to himself when he started straightening it up. "At least this visit won't be boring."

A shadow crossed his features. Even this visit couldn't make him forget his troubles for long. Work was a lot more stressful than it had been in the past and nothing had been going right lately. Maybe he only needed a chance to regroup. A vacation could do him good. He'd hoped talking to Nicole might help him and his sister, but she obviously had far too much going on in her own life right now. He couldn't put his problems on her, as well. He'd have to handle this on his own.

* * *

NICOLE WOKE up to the smell of something burning. Reluctantly, she climbed out of bed and opened the bedroom door. Looking over at the stove, she found Billy frantically stirring something in a frying pan. "What are you doing?" she asked, coughing on the smoke that filled her apartment.

"Cooking breakfast."

Nicole stared at him incredulously. "But you cook worse than I do."

"Practice makes perfect," he smiled.

"Well," she said, dropping down onto the couch, "I suppose if I survived some of your earlier cooking experiments, I can survive whatever it is you've tried this time. You must have improved a little." Sniffing the air, she screwed up her nose. "I hope."

"Oh, ye of little faith." He gathered the food and joined her in the living room.

"If you woke up to what I'm smelling, you'd be a little short on faith, too." Light streamed in from the balcony doors, reflecting off a glass vase and sending color dancing across the walls. She watched them for a moment before glancing back at the balcony. "Did the wolf show up?"

"Yeah, I saw him. You know, it was funny, he looked in the direction of your room first, then he turned and looked at me for a second and then he left."

"I guess he decided I was in good hands," Nicole mused. "He obviously didn't smell your cooking."

Billy smiled and shook his head. "You know, your life is a lot more interesting than I remember it being."

"Maybe if you visited more often, you'd know exactly how interesting my life is. I guarantee you'd never suffer from writer's block again."

Billy shrugged, handing Nicole a plate of food which included hash browns, toast, and two sausage links. The toast was the only thing that wasn't burned. "You know, I don't really write anymore. I never even finished that book I was working on. I've been too busy with my research."

Nicole laid a hand on Billy's arm. "Are you happy?"

"Yeah, of course I'm happy. As happy as anyone ever is, I suppose," he responded. "I love my work. I actually get paid to study ancient literature. What could be better than that?" He attempted a grin, but it was more of a grimace. He escaped to the kitchen, putting some pans in the sink. By the time he returned with his own plate of charred victuals, he'd regained his composure.

Nicole studied his face. Whatever emotion he'd been feeling a few seconds ago was no longer evident. "I want to let you know I'm glad you're here. I've really missed you."

"I've missed you, too." His expression softened again.

"I'd like you to tell me what's going on with you. I want to help."

"I'm fine. I'm just a little stressed. Eat your food."

Nicole wrinkled her nose, poking her fork around on the plate. Billy couldn't help laughing at her pained expression.

Maybe it was stress bothering Billy, but she suspected it was more than that. It wouldn't do any good to press the point right now though. Better to change the subject "I think I'd like to sell the house."

Billy nearly choked. "What? Why? You love that place." He always assumed Nicole would end up living there. Billy was established with a good job and Nicole still had friends in this town.

"I know, but it's too big for me, and I can't afford to keep it. I have enough bills to keep up with. My financial aid only just covers everything for this place."

Billy suppressed a shudder of shame. He hadn't thought of what the house was costing her. The mortgage was paid, but there was still property taxes, insurance, and utilities. "Then I'll take it." The words fell out of Billy's mouth before he'd had a chance to think about them, and he immediately wished he could take them back. What did he need with that old house? Why should it matter what happened to it? It was just a house. He should let her sell it and keep the money for school.

"Are you sure you want it?"

He wasn't sure. He wasn't sure about anything right now, but he just couldn't let it go. No matter how little sense it made, he couldn't let himself think about the alternative. "Yeah, I'll take it."

"Does that mean you'll be visiting more often, since you'll have a place here?"

"Maybe." He grinned. Every time they talked over the

past few years Nicole tried to talk him into coming back to Connecticut. Now it looked like he was doing the job for her. He hoped he knew what he was getting himself into.

* * *

THE AGGRAVATED MUTTERING GREW LOUDER. Six none-too-happy people sat around the long meeting table, complaining about an unscheduled Sunday meeting.

Rodney came into the boardroom and sat at the head of the table, his bright yellow and orange shirt in stark contrast to the dull gray and brown worn by those seated around him. He lifted his feet onto the table, cleared his throat loudly, and the grumbling slowly died down. "I know everyone has other places they'd rather be right now. Unfortunately, we have some business which needs to be taken care of. We have got to get rid of anything which might prove detrimental to this company's image. In case you didn't realize, I'm going to trial soon."

Before he could say anything more, there was a knock at the door and the secretary stuck her head into the room. "Mr. Steagel, you have a call."

"Tell them I'm busy."

"It's the president, Mr. George Steagel, sir.

Rodney took his feet off the table and stood up. "I'll take it in my office."

He hurried into the adjoining room and pushed the 'on' button on the side of the video screen. George Steagel immediately appeared. Unlike his nephew, the older Steagel was dressed in a pinstriped suit. His hair was clipped short and his appearance was absolutely pristine. He didn't look happy.

"Uncle George," Rodney stammered. "This is such a surprise. I wasn't expecting—"

"Save it, Rodney. I've heard all about your latest legal problems."

"It's just a misunderstanding."

"For your sake, you'd better be telling the truth, because I'm not going to help you this time. I'm tired of bailing you out every time you get into trouble. This time, you're on your own."

13

"Never mind. I'll be back by tomorrow." Billy hung up the phone with an aggravated sigh. Calling the airport, he booked the next flight home.

"Leaving so soon?"

Billy turned to find Nicole standing behind him. "Yeah, there's a problem at work I need to handle."

"You haven't even told me why you showed up to begin with."

"What, a guy can't visit his sister without a reason?"

Nicole raised an eyebrow but didn't say anything.

"You're right," he said, the smile disappearing from his face. "I haven't been known to do it in the past." He suffered a surge of guilt. "I wanted to see how you are. I wanted to surprise you."

"Are you sure that's all there is to it?"

"Yeah, it is...well, I have been a little stressed lately, but there's no sense in going into that now. You've got enough to worry about right now." He leaned over and kissed her on the cheek. "Don't worry about my problems."

She didn't like Billy's glib response, but she knew there'd

be no convincing him to talk about his problems when there was so much going on in her life. "Just promise you'll talk to me when everything here blows over."

"You've got it." He gathered his belongings, and with one last glance, he was gone.

"Well, that was strange." Nicole straightened the room up out of habit. "I wish I knew what was bothering you," she muttered to the empty room. She shook her head in annoyance. She'd just have to figure out what was wrong with Billy later. Picking up her car keys and books, she left for school.

* * *

He watched from the shadows as the boy, Billy, got ready to board his plane. A smile played across his lips. A brother. This could be useful, especially if Artemis was unable to deliver on some of his promises. He made a mental note of where the boy was traveling to, picking that information, along with a few other choice tidbits, easily from his mind.

He contemplated his next move while other travelers bustled about the crowded airport, completely oblivious to his presence. A woman drew her sweater a little tighter around her shoulders when she walked by, a shiver rippling through her body. His smile broadened.

The smile quickly dissipated when he smelled the presence of a nearby dog. Glancing over, he saw a Seeing Eye dog, leading a man through the lobby. The dog paused, sniffing the air around it, unable to pinpoint the cause of its unease, but it obviously knew something or someone it didn't like was nearby. It began to bark, a low, growling woof. He narrowed his eyes and sent a low, telepathic growl in the direction of the dog's mind. Instantly, the dog grew quiet, searching wildly in all directions. He sent one last growl and was immediately rewarded by a startled whimper from the dog. He grinned when the dog hastily led his master away from the area.

He cast one last, contemplative look at Billy's plane before turning to go. Yes, this could be very useful knowledge, indeed.

* * *

NICOLE REMINDED herself to keep her speed down when she passed a school zone. She didn't usually drive to class, but it was supposed to rain later, so she'd thought it would be simpler to drive. Besides, all the attacks were taking their toil. Her nerves couldn't take walking today. She surveyed the trees and flowers growing along the road. She'd driven down this road many times, walked it even more, and she'd never taken the time to check out the scenery surrounding it. Why she'd taken notice now, she didn't know. She'd been noticing things a lot more lately, as if the outside world was becoming more real.

An image of David's face came unbidden to her. She could see his dark hair, and beautiful blue green eyes which seemed to read her very soul. With an effort, she pushed these thoughts away and concentrated on the road.

Movement in the rear view mirror caught her attention. She saw a man crossing the street behind her, but when she looked at him, she had the eerie sensation he was staring at her through the reflection in the mirror. She was almost positive it was the man she'd seen outside the diner a few days ago. He was wearing the same sunglasses, even though it was cloudy. The traffic around her forced Nicole to take her attention away from him for a moment, but when she looked back in the mirror he was gone. She checked the side mirror. No sign of him there either.

A shiver ran down her spine. Where could he have disappeared to so quickly? The light ahead changed from green to yellow, so Nicole put light pressure on the brake pedal.

Nothing happened. She pressed harder, and still nothing happened. Frantically she tapped the brakes several times.

To her horror, a group of children started to cross the road at the crosswalk in front of her. The police officer directing traffic motioned for her to stop. With no time to warn them, she yanked the wheel to the right and the car swerved up onto the sidewalk. People scattered in every direction, and some screamed as she tried to avoid hitting anyone Bracing herself, she pulled the emergency brake. Her body whipped back and forth when the car jolted to a halt, and she found herself staring at the tall oak tree she'd almost ran into while she was busy avoiding pedestrians. Another second, and she would have hit it. With a loud exhalation of breath, she let her head fall against the steering wheel.

Nicole jumped when loud tapping sounded on her window and her neck and back protested the additional sharp movement. Her heart was still beating uncontrollably and she turned to find the worried face of a police officer staring at her. He said something, but her sluggish mind refused to follow his words. She forced herself to focus. "Huh?"

"Are you okay, Miss?"

She reached over and rolled down the window. "Yeah, just a little shaken. My car wouldn't stop. The brakes didn't seem to work."

"Have you had problems like this with your vehicle before?"

"No, sir. If I had brake problems, I wouldn't be driving it now. After this, I'll probably never drive again," she added with a slightly hysterical laugh.

"What's your name?"

"Nicole Cameron." He wrote the name down in a notepad.

"Cameron... weren't you the woman who was attacked outside your residence recently?"

"Yeah, that's me." She managed a weak smile. *Great, now everyone seemed to know who I am.*

"Miss Cameron, I think you should probably get yourself checked out, and your vehicle definitely needs to be checked out. I'll get someone to drive you to the doctor's surgery, and we'll take care of the car. Considering all that's happened lately, I don't think we can be too careful." He motioned to a second officer to join him. "Officer Clark will take you to get checked out."

Nicole tentatively got out of the car, aware of the fact that every muscle seemed to be sore. She just managed to avoid moaning when she straightened out. "Thank you, Officer..."

"Grimaldo, Tony Grimaldo."

"Thank you Officer Grimaldo." The two shook hands, and Nicole followed the younger officer to his car.

* * *

"Does this hurt?" The doctor moved her arm back and forth and pressed the skin in several spots.

"No."

"Can you rotate your neck for me? Any pain or soreness?" Nicole rolled her head around in a circle, realizing that she wasn't feeling any of the pain she'd had when she'd first stopped the car. "It feels fine."

"Okay, it looks as if you're in pretty good shape. All the tests are showing no problems. Unless there's any pain anywhere, I'd say you're fine to go."

"Great." She jumped down from the gurney and grabbed her things. "I don't suppose I could get a note to take to class. The teacher has a really strict attendance policy."

"Sure. Just see the secretary on your way out."

"Thanks." Nicole headed out, stopping by the front desk to get her note, before she headed towards the diner. She was starving. She started to walk down the street, crossing at the lights. All the normal sounds surrounded her, cars on the street, birds singing, the wind rustling some leaves, and footsteps echoing lightly behind her. She frowned at the even sound of the steps. They never got any softer or louder, as you'd expect when people were walking in different directions on the sidewalk. These footsteps stayed at the same volume, with the same pattern. Nicole slowed down and the footsteps slowed down.

A little on edge, she glanced over her shoulder, but there was no one there. She quickened her pace, not feeling so hungry anymore. She would be a lot happier once she got inside a building.

ARTEMIS DUCKED back into the shadows and waited for her footsteps to start up again. He couldn't risk being seen by anyone who might be watching her, but he needed to find a way to approach her. He used to be much better at this. If only she would go somewhere which wasn't so out in the open. After the incident with the car, she went out for lunch, then headed for the school. Both were accessed by side-walks a good distance from buildings. The library was no better, surrounded by an array of sidewalks and sapling trees that couldn't hide a squirrel. When he thought she might be done, she turned and walked to a couple of down-town stores. How many places did one person have to go in a single day, anyway? They must have covered every inch of this wretched town by now. The rain started to come down, sending people scampering for cover, yet Nicole hardly missed a step. He frowned. With everyone leaving the streets, he'd be spotted more easily. He needed to end this, and soon. He tried to hold back his enthusiasm when he saw her change direction, heading towards her apartment building. Now was his chance.

NICOLE RESTED a hand on her chest where the necklace lay, holding it through the wet material of her shirt. What a day. Billy left town, her car freaked out on her, and now she was being followed – in the rain, no less. She glanced nervously over her shoulder as she walked down the sidewalk to her apartment building. She regretted leaving the cell phone at home.

She saw movement in the shadows and knew someone was there. It had to be him, the man with the sunglasses. At first, she hadn't been sure he was following her, but he seemed to keep popping up wherever she went today. She saw him near the diner, the library and various other places. Then there were the footsteps. She kept hearing footsteps wherever she walked. She refused Meg's offer to give her a ride home from the diner. It was a big inconvenience for Meg. Nicole had more classes and errands to run. This was

Meg's short day. She couldn't ask Meg to hang around and drive her around everywhere. Now, Nicole wished she had taken her up on the offer. She could sure use some company right now.

She hurried the last few steps to her door and forced her shaking hand to push the key into the lock. It finally slipped into the keyhole, but before she could turn it, another hand came to rest on her hand. "Miss Cameron?" A deep voice spoke near her ear.

She snatched her hand away, jerked around and saw a man and she quickly realized it was the same man she'd seen outside the diner and in her rear view mirror this morning.

He had dark, brownish red hair, and was wearing a light-colored leather jacket. Nicole breathed in sharply and inhaled the scent of new leather. Dark, almost impenetrable sunglasses completed the look. "I'm sorry I frightened you," he said, although his tone seemed less than sincere.

"What do you want?" She was amazed by how calm her voice sounded. In reality all she wanted to do was run away or scream.

"I have something to tell you. If we could just go inside." He gestured toward the door.

"I'm listening." She snatched her keys from the lock and turned her back completely away from the door.

"He chuckled lightly. "You're just like your father, you know. Your real father, that is."

"What do you know about my father?" She silently chided herself for letting her voice betray her interest.

"More than you, I'd wager."

"That wouldn't be difficult. If you know the man's name, you're one up on me." She forced lightness into her words, eager to be in her apartment and away from this stranger.

The man leaned forward and took off his shades. His face was inches from hers, and she could stare right into his eyes. She blinked. She could have sworn his eyes were blue, but now they seemed violet. No, green. She couldn't be sure. They seemed to be changing color right before her eyes. It was hypnotic. "I know that and much, much more."

"What do you want?" she demanded again. The sound of people walking down the hall reached her ears.

The man turned his head in the direction of the noise. "Another time." He looked back to her, smiling before he put his sunglasses back on and walked away.

She waited until he was out of sight before she hurriedly unlocked and opened the apartment door. Only then did she let herself breathe again. Her heart nearly beat out of her chest. She leaned against the closed door for a second before she locked every lock, including the night latch and chain.

She wished silently for David's presence, but she wasn't sure if she should call him. After the events of the day, her brakes failing and then the strange man coming to her door, she didn't think he would mind if she did. She lifted her hand to her mouth to stifle a yawn. She was exhausted. Maybe she'd just lie down on the couch for a few minutes and relax. Then she would call David.

14

The ringing of the phone pierced through the thick veil of sleep and woke Nicole. She sluggishly reached for the phone, anxious to stop the irritating noise. Batting her hand around blindly, she finally made contact with the phone. "Hello," she mumbled into the receiver.

"Hey Nicole, it's Billy. Did I wake you?"

Her eyes drifted shut, despite how hard she worked to keep them open, and she sat up to keep herself awake. "Yeah, I guess I dozed off. Where are you?" Sitting up had helped, but she was still struggling to concentrate.

"At my apartment. I just called to tell you I got home okay and to check how you were doing."

"It's been a rough day, but I'm fine."

"What happened?" he demanded.

Nicole considered her next words carefully. She didn't want to worry him. "I had a little trouble with my car."

"What kind of trouble?" Billy asked sharply.

"Oh, just a difference of opinion really. I wanted it to stop, and it didn't want to."

"What? I'm coming back on the next flight." She heard him unzipping a suitcase, and then opening drawers.

"Don't be ridiculous. I'll be fine, and you have work to do." A knock sounded at the door. "Listen Billy, someone's at the door. I've gotta go, but don't worry. I still have David and the wolf to take care of me."

Billy reluctantly let her go after she'd promised she would be more careful and call him if she needed anything. Dragging herself off the couch, she hurried across to the door and turned the doorknob, but for some reason, the door didn't open. She tried again with the same results. Studying the door more closely she realized that the main lock, the dead bolt, and the chain were all in use. She fumbled with the locks. When had she done that? She hardly ever locked her door, and she usually only used the main lock when she did. Still trying to figure it out, she opened the door.

* * *

WHEN NICOLE finally opened the door, David's expression darkened even more once he got a good look at her. Her eyes were hazy, her hair was a mess, and there was the imprint of her watch band on her cheek. "You don't look so good."

Nicole pushed the door shut behind him . "Gee, thanks." She collapsed onto the couch. "I don't know why I'm so tired. I must have fallen asleep on the couch earlier, but I never take naps, and I don't even remember locking the door." She yawned.

David turned her head toward him, his hand gentle against her face, and gazed into her eyes. "Nicole," he began softly, "could you tell me what happened after your car's brakes failed?" Mark Stephenson had told him she was fine after the accident, had just had a couple of aches and pains. So what was causing this lethargy? He should have kept a closer eye on her, or at least been her to see how she was before now.

He watched her struggling to recall her day. "I... uh... they took me to the doctor, but he said I was fine. Then I went to the diner... I think. Yeah, I went there and a few other places. Then I came here."

"Did anything else happen?" At least he could rule out physical injuries as the cause of her current state.

"I... I don't know. Everything's so hazy." She stared into his eyes, trying to focus. As she watched, she thought she saw the color of his eyes change. She blinked a couple of times. No, his eyes hadn't changed, it had just been in her imagination, but for a second there, it seemed so real. The image of another man's face came to mind, his eyes changing color hypnotically. Before she could get a firm grasp on the memory, it slipped away.

"Here, drink this." David pressed a cold glass into her hands. She stared stupidly at the glass for a minute, then lifted her gaze to David's face. She hadn't noticed that he'd left her side and gone into the kitchen. What was happening to her? Just earlier, she'd been thinking how observant she was getting. She'd even noticed those footsteps echoing behind her.

She stumbled over that thought. What footsteps? She couldn't remember any footsteps. Had she heard footsteps today? Why couldn't she remember? She drank the water quickly, trying to clear her head.

David took the empty glass from her fingers, his hand lightly resting against hers. He stroked the back of her hand, comforting her. "Do you want any more?" he asked softly.

His words triggered something in her mind. "... *much, much more.*" She processed the words slowly, careful not to force the memory too quickly and risk losing it. The words combined with a vision of color-changing eyes in her mind. She rubbed at her eyes, willing the fogginess from her brain.

Piece by piece, she began to remember. The eyes had been hidden by sunglasses, despite it being cloudy and starting to rain. She recalled walking through the rain, and knew he was following her. Those had been the footsteps she'd heard. An image of the man fragmented at first, began to coalesce in her mind until she could see him quite clearly. The man wearing the sunglasses had followed her all day. After she'd walked home in the rain, he'd approached her apartment door, claiming to know her father. Her real father.

She lifted her head to stare at David, realizing her mind was completely clear. She was wide awake, felt energized. Quickly, she described the man she'd seen to David, telling him everything that had happened. "I don't know why I couldn't remember it before."

A deep furrow between David's eyebrows caught her attention and she realized he hadn't said a word since she'd started talking.

David berated himself for letting her out of his sight for so long today. He should have been there for her. He couldn't bear the thought of something happening to her. Drawing himself back from his thoughts, he looked at Nicole and noticed her eyes had settled on him.

Her eyes were so beautiful, revealing far more emotion than she'd ever allow her words or actions to exhibit.

She settled her warm hand on his arm and his self-control nearly snapped. Just the sensation of her fingers on his arm was enough to have him wanting to draw her into his arms and capture her lips with his. Her skin was so beautifully soft, what he wouldn't give for the chance to explore it more thoroughly. He forcefully pushed back his desire and reminded himself of the danger she was in. This was no time to get carried away. "Where's Billy?"

"Billy? Oh, he had to fly out this morning. He got a call from work about some job that couldn't wait, and he caught the first flight out."

"You shouldn't be here alone," he heard himself say. "It isn't safe. Why don't you come and stay at my place? I have plenty of room." He told himself the only reason he wanted her to stay under the same roof was for her protection, but he knew it was a lie. Realistically, he could protect her perfectly well here at her apartment as the black wolf. Shoring up his argument, he conceded that she was more likely to be attacked here at the apartment, whereas nobody would know she was staying at his place.

"I appreciate what you're trying to do, but you don't have to worry about me. I'll be fine."

"Nicole, I'm going to worry about you, no matter what. Nothing is going to change that. It would kill me if anything happened to you."

A painful lump lodged in Nicole's throat. Could she possibly believe he cared so much about her? How could he? They'd only known each other such a short time.

David lifted his hand and ran his fingers along the edge of her hair. She instinctively pressed her face closer to his stroking hand, and goosebumps erupted in all directions from the contact. She was amazed at what he could do to her with such a simple touch.

David sighed. If only she knew what she did to him. "But I know how stubborn you are." He leaned in, resting his forehead against hers. "If you see that man again, or anything else happens, I want you to call me. Anytime, day or night. Promise me you will."

"I promise," she whispered, her heart beating faster. His breath was warm against her skin, mingling with her own breath when he spoke.

He reluctantly removed his hand from her face and stepped back. She admonished herself for wishing he would never move away. She knew nothing about his past. He never talked about his family or where he was from. She couldn't do this to herself anymore. She had to have some answers. "Are you ever going to tell me something about your past.?"

David gave her a tired smile. It was time he told her something about himself. In the beginning, he hadn't planned on staying around for long, but now... she deserved some information. "I you could say I'm sort of a security consultant."

Nicole's jaw dropped. He'd actually told her something. "A security consultant? How did you get into that business?" she asked hesitantly.

His smile broadened. He could see how excited she was, yet she seemed afraid to reveal it, afraid she'd be disappointed, and he'd clam up again. It amazed him that he could pick up on all that, but he knew it was true. He felt as if he knew her so well, and it was time she had a chance to learn about him. "I guess you could say I had a unique perspective to provide." He wasn't sure if it was wise to tell her the truth, but now was as good a time as any. And this part would be a lot easier for her to believe than most of his past. "I used to be a thief." He waited a moment, trying to gauge her response. She seemed surprised, but he didn't see any condemnation in her eyes. "You see, I left home when I was very young. I'd had a falling out with my folks, and I decided to try and make it on my own, set my own rules. You probably know how it is."

She offered an understanding nod. It reminded her of what had happened to Billy. No wonder they got along so well. She leaned in closer to listen to his story, endeared by the emotion in his voice, the way he said certain words, as he spoke about his past and his family.

"I ended up living on the streets for a while," he said. "It wasn't pleasant. There was never enough to eat. The winters were cold. The other kids, mostly orphans or runaways, like me, were bitter and cynical. We learned that if we stole things, we ate. Eventually, I tried to rob this one rich guy, but he caught me. I thought I was dead, but he ended up hiring me. He put me in charge of making sure his home was burglar proof, and in return, he let me stay there for free. He figured a thief would know how other thieves think, and therefore, I'd be perfect for the job."

"He wasn't afraid you'd try again?"

"No." David shook his head. "He knew I was terrified of him." He chuckled. "He knew."

"How old are you?"

"Huh?" She'd caught him off guard again and he stared into her soft eyes. They were so gentle, so kind.

She smiled at him. "I asked how old you are. You've been through so much, and yet you don't seem very old."

"Looks can be deceiving."

"And are they, in this case?"

He wanted to tell her everything, but he couldn't bring himself to do that just yet. "You could say that," he hedged.

"So how old are you?" She leaned forward, resting her chin on the palms of her hands.

He swallowed hard. Her movement had brought her upper body closer to his, giving him a perfect view of her cleavage. He inhaled sharply and caught the fruity scent of her shampoo which only made things worse. She was killing him, and she didn't even know it. She smiled up at him innocently and he could feel his pants grow tighter while he fought to focus on the conversation. "Older than some, not as old as others."

"What kind of an answer is that?" She fisted one hand and punched him in the arm, then sat back.

"A truthful one." He shrugged.

"Okay, well as long as we're being truthful…" She smiled mischievously.

He groaned. "I don't like the sound of that."

Nicole laughed, and he glowered at her, which only made her laugh even more. "Are you older than me?" she asked after her laughter subsided.

"Yes," he answered easily.

"Are you older than John?"

He didn't like this game. "Yes."

She saw the muscles tensing in his neck and the wary expression in his eyes and decided to cut him a little slack. "Are you older than… Dick Clark?"

He laughed. "No one's older than Dick Clark."

Nicole's smile broadened and she was pleased to see that he'd relaxed a little bit. "Well, however old you are, you certainly have a lot of time to spend hanging around with me."

"Are you complaining?" He tried not to show how important the answer was to him.

"No. I'll admit, you have come in handy a time or two." *And every day, I look forward to seeing you,* she added silently.

"Now, now, we wouldn't want you going out on a limb. You might fall."

"If I did, you'd just catch me."

They both laughed. Nicole was glad to see him more relaxed again. Maybe now she could get some more answers out of him, or would it be wise not to try again right now? Nicole didn't want to push him too far, but curiosity finally won out. "Seriously..." she began.

"I hate that word."

She ignored him and continued. "How do you have so much time available to spend with me?"

"Do I spend a lot of time with you?" He smiled, his eyes wide with innocence.

She glared at him, but it quickly morphed into a grin. Even though he aggravated her, she enjoyed it. Before she could think of a response, the phone in her bedroom started ringing.

"Your phone's ringing," David announced, and she offered him a wry grin.

"Saved by the bell." She bounded up off the couch and headed in the direction of her bedroom.

"Hello?"

"Hey, it's Meg. How ya doin?"

"Oh, I'm fine."

"Oh, really? Is that why you didn't tell me about your car accident?"

Nicole sighed. She'd completely forgotten about what happened with her car when she went to the diner to meet Meg for lunch. She'd been too preoccupied with the man following her, but she couldn't tell Meg that. It would just make her worry even more. "There's nothing to tell. My brakes didn't work. You know how old that car is. It's older than me."

"Is that what the police said?"

"I haven't heard from them yet."

"So, you don't really know what happened, do you?"

"Well, no." Nicole pushed back her own fears and speculations. She couldn't let herself dwell on them right now, or she wouldn't be able to leave the apartment.

"Nicole, this isn't a one-time thing. You *know* that! Someone is trying to hurt you, maybe even kill you!"

"I know, I know, but I'll be okay. Stop worrying so much." she said, hoping to convince herself as much as Meg.

"You know I won't, but I guess I'll back off for now. Just promise you'll be careful."

"I promise. Look, can I talk to you later?"

"Yeah, I guess"

"Bye."

"Bye." She put down the phone and walked across to the bedroom door. David was sitting on the couch with his back to her, his ankle resting on his knee, and his arms were crossed. He turned to her when she stepped into the living room and smiled, and she rested her crossed arms on the back of the couch. "You know, until just now, no one but me has ever heard that phone from in here, because of how quietly it rings. It's kind of a running joke between my friends and me. But you did? How?"

He shrugged. "The same way you do."

"Why do I get the feeling you're keeping something from me?"

David got to his feet. "Because you're a very smart person. I have to go." He walked over to the door with Nicole following closely behind. "I'll see you later."

She lifted one eyebrow. "You're just going to leave?"

"Yep." He grinned. "Bye." He leaned forward and pressed a lingering kiss to her forehead. He pulled back slowly and removed his hand from her shoulder, then slipped out through the door, leaving before Nicole could say another word.

* * *

"YOU DIDN'T SEE the look in her eyes. Someone tried to make it so she wouldn't remember, so she couldn't remember." David turned away from the patio doors and started pacing the floor.

Mark sat in a leather chair in the corner of the room, watching David pace. "Is that possible?"

"Richard told me stories of those who managed to manipulate memories, but he said it takes someone with a great deal of power to do it." This was just what he needed – another threat to Nicole. Who could it be? Whoever they were, they knew exactly who she was, and knew her family – but that didn't narrow the field down much.

"Yeah, I seem to remember hearing some stories about the ability, now that you mention it, but why would anyone want to make Nicole forget she'd seen them? Why would anyone be approaching her at all?"

"I don't know. Do you think it's got anything to do with the threats Richard received before his death?"

"It's a possibility." Mark contemplated who could have been behind those threats. After all these years, he was no closer to an answer than he had been back then. And if these two incidents were connected, he couldn't begin to know where to start.

"She also said the guy's eyes seemed as if they were changing color."

"Hmmm, that sounds like some type of illusion. If anyone was powerful enough to get into a person's head and manipulate memories, it would only be a small chore to make someone see what they wanted them to see."

"I guess that makes sense."

"Either way, there's not much you can do until he shows

himself again, and for goodness sake, stop pacing! It's like watching a tennis game."

David plopped down into a nearby chair. "Sorry. I feel like I should be doing something."

"I know, but aimless worry and guesswork isn't the answer. Maybe Mara knows something. She was friends with Richard's father, before Richard was even born. She's known their family for a long time."

"I didn't realize she was quite that old." Despite his worry, David's interest was piqued by the prospect of learning something from Mara.

"Oh, I think that's barely scratching the surface where Mara's concerned." Mark thought back on snippets of conversation he'd heard over the years. From conversations which stopped abruptly when he entered the room, to vague references to situations past, he'd heard his fair share of names from the history books, as along with other hints regarding the vast complexity and longevity of Mara's past. "I overheard a conversation once when she was talking to Richard about political situations in fifteenth century Europe. She seemed extremely well informed about the topic."

"Really?" It could certainly explain how she was so knowledgeable about everything. "I'll go and talk to her."

15

Mara finished lighting the lavender incense and turned the door handle. She opened the door and smiled at David's surprised expression. His hand was raised, but he hadn't knocked on the door yet. "How did you know I was here?" he questioned.

She shook her head. "All the years you've known me, and you still have to ask? Come on in." She motioned for him to sit on the couch.

David smiled and shook his head, settling onto the couch. "When are you going to teach me how you do that? I didn't even tell you I was coming by."

Mara sat in a nearby chair. "I've tried. You just don't have the patience to learn."

He fidgeted. Sometimes he still felt like the kid he'd been when they first met. He occasionally felt like that with Mark, too, but not as often. "I suppose you know why I'm here then, too?"

"Yes." Her expression darkened, her eyebrows drawing together, creating several creases in her smooth forehead. "I'm afraid I don't know who this person is that you seek. I have sensed his presence for a short time, but he's very guarded. He's found some way to block himself from my mental probing. I sense his powers are strong, yet somehow false."

"You mean, he's not as powerful as he seems?"

"Not exactly. He is exceptionally old and extremely powerful. Never doubt that. But there's an unnatural strength in his abilities. I have yet to pinpoint what it is." Mara was certain it had something to do with the dark presence she'd sensed, but she didn't tell David that. There was no sense in worrying him even more. She'd almost missed sensing this other person David sought. The dark presence was occupying much of her time and energy. If this man hadn't attempted to use his powers on Nicole, he would probably still be hidden from Mara.

"I need to find out who this guy is, before he hurts Nicole. Is there anything else you can do?" David was even more worried than he'd been before. If this person was strong enough to evade Mara's powers, and he was after Nicole it wasn't good.

"I'm doing all I can. I've only been aware of him since he first approached Nicole, and he has strong barriers in place to protect himself. It will take some time to get through them. I'll keep trying until I learn something useful. I'm also making some inquiries among our community. So far, they haven't yielded any useful results, but that could change. I'll let you know if I learn more. In the meantime, you should be very careful, David. This man is not what he seems. I don't think he's an immediate threat to Nicole. This other enemy of hers is the one you should focus on for now, but keep your eyes open all the same."

David let Mara's words sink in. This wasn't the kind of

news he'd been hoping for. He released a disappointed sigh and stood to leave.

Mara looked up at him, wishing there was something more she could do. There was so much worry in his eyes, and she imagined even more worry was hidden from view. She couldn't remember him showing this much emotion since Richard's death. The few times she'd seen him since then, he'd been an emotionless shell, everything shut off.

Now, everything was different. He was more like the person he'd been before, and it wasn't hard to figure out why. "You have feelings for Nicole, don't you?"

He looked into her eyes and offered her a weak smile. "Yeah, I do."

Mara got to her feet and took his hands in hers, staring deeply into his eyes. "Things have a way of working themselves out. You just need faith. It's a very powerful force, you know." She prided herself on being able to say those words with conviction. But then, it was always easier to inspire faith in someone else than it was to make oneself have faith.

"I know. I need to be going. I don't want to leave Nicole unguarded for any longer than necessary." He'd already been gone too long, and he needed to fill Mark in on Mara's advice. He wondered if Mark would be at home or at work. He didn't have time to go searching for him, but there was another way. He hadn't done that in a long time, though.

"All right. I'll let you know what I learn."

"Thanks."

Mara shook her head dismissively. "It is nothing."

David took his leave, hurrying down the stairs and getting into the car. He sat back in the seat and leaned his head against the headrest, closing his eyes. If he was going to try this, it might as well be now. Taking a few deep breaths, he concentrated on Mark's face, calling his name silently in his mind. He repeated it a few times, before he exhaled loudly and opened his eyes. This was hopeless. He was obviously too out of practice to make it work.

"No, you're not. You're just impatient."

David straightened up. *"You heard me?"* he thought.

"Yeah. Don't sound so surprised. Now, what did you want?"

"I wanted to tell you what I learned from Mara. She doesn't know who this guy is. She hasn't been able to break through his mental barriers. She doesn't think he's an immediate threat to Nicole, but she told me to watch out for him."

"Understood."

David was a little relieved. The more people watching out for Nicole, the better. He couldn't let anything happen to her. He suspected he might be falling in love with her. It was so soon, but she made his desire flare with just a look. Just thinking about her made him crazy.

"David."

"Yeah?"

"You really have been away from other people for far too long. You're not paying attention to where your thoughts are going. Unless, of course, you wanted me to know what you'd like to do to Nicole."

David suffered a surge of embarrassment.

"I didn't think so," Mark continued. *"Have you forgotten everything we taught you?"*

David rubbed the back of his neck. He remembered those lessons all too well. They had been ground into him.

"Then try using them. With this powerful werewolf after Nicole, you can't afford for your thoughts to be out in the open."

"I know – and will you stop doing that! I didn't like it when you two used to do that to me, and I certainly don't like it now."

"Then do something about it. Block your thoughts. You know how to do it. Now, if that's all you need, I have work to do, and I

can only concentrate on two conversations simultaneously for so long."

"That's it."

"Okay. I'll talk to you later."

"Okay."

David carefully closed the connection and turned the key in the ignition. Still, as he drove away, he made sure to watch out for what he thought.

* * *

NICOLE LEANED AGAINST THE RAILING, the wind blowing her hair and making her nightgown flap against her legs. The gibbous moon lent a magical glow to the night and it shone on her upturned face. She fingered her necklace, comforted by its warmth and thinking about everything which had happened lately.

Her thoughts kept returning to David. He'd become an important part of her life, and she cared about him deeply. She'd tried hard not to, but she had the nagging suspicion she could be falling for him. She couldn't imagine her life without him in it.

She sighed and propped her elbows up on the railing, resting her head on her hands. She shouldn't have let things go this far. She was only going to get hurt when things didn't work out. Things couldn't work out. Something would happen, and all her dreams would crumble. It had happened too many times in the past for her not to believe it would happen again. The only one she let herself depend on was herself, and to some extent, Meg.

Of course, Meg could always leave at any time. She often talked about wanting to travel, she was a free spirit who had been held back for too long. Someday, she'd break free and leave this town, and Nicole would truly be alone.

She pushed away from the railing and went inside. She walked in and out of each room three times before she accepted the fact that she needed to get out of the apartment for a while. Given all that had transpired in the past week, taking a walk alone at night was not exactly the wisest choice she'd ever made, but she didn't care. She needed to get out. Her future was uncertain, a jumbled mess with no relief in sight. She wasn't in control of her own life, and maybe she never had been.

She could hear David's warning voice, along with Meg's, but chose to ignore them. Staying in the apartment was making her crazy, she needed to get outside and clear her mind, try and figure out just exactly where her life was headed.

She walked without conscious knowledge of her surroundings. She stared ahead, unseeing, forcing her feet to take one step after the other.

A cricket chirruped and for the first time since leaving the apartment, she glanced around. She was stunned to find she was walking on grass, rather than cement, and there were trees surrounding her instead of buildings. Nearby, she heard the sound of running water. Somehow, she ended up in the woods near the river. The moon shone down over her surroundings, casting shadows but still providing enough light to see reasonably well. She noticed a tree root, raised slightly above the ground. She looked, really looked around and confirmed her suspicions. She knew this spot, and she knew that tree root. It was the same one which tripped her the last time she'd entered these woods, when she'd been running for her life. This was where she'd first seen the black wolf.

A strange sensation swept over her, as if energy was vibrating all around her and even through her. The air all around her seemed electrically charged. She noticed light from the corner of her eye and looked down at the pendant between her fingers. If she didn't know better, she would have said it was glowing. She blinked, dismissing what she'd seen. After all, it was probably just a trick of the light. But the glow grew brighter, encompassing the necklace and entering her fingertips. Soon, her entire hand was glowing as well. The necklace dropped from her fingers, but she hardly noticed. Her eyes were focused on the light traveling up her arm and beyond, until her entire body seemed to be glowing. She remained motionless as the light grew so bright, it became hard to see anything else.

Abruptly, panic overwhelmed her. She began running blindly, groping for something familiar, something solid. She stumbled through the woods, running into several branches and bushes before she fell to the ground. She curled up in a ball, afraid to move anymore, and concentrating on the grass beneath her. It was the only proof she had that anything around her still existed

Her breathing slowed and she refocused her other senses. She could still hear. Animals were moving in the night. Water was running, very close to where she lay. She could feel the wind on her face, blowing through her hair.

The panic subsided, and she noticed the strange light was dimming. It gradually lessened until she could see the trees and bushes around her again. She pushed herself up from the ground shakily and leaned over the water, looking at her reflection. She appeared the same as she always had, but something did seem different. There was an almost ethereal glimmer in her eyes. She began walking quickly through the woods, hurrying back towards the apartment.

As she walked, she noticed that all her senses had been amplified and her skin seemed more sensitive than normal. Everything looked more... *real* than it ever had before. It was both energizing and frightening at the same time.

She hurried into her apartment, grateful when the feeling finally dulled a little. It didn't disappear completely, but it certainly wasn't as strong as it had been in the woods.

She got ready for bed and let the wolf in through the balcony doors. By the time she fell asleep, she'd almost managed to convince herself she wasn't crazy.

NICOLE REMINDED herself for the third time to pay attention to the professor. It was a useless endeavor. Even though she'd finally managed to put the events of the previous evening out of her mind, there were still thoughts of David to distract her. She thought about him walking with her, watching movies, yelling on the roller coaster and laughing at how small everyone else looked from up on the Ferris wheel. She remembered how it felt to talk to someone about the things on her mind and know he really cared. His forehead pressed against hers, his lips on her fingers, his arm around her, all those memories played repeatedly in her mind. His face and touch were burned into her memory, and she could see him as clearly as if he was standing before her now. She heard his low, gentle voice murmuring in her ears and she could smell the soft aroma of his shampoo and aftershave.

Damn, she was doing it again. Why did she have it so bad suddenly? She'd thought about David a lot lately, but not this obsessively. Maybe it was stress. Maybe it was because he'd finally told her a little bit about his past.

Great, now she was distracted trying to figure out why she was distracted. There was no way she was going to know what their next assignment was if she didn't knuckle under. With that in mind, she managed to pay a bit of attention to the last five minutes of the lecture, at least enough attention to get the assignment copied down from the board. It had to count for something, didn't it? Considering the state her mind was in, she considered herself lucky to have managed that much.

Things went much the same way all day. Everything reminded her of David, and she was constantly losing herself in thought. Even Meg commented on her distraction at lunch.

Nicole pleaded fatigue and escaped to the library, even though she doubted she'd get much work done. She was right. It took three attempts to finish one math problem, and it wasn't even a hard one. She decided she should probably just do some reading. She could usually lose herself in a book, but even that was a futile effort. She finally gave up after reading two chapters of her book without the least idea what she'd read.

Maybe she should just accept she wasn't going to get anything done today. This might just be a blown-off day. Deciding that was all she could really do at this point, she threw her books in her backpack and stood to go.

Only then did she see her obsession, in the flesh. David walked slowly across the library towards her. His eyes held hers with such intensity, she suspected she might shatter, but she was helpless to look away. Taking her hands in his, he placed a light kiss on her fingers. Her legs grew weaker and her heart beat swiftly, her breaths getting shorter. Warmth filled her body, but this time, she didn't fight it. She embraced it. "If you keep doing stuff like that, I'll fail the semester for sure." Her voice betrayed her, coming out slightly husky, and she leaned against the table to stay upright.

He smiled. "Am I interrupting your study?"

"Yes." She smiled back.

"Then I'll leave."

"You intrude on my thoughts whether you're here or not." She spoke honestly, unable or unwilling to filter her words. She couldn't quite figure out which it was.

His breath caught. "Ah, quite a dilemma. I seem to have the same problem. What shall we do?"

"If I knew that answer, I wouldn't be daydreaming during lectures."

He was shocked by her honesty and a momentary surge of courage filled his chest. He continued without hesitating. "Would you have dinner with me tonight?"

As soon as the words were out of his mouth, he wondered if he should have spoken. He wanted to do something special for her birthday today. She didn't know it was her real birthday, she'd been too young when her parents died and she got put into the other home, but he needed to do something all the same. What if it was too much, too soon? *It was only dinner, though.*

Nicole seemed momentarily at a loss for words and he cursed his recklessness. What if—

"Yes."

The single word had his heart skipping a beat. He smiled broadly. "Great. Is seven good?"

"Yeah, that's fine." She could hardly believe it – she had a date! David had asked her out!

She lifted her backpack, but David quickly took it from her. "I'll carry that."

"If you insist." He put his arm around her, and she

leaned into him, wrapping her own arm around his back. She might regret it later, but for now she just couldn't help herself. She loved being with him, and he made her feel good. "Where are we going tonight?"

"You'll find out tonight."

"But I need to have some idea of how to dress."

"Nothing too fancy. You can wear what you have on, if you want, or you can dress up some."

She smiled, thinking of the one dress she hadn't had the chance to wear yet. "Okay then, I think I know what I'll wear."

"What?"

"You'll find out tonight." She lifted her chin defiantly. She could keep secrets, too.

David laughed. He almost felt giddy. The walked the rest of the way to her home in companionable silence. As they stopped on the steps, he handed her backpack to her and kissed her hand. When his eyes looked up at her from over her fingers, a shiver ran through her. She could feel his warm breath on her hand as he said, "Seven," before standing to go. Glancing over her shoulder several times, she walked up the last couple of steps and entered the building. She could hardly wait for seven to arrive.

16

Nicole smoothed down the material of her dress for what seemed like the hundredth time. It was a short black dress which tied around at the back, pulling the material tight across her breasts and showing off her trim waistline. It had short, gathered sleeves which didn't quite cover the straps of the lacy black and red bra she wore, and came to the top of her knees when she stood. It was considerably higher now when she was sitting, and she found herself watching to see if David would show any signs of having noticed. Her hair was loose and flowing down her back.

David sat quietly beside her, driving them to some unknown destination. He hadn't even give her a hint as to where he was taking her. She didn't mind though, because she was still savoring the appreciative looks he'd given her when she first opened the apartment door.

The road curved through another patch of dense forest. At the edge of the trees she noticed a large stone wall and then a tall metal gate. David drove up to the gate and reached for a remote control which was attached to the sun shield above his head. At the press of a button, the gate opened, revealing a magnificent scene beyond. At the end of a long driveway rested a huge house. No, house wasn't quite the right word for it. Mansion even seemed inadequate. Nicole was looking at what appeared to be a veritable castle. It appeared to be at least three stories high with turrets at each of the four corners. The outside was white brick with arches visible on every floor. The house even boasted an indented parapet. Yes, castle was the right word for it.

The car came to a stop near the front door. Nicole waited as David opened her door and helped her out, her eyes never leaving the building. She took a step toward the structure, awed to be witness to such a sight.

"Well, what do you think?" David's voice spoke near her ear.

"It's beautiful!" she breathed.

David smiled broadly at her reaction. "I'm glad you like it. Come." He ushered her inside with his hand against her back.

She wouldn't have though it possible, but the inside was even more magnificent than the outside. There was wall to wall carpet, rich tapestries, and a mural on the domed ceiling of the front room. "Welcome home."

David watched her as she walked around with her head tilted up, staring at the mural. She turned around in a circle in order to see it all. Reluctantly, it seemed, her eyes left the mural and studied the rest of her surroundings. A hesitant hand reached out to one of the tapestries on the wall, barely touching it with her fingertips. "You live here?"

He nodded.

"Now, I wish I had come sooner."

"Would you like to see the rest of the place?"

She laughed. "I'd love that, but I do have a paper due next week."

"I'll give you the nickel tour." Nicole took his proffered arm and followed him throughout the house. David watched her expressions the entire time. He even tried to tap into her thoughts and senses, but he couldn't pick up anything. Either he was rustier than he thought, or she had some powerful barriers.

He didn't think the first alternative was the case. He'd been noticing that he'd picked up on a number of stray thoughts from people, ever since he'd first tried using telepathy again. He was hearing things without even trying, in fact, since his old filter wasn't in place. Which meant it must be a barrier. Why would Nicole need barriers that strong, though? Few people were so guarded that not even a few thoughts strayed to the surface, but he wasn't hearing a thing. It seemed particularly strange, given she seemed reasonably comfortable around him. He sighed. It just meant he'd have to continue watching her actions to get a handle on how she was feeling. No cheating for him.

He shifted his concentration and tried to figure out how she was dealing with everything. She seemed awestruck by the grandeur of the house, but it didn't seem as if she remembered anything about the place. It had always been a long shot. After all, she was young when she'd lived here, but he'd hoped it might spark something. If she remembered something from her past, it might make it easier to tell her the truth. No matter. Maybe just being here, whether she remembered it or not, would make her feel more at ease. She had loved the place as a child, and if it made her more relaxed to be here, with him, then it was worth it.

Besides, he wanted to spend the time with her – not only because it made it easy to protect her, but because he enjoyed being around her. He looked forward to seeing her and talking with her every day and he was beginning to let himself believe she felt the same way. She certainly seemed to, but was this wrong when he was so much older than she was?

Then again, Richard had been a lot older than Caroline. She hadn't been much older than Nicole when they first met, and they'd been blissfully happy together. Maybe he and Nicole could have something.

"And here's the dining room." David held open the door for Nicole and waited for her to enter ahead of him.

She was surprised by what she discovered beyond the door. She'd half expected to see one of those long tables, the type a person had to shout across to be heard and where you needed to stand up to pass the salt.

What met her eye was a small table, set for two, with a small bouquet of flowers sitting between two plates of pasta and chicken. The entire room had been filled with candles, casting a romantic glow on the scene. David pulled out a chair for her, his hand brushing her arm when he pushed the chair closer to the table and seated himself beside her.

They kept the conversation light while they ate. Once they'd finished, Nicole dabbed her lips with a napkin and asked the question which had been on her mind all night. "So, tell me, how did you end up living in a place like this? Did you rob a bank, or just inherited it?"

He lifted one eyebrow. "Those are my only two options?"

"Unless the security consultant business pays a whole lot better than I thought."

"Not really." How much should he tell her? He wasn't certain.

She glared at him. "Ambiguous as always, I see."

David raised his glass in a mock toast and downed the rest of its contents. "More juice?" he asked, standing.

"Please." He filled their glasses and took a deep breath. "I guess you could say I inherited it."

"From who?"

He sat back and stared at her over his glass. "From the best friend I ever had."

"I'm so sorry." She placed her hand over the top of his.

"It's okay. He died a long time ago. He was like a father to me and when he died, I started taking care of the place. I don't even stay here most of the time. I have another place about an hour away. I've been staying here lately, because it's closer to town."

"Why do you need to be closer to town?"

He raised the same eyebrow but didn't voice the real reason – that he needed to be near her. Instead he said, "I have some things to take care of in town."

"But isn't it expensive keeping up two places, especially with one being this big?"

"Yeah, but I couldn't get rid of the place. Richard loved it."

"Richard?" The name sounded familiar. Nicole glanced around the room, experiencing another wave of déjà vu. She'd pushed it aside all evening, but she was certain she'd been in this house before. Abruptly, she could hear the sounds of laughter. For a second, the room looked different, daylight streaming in through the window. She could smell cookies baking in the oven.

"How much longer 'til they're done?" she heard a child's voice demanding.

"Not too much longer," a woman answered.

"Nicole?" David's voice broke through her thoughts. The room returned to normal, and she had to blink back some dizziness from the abrupt change. "Nicole, did you hear me?"

"Uh, no. I guess I drifted off somewhere else."

"Where to?"

She shook her head. "Oh, it's nothing important. What did you say?"

David didn't seem convinced, but he didn't persist. "I asked if you wanted to go into the den."

"Sure."

David blew out the candles and led her through to the den. Soft music was playing on the stereo . He took a deep breath. Get to know her. Mark had told him to get to know her.

David watched her, standing across the room. She was a vision. Her hair was full and sexy, the ends reaching just above her breasts, and that dress gave him a great view of her sensational legs. He was getting harder with every second he stood gazing at her.

Mark's words flew right out of his head. He walked across to her, taking her drink and setting it on the end table with his own.

Before she knew what he was doing, he'd slipped her glasses off. "Oh, I don't think that's such a good idea. My eyes are pretty bad," she protested.

He put her glasses on the table beside their drinks. "They look good to me."

She inhaled a shaky breath. His voice was filled with what sounded suspiciously like desire. "You know what I mean."

"What do you see?"

"You, only you're blurry."

"How close would I have to be for you to see me clearly?" he asked. He took a step toward her. "This close?"

She forced herself to keep breathing. There was no mistaking the desire in his voice now. "A little closer."

He took another step toward her. Now they were almost touching. She could see him perfectly clearly. Regardless, she found herself saying, "A little closer."

He took another step toward her. Their faces were mere inches apart now. This time when she opened her mouth to speak, she wasn't alone. They spoke simultaneously. "A little closer."

David started to close the remaining distance, but an instant before his lips would have met hers, she ducked away. "I love this song. Let's dance."

Nicole reached for her glasses and slipped them back on. "Come on." She took his hands and led him to the center of the room. "You can dance, can't you?"

"Can I dance? Of course I can dance." He proceeded to do some dance moves which were throwbacks from the seventies.

She tried unsuccessfully to keep from laughing.

He stopped and offered her the most innocent look she'd ever seen. "No?" He shrugged. "Okay." He grabbed her hand and spun her around a couple of times before lowering her into a dip. "Better?"

Still draped over his arm, she responded. "Better."

He lifted her up and pulled her close to him, close enough to feel her breath on his neck. He held her so tightly, he could feel her heart beating. Every inch of her was pressed against him, leaving little question about how turned on he was. He lowered his head, brushing his lips lightly across hers. Nicole's eyes closed and he could feel her trembling.

The shrill ring of the telephone stopped his movements. With a growl, he stepped away and answered the phone. "What?" he demanded abruptly. "No, I'm sorry. She's right here." He handed the phone to Nicole. "It's Mar— er... Officer Stevenson."

She took the phone from him. "Hello," she answered distractedly, her voice sounding a little shaky.

"Hello, Miss Cameron. I called to let you know we have the results from the tests on your car. Your brake line was cut, and the lug nuts had been loosened. If you'd driven the car much longer, the tires would have come off."

"You're sure?"

"Positive. Miss Cameron, you need to be very careful. Someone is going to a lot of trouble to get rid of you."

"Yes, of course. I'll remember that. Thank you for calling." She hung up the phone with a soft click and tried to clear the buzzing from her head. "I should go. This was a lovely evening."

He blocked her movements. "Whoa, wait a second. What's the matter? What did he say?" He'd heard every word the two had said, but he wanted to hear it directly from her.

"Oh, it's nothing. My brake line was cut, and my lug nuts were loose. Said my tires could have fallen off at any minute. Could happen to anyone." She walked past him towards the door.

"Ah, Nicky, don't go," he begged softly.

She stopped walking. "What did you call me?"

David walked up behind her and put his hands on her shoulders. "I called you Nicky; you know, it's a nickname for Nicole, generally used by close friends. It's like when you call Meghan, Meg, or me, Coverton. Same concept. Now please, don't go."

She didn't say anything, didn't turn around. She just stood there. Finally, he couldn't stand it any longer. "Is it so difficult for you to let someone get close to you?"

A shudder rippled through her limbs. She covered her face with her hands and shook her head. "Everything's so confusing right now. It's all happening so fast."

He pulled her into his arms and held her tight. "I really think you should stay here tonight. It's not safe for you anywhere else, and I've got plenty of room."

It felt so right to be wrapped in his arms. She inhaled deeply and smiled smiled when she recognized his familiar scent. She hadn't intended to agree to his request, but just then, there was a loud clap of thunder outside and the sound of pouring rain. She tightened her hold on him. Why did it have to storm tonight? She hated storms, they always made the nightmares worse. After her heartbeat slow down a bit, she pulled back just enough to look up at him. "I think I could be convinced to stay the night."

"And what would it take to convince you?"

"Well... have you got cable?"

He laughed. "Yeah, I've got cable."

"Then you've got yourself a boarder, but only for one night, okay?"

He smiled and hugged her tight. "Okay."

They stayed up, watching several old movies. It was after midnight before they finally headed to bed. David gave Nicole one of his t-shirts to change into and showed her to one of the guest suites. It was the room right next to his, she noted. The surroundings were sumptuous; each guest suite had a sitting room, bedroom, and bath, fully stocked, so she had everything she could possibly need for the night.

She stepped out onto the balcony and gasped. To her right, a staircase curled downwards to a grassy meadow which led to an expansive garden, but just to the left of the stairs was a substantial drop off. The ground there was rocky and slanted down to the shoreline of a small lake. It was truly the most beautiful place she'd ever seen.

Nicole slipped beneath the covers of the bed, loving the sensation of the silk sheets against her bare skin. She heard David getting ready for bed and imagined what he must be doing. She could discern when he slipped into his bed, and she imagined him lying there, beneath his own silk sheets.

She considered how easy it would be to walk into his room right now. Would he stop her if she did? She had to stop herself from acting on her thoughts. Images of what she would do if she had the courage to go in there played through her mind as she drifted off to sleep.

* * *

"No!" Nicole shrieked, sitting up in the bed. A loud crash of thunder was followed immediately by a bright flash of light-ning which filled the room with light.

She could still feel the vibrations from the thunder, as the room was again left in darkness. Her breathing started to slow, the momentary rush of adrenaline dissipating. The nightmare was still sharp in her memory. It seemed almost as though she was still stuck in it, but she could probably thank the ongoing storm for the sensation. The nightmare was pretty much the same as always, with flashes of light and sound and the sensation of being jolted around, but this time there'd been something different. She'd heard a man laughing and she could remember it clearly. A man had been laughing. She didn't remember ever hearing it before, but was that the only difference? She searched her memory for any other changes. She tried to focus on her surroundings, but they proved too elusive. It was right there, at the edge of her memory, but she was too far removed from the nightmare now to hold onto the details.

She sighed and swung her legs over the side of the bed. She could still hear the rain coming down hard outside. She made her way downstairs as quietly as possible and searched around for the kitchen. She needed coffee and some time to think. Luckily, her memory of the house tour proved better than that of her dream. She turned the radio on low and put some coffee on. The storm and the nightmare had left her on edge. She hadn't been this on edge in a while. She knew it was a mistake to let herself get used to having the wolf around. Now, she was forced to deal with the nightmare on her own, during a storm, in a strange new house. Was it any wonder it was affecting her so much?

She could go to David, but she didn't want to wake him, not for this. It was just a nightmare after all, a nightmare which had plagued her all her life. She poured a steaming mug of coffee and took a grateful sip, enjoying the aroma.

David walked soundlessly to the door of the kitchen and leaned against the jamb, watching Nicole take several sips of coffee. He almost stopped breathing right then and there. She was a sight. Her hair was all tousled, and she was gently swinging her leg as she sat at the counter. And his shirt definitely looked better on her than it did on him. "You look damn sexy wearing my shirt." he heard himself say. Yesterday he would have chided himself for saying something like that, but it was too early in the morning, and he was past the point of caring.

Nicole looked up in surprise. She hadn't heard him approach, but then she never did. His words registered in her brain and she admitted to herself it felt good to hear them. Her eyes ran over him, starting at his bare, muscular chest and moving down to the green drawstring pants he was wearing. "I'll keep wearing your shirts if you keep not wearing them." The words were out of her mouth before she could stop them.

A smile tugged at the corners of his lips. "Personally, I think it's a fair deal."

Nicole smiled back. She'd never been this outspoken with anyone.

In the background she heard the radio, a news piece momentarily catching her attention. *"Family of four died in the late night plane crash,"* the newsman's voice said. She went cold, the man's voice fading away. A loud clap of thunder boomed and the room was lit up by a flash of lightning. A different room replaced the room she was sitting in.

No, not a room, not really. There were seats in front of her and others beside her. Something clicked in her mind, and she suddenly knew where she was. This was an airplane. She was in an airplane. As fast as the vision appeared, it was gone, and she found herself back in the present.

Warmth from the coffee cup heated her hands, and she could sense a presence beside her. Her eyes blinked open and she found David standing beside her.

"What happened?" His eyes conveyed his concern.

"I was in a plane. In my nightmare, I was in a plane." It was all starting to make sense now. She reached out and clutched his arm, her excitement growing by the second. "Don't you see? I'm starting to figure it out." She put the coffee cup down on the counter and jumped off the stool, throwing her arms around David's neck. "I'm starting to remember. Maybe now I can finally get rid of these horrible nightmares once and for all. I can figure out why I was having them in the first place." She pulled back and gazed into his eyes, and, in her excitement, she finally had the courage to do what she'd been too afraid to do up until now. She kissed him.

17

David's mouth dropped open in surprise when Nicole pressed her lips to his and she tentatively ran her tongue over his lips and teeth, quickly gaining confidence when David wrapped his arms around her back and groaned.. Recovering from his initial shock he met her tongue with his own, matching her desire completely.

Nicole was overwhelmed the emotions coursing through her body. She was aware of every touch, every kiss, every heartbeat – yet everything seemed surreal at the same time. She couldn't quite believe she was kissing David.

She lifted her hand rubbing experimentally over his arm and shoulder, gently clasping the back of his neck before she slipped her fingers upwards and ran them through his hair. David's hands were on her back, holding her tightly against him and creating a protective circle of warmth and strength. He drew her even closer, and her bare leg rubbed against his pants, and her arm rubbed across his bare chest, reminding her of how they were dressed. All that separated them currently was a thin layer of clothing.

Anxiety rushed through her limbs. She wanted him so much it scared her. How could one person make her feel so much?

He slowly ended the kiss, and pulled her even closer to him. He held her tight, allowing their breathing to slow. "Wow," she heard him whisper.

She thought that pretty much summed things up.

David felt her trembling and pulled back just enough to gaze down at her. Her eyes were filled with passion, but he could see something else there. She was nervous and perhaps a little confused, and she was trying not to show it. Remarkably similar to his own emotions, as a matter of fact. He still couldn't get a clear fix on what she was thinking, but he was past the first barrier. He could *feel* her emotions.

He raised a hand and gently traced the side of her face. She trembled even more, her eyelids fluttering closed. "I left sweat-pants and a shirt in you room. They're probably going to be a little big on you, but they should work. Why don't you go change while I cook some breakfast?"

She nodded, but rather than letting him go, they came together for another kiss. Nicole suspected their very souls were melding together. She kissed from his mouth across to his face and neck. His flesh was so warm to the touch and she moaned softly when his lips trailed down over her neck. Their kisses became more frantic, their lips moving from place to place until their mouths found each other again. She shuddered, breathless and emotional.

Their kisses slowed, their lips barely touching, their breathing heavy. David held her tightly, his hands clenching as he let out a ragged breath. "Can you make it to you room?" he asked.

"I don't know." Her legs were like rubber. She wasn't even sure she could stand on her own.

He smiled and kissed the top of her head. "Come on. I'll walk you to your room."

They'd only taken a couple of steps before they stopped and started kissing again. They continued this way, kissing, taking a few steps, then kissing again, all the way up to Nicole's room.

By the time they made it to her door, she knew her legs weren't going to hold her for long. David kissed her hand just before she slipped into the room. She pushed the door shut and leaned against it with a sigh. "Wow," she mouthed to the empty room. She stumbled across and collapsed onto the bed with a laugh. She could get used to staying at David's.

* * *

Nicole sighed and touched a finger to her lip, closing her eyes.

An enthusiastic Meg leaned in closer. "So? What happened next?" she demanded.

Nicole smiled her eyes still closed. "We ate breakfast and he dropped me off at my apartment, so I could get changed before class." She opened her eyes and looked across at her friend. "He wants me to keep staying at his place. I told him I'd think about it."

"Is that what you want to do?"

"I don't know. Staying at his place would probably be the wise choice considering all that's going on, but I don't know if I should. It's strange, I felt so comfortable in that house," she mused. "It seemed as if I'd been there before. A few times when David was showing me around, I had the strangest impression that I knew where we were going, as if I almost knew which room would be next. Then, during dinner, I thought I heard voices, and the room seemed to look a little different to how it actually was."

Meg's eyebrows pulled together. "Maybe you were picking up on vibrations left by the previous owner."

"Maybe, but that doesn't explain why I would feel as though I'd been there before."

Meg shrugged. "I don't know. I think you're right about it being the smarter choice to stay there, what with the trial in less than a week and all, but you've got to do what's right for you."

"There's another thing to consider. If I stay there, what will happen to the wolf? It seemed so strange not having him there beside me last night, but it's not as though I can tell a wild wolf where I'm at."

"I'm sure he can take care of himself, and maybe he'll find you again. After all, he did it the first time. I think you need to focus on you, on what's good for you."

"I guess you're right." Nicole studied her hands while she thought, then her eyes glanced at her watch out of habit. Her eyes widened. Had that much time really passed since she'd sat down to talk with Meg? She'd obviously been talking for a lot longer than she'd intended. She still had a ton of things to get done today. "Jeez, look at the time, I guess I'd better go."

They stood up and Meg wrapped Nicole in a big hug. "Call me if you need anything." She followed Nicole out of the diner and reached absentmindedly into her pocket for her keys. Meg quickly patted the rest of her pockets and fished around in her purse. "I think I left my keys in the booth. I'll be right back."

"Oh, I'll just go on ahead. I'll see you later," Nicole said.

"Okay, I'll see you later."

Nicole watched Meg disappear back into the diner before she turned and started across the street.

Tires squealed loudly on the pavement, drawing her attention. She turned just in time to see a car flying down the street, headed directly towards her. Nicole knew instantly that there was no way she could get out of the way in time.

Unexpectedly, a bright light blinded her and a strange tingling sensation spread over her limbs. Her entire body seemed both weightless and heavy simultaneously.

The strange sensations dissipated, and the bright light dissipated, revealing that Nicole was on the opposite side of the road. The speeding car had already driven well past where she'd been when she first saw it. She sank down onto the ground dropping her face into her hands.

The first cohesive thought she had was when a hand came down to rest on her shoulder.

She looked up to discover Meg watching her worriedly. "Are you okay? You don't look so good," Meg stated.

"I think so. Did you see what happened?"

"Nope, you were already sitting over here when I came out of the diner."

"Oh," Nicole sighed, disappointed.

"What happened?" Meghan sat beside Nicole on the grass.

"I'm not sure. One minute, I'm about to get hit by a car. The next, I'm standing over here on the other side of the road."

"Oh, my God. You mean, you had another near miss?"

"Yeah, and I've made a decision. I think I'll stay at David's for a while."

* * *

"WHAT DO you mean you couldn't kill her?" Rodney jumped up from his chair and leaned his fists on the desk. "You're supposed to be a professional, and you couldn't kill one measly girl?"

The man dressed in black moved nervously from the door to the chairs positioned in front of the desk. "That wasn't just some measly girl you asked me to kill. She isn't human, I tell you. I waited for her outside the diner, just like you said I should do, but when I was just about to hit her, she changed into some kinda animal. It was a wolf, I think."

"She changed into a wolf?" Disbelief was evident in Rodney's voice.

"That's what I'm telling you! Look, you explain it. One second she was standing in the middle of the road. The next, a white wolf was jumping out of a blinding light, landing on the other side of the road. And when I looked back in the mirror, it was the girl who was standing on the side of the road."

"You idiot! The girl didn't change into a wolf. You were just seeing things!"

"I didn't just see nut'in," the man responded. "There are *paw prints* on my car."

Rodney was momentarily shaken. He shuffled some papers on his desk and tossed them into a drawer to try and disguise his nerves. "Look, my guys have reported seeing a wolf around her. That's probably what you saw. Now, get out of here," he snapped.

The man left Rodney's office quickly, seeming none too convinced by Rodney's explanation. Rodney plopped down into his chair and propped his feet up on the desk. Pushing the man's story from his mind, he turned his thoughts to what he was going to do about Miss Cameron. She was proving far more difficult to eliminate than he had first envisaged.

A figure moved in the shadows in the corner of his office. "If you truly want to rid yourself of these nuisances, you cannot allow your emotions to cloud your judgment."

The menacing voice reached Rodney from across the room, even though it was barely speaking above a whisper. Rodney shivered. Not for the first time, he wondered at the wisdom in listening to this shadowy man. He didn't trust him, not one bit, but he couldn't get out of this situation without some help. He was in too deep this time.

"And you'd best remember that."

Rodney's eyes widened. Was the voice just adding to his earlier words, or had he responded to Rodney's thoughts? It wasn't the first time Rodney had asked himself that question. It was eerie the way the voice always seemed to respond to unspoken words.

Although he was hidden by shadows, barely visible in the dark office, Rodney could see the corners of the stranger's lips curve up in an unnerving grin. It only served to underscore his belief that this man could read his mind.

"What am I supposed to do? I've tried every way I know to get rid of her! I don't even know why you're so focused on that. Even if I do get rid of Nicole Cameron, there's still the pictures to get rid of."

The figure clucked his tongue a few times and shook a dark finger. "Oh, ye of little faith." A small object came flying out of the shadows, landing on the edge of Rodney's desk. It rolled across the desk, stopping in front of Rodney.

He stared at it in wonder. It was a film canister. Turning it over in his hand, he read the word 'Evidence' printed on a sticker which had been placed on it. "How did you get this?" His luck might be turning, after all.

"That is not important. What is important is that you get the girl. Now, if you can't handle that simple task on your own, I'm afraid I'll have to take care of that myself as well. And if I have to do everything on my own..." He let the threat hang in the air.

Rodney understood precisely what he was saying. If he couldn't kill the girl, he was of no use. He didn't know why this man had taken such a keen interest in Nicole Cameron, but it wouldn't be wise to disappoint him for much longer. Rodney would much rather face court than this dark man's wrath. He thought carefully. He had to find a way to take care of this, and quickly.

A thought occurred to him – maybe he could kill two birds with one stone! He chuckled to himself. Soon, one way or another, Nicole Cameron would be out of his way – forever.

* * *

"Artemis." The voice echoed in his head and he turned toward the nearby shadows, seeing the almost imperceptible movement.

A moment later, a figure took shape in the shadows beside him and the usual shiver ran up Artemis' spine. In his many years, he'd never met anyone who moved as quickly or stayed so easily hidden from perception.

"What's wrong?" the figure questioned.

"Nothing, I'm fine."

"Really? You seem a little on edge."

"I'm just a little anxious to be done with the whole thing. If anyone found out —"

"No one is going to find out, unless you tell them. The

girl doesn't remember, and Richard isn't talking." He laughed quietly.

"But if someone did find out, I'd be dead. You know how everyone cared about Richard. He was some kind of hero to them all." Artemis spat out the words. He'd never understood why everyone always clambered to Richard. What had made him so special?

"Richard stood in front of you. He prevented others from seeing what you could really do. Soon, you can take your place of honor. You'll have the power you always deserved."

Artemis almost licked his lips at the thought. He would be the one in power, he would be the one people turned to for advice. He would get all the attention. He had a few more things to take care of, and it would all be his.

"You know what you must do."

Yes, he knew what he had to do. He just had to convince the girl to trust him, before it was too late.

18

D avid knocked on the door and waited. When Mark answered the door he seemed surprised. "What are you doing here?"

"You invited me to come over. May I come in?"

"Of course." Mark focused on the smile on David's face for a second before he led him into a small den. Sketches lined every wall and covered every flat surface.

David studied the many faces the drawings portrayed. Some he recognized, others he didn't. One thing was certain, they were extremely realistic. "I'm glad you haven't given up your sketching. You're very good."

"Actually, I did give it up for a while." Mark surveyed his sketches. He'd stopped after the funeral, not being in the mood to sketch after that. He didn't really know why he'd finally decided to sketch again, one day he'd just decided to pick up a pencil. Now, he spent every free minute – of which there were few–sketching. "I only recently picked it up again. So, what's up?"

"I wanted to let you know Nicole is going to be staying with me for a while."

"Really? So, the prodigal daughter had returned home." Mark had wondered how long it would take, although admittedly, he hadn't thought it would be so soon

"Yeah, it seemed like the logical thing to do, considering all the threats."

Mark nodded. David's house was the safest place for Nicole to be, the house and grounds were like a fortress, and thanks to David, it had one hell of a security system. "You know, you could have told me this over the phone or through telepathy, now that you've gotten the hang of it again. Why the visit?"

"I wanted to see how you were doing."

Mark stared at him dubiously. "And?"

David laughed. He'd never had been able to keep anything from Mark. "And Nicole kissed me."

"Really?" Mark grinned. This news explained the good mood David was in.

"Yeah, she kissed me the other morning. She was excited about something she figured out and she just suddenly kissed. We haven't really talked about it since, but she finally seems to be comfortable enough around me."

"How do you feel?"

David couldn't help the grin which lifted his mouth. "Good. Nervous, but good. It was amazing. I've never felt like this before, it's like the air was charged between us. Is that normal?"

Mark shrugged. "Does it matter?"

"I guess not. I guess I'd better go."

"It was good seeing you." Mark held out his arm, but David unexpectedly pulled him into a hug, instead. Mark stood stock still, unaccustomed to such physical contact.

"Thanks for being such a good friend to me."

"No problem."

* * *

"NICOLE? NICOLE!"

Nicole came to a stop at the door of the library and turned as John came rushing toward her.

"Hey Nicole, where are you headed?" He glanced around the library foyer nervously.

"I'm going by the SES meeting hall, then, I'm headed back to my apartment." She'd already taken some of her things to David's the day before, but there were a few more items she needed if she was going to be staying with David for a while.

"Why are you going by the meeting hall? There isn't a meeting today."

"I know, but I had a message on my machine saying I'd left a notebook there."

"A message?" John seemed puzzled. "Who from?"

Nicole shrugged. "I don't know, to be honest. I didn't recognize the voice, and he didn't say. He just said to come by at five, so there'd be someone to let me in."

"I'm coming with you," John announce decisively.

"John, that's not nec—"

"Nicole, the film has been stolen from evidence."

"What?" The color drained from Nicole's face.

"Susan called me about an hour ago and told me. She wanted to warn you. I've been searching for you ever since. Given what I've just told you about the film, I think this entire situation with the meeting hall sounds a little too strange."

"Yeah, maybe you're right, but we're both probably being paranoid."

"If you're going, I'm going," John announced firmly

Nicole held up her hands. "Hey, you've got no argument from me."

It only took them a few minutes to reach the meeting hall. Nicole glanced down at her watch as they reached the steps and saw it was 5:01.

A wave of nausea hit her abruptly. John took a step forward, ready to mount the stairs, but Nicole's hand shot out to stop him. It might just be extreme paranoia, but so much as a single step further made her feel sick.

"This isn't right. We've got to get out of here, right now." Nicole backed up a couple of steps.

One look at the panic in her eyes, and John was swiftly following her. They started to run from the building but had only gotten a few feet before a rumbling sound erupted inside. They glanced at one another and simultaneous ran faster.

A blast of heat knocked Nicole to the ground. She lifted her head, searching for John and realized he'd made it a little farther than she had and been knocked to his knees by the blast. She watched him lift his arms to protect his head from a shower of debris. Her ears were ringing and if she'd been able to piece together a single coherent thought, it would have occurred to her that she was also in danger of being hit by the debris. Instead, she watched as the fragments of the building landed all around her, until a sharp pain at the back of her head made everything go black.

NICOLE WAS SORE ALL OVER, especially her head. "Is she going to be okay?" she heard someone ask. The voice sounded familiar, but with her head throbbing, she couldn't place it.

"Yeah, she'll be fine." This voice was closer to her. Even with the throbbing, she knew it was David's voice. "You hear that Nicole? Be fine."

His words echoed softly in her head, and she was sure, with an absurd level of certainty, they hadn't been spoken aloud. Nicole slowly became aware of small gravel rocks, biting into her back and legs. Through a haze, she could recognize that her head and shoulders weren't on the ground. Something gently rubbed the sides of her head and the headache began to decrease. A warm sensation began to spread through her body, slowly easing the pain. Once her head had cleared considerably, she attempted to open her eyes. She blinked several times at first, blinded by bright light until her eyes adjusted. David's face slowly came into focus. "Welcome back," he said, smiling.

She smiled back. She was already feeling a lot better and being in David's arms definitely helped. His arms were warm, strong, and comforting. She surveyed the surrounding area as much as she could without moving her head. Pieces of brick, shards of metal, and slivers of glass were everywhere. "Where's John? Is he okay?" she demanded.

"He's fine, he has a few cuts and bruises. He filled me in on everything that happened, and he's gone to call the police. His phone is lost somewhere in the rubble."

Nicole heard footsteps and tried to locate their source, catching sight of John before dizziness overwhelmed her for a minute.

"Are you okay?" she heard John ask.

"I'm fine." Nicole propped herself on her elbows, ignoring the pain. "Just a few bruises and a headache."

The worst of the dizziness passed, and Nicole started to stand. Four hands instantly reached out to help her. She accepted the help without complaint, knowing that despite her bravado, she probably couldn't stand without it.

"Can you walk?" David asked.

She tested her balance, leaning her weight on one foot, then the other. "I think so." Resting a hand on David's arm, Nicole slowly took a few steps. Her balance was a little shaky, but everything seemed to be in working order.

"Hey, your glasses are here." John bent down and picked them up.

Nicole was stunned. Her hand flew to her face, where her glasses should be. Sure enough, they were missing. Her eyes grew wide and she turned her head from the billboard sign at the end of the street, to cars which were driving a couple of streets down, then to the crowd of people gathering, and finally to John and David's worried faces.

It was all completely clear. Everything was as clear as if she was wearing her glasses – clearer, in fact. Her gaze returned to David and she saw the expression in his eyes. It was as if he had already known what she'd only just discovered.

Silently, David took the glasses from John, without taking his eyes from Nicole's. He needed to get them away from this place, away from all these people.

He was still a little unnerved by the strength of Nicole's emotions which had been pounding him ever since he'd got here. He wasn't used to feeling someone else's feelings so strongly. She was confused and terribly scared. He needed to get her back to the house and let her rest and regroup. "I'm going to get Nicole out of here," he told John. "When the police arrive, I want you to find Officer Mark Stevenson, and tell him everything you told me. Don't talk to anyone else but him. Do you understand?"

"Yeah," John responded immediately. It was obvious he

was confused, but the tone of David's voice didn't leave room for discussion.

David led Nicole to his car.

Almost all the pain and dizziness had gone, but Nicole was on edge. Her skin tingled, and her senses were heightened, just like they'd been in the forest. And strangely, she could *see*. "Where are we going?" she demanded.

"We're going to my house. I think you should lie low for a few days."

"I need some things from my apartment."

David glanced over at her. Her eyes were wide, her gaze darting back and forth as if she couldn't settle on anything. She was holding herself stiffly, as if she suspected if she moved, she could shatter. He couldn't tell if she was in shock or terrified right now. Her emotions seemed to be incredibly confused. He finally decided she was probably a mix of both. "Okay, the apartment is on the way."

Nicole waited for the car to stop before she opened the door and rushed out. "I'll be right back."

"I'll come with—"

"NO!" Nicole interjected. She took a deep breath, tried to calm herself. "Please. I just need a few minutes to think. I'll just be a few minutes, I promise." Nicole rushed up to her apartment and started grabbing anything she thought she might need. After all, she didn't know when she'd be able to come back here again. She surveyed the room for a minute and sank down onto her bed. What was happening to her?

"Going somewhere?"

Nicole jumped. The man with the strange eyes strolled into her bedroom, but instead of being afraid, Nicole got angry. "What the hell are you doing in my apartment?"

"Such hostility. I'm here to help you."

Nicole stood up. "I don't know what you know or think

you know about my father, but I'm tired of all these games."

The man's smile faltered. She shouldn't have remembered meeting him before. If she managed to remember that, she might remember... well, he'd have to make sure that didn't happen. It would ruin everything. He took off his sunglasses and stared into her eyes.

Suddenly, Nicole's head start to hurt again, and the pain slowly spread through the rest of her body. Everything became blurred, everything except the man's strange eyes. Their color changed creating a hypnotic pattern she couldn't draw her gaze away from. She found herself lost in those colors, forgetting everything but the color. Then, even his eyes blurred.

She heard a noise, somewhere off in the distance. It was soft at first, but it slowly grew louder. Nicole focused on the sound, unable to grasp any other coherent thoughts.

The man's shadowy image left the room, but she couldn't move. She had no thoughts or abilities to do anything. Her willpower was gone, leaving only perception. All she could see was a blur, and all she could feel was pain.

The sound grew, stopping only after another blurry figure entered the room, his footsteps pounding. Nicole suspected her head was going to explode, his every step seemed like a sledgehammer slamming into her brain.

Something settled on her shoulder and it felt like a thousand knives, cutting into her skin. Her throbbing head was filled with a sound so loud, her hands flew up to cover her ears, to try and protect herself. With the sound dulled, she realized what she was hearing was a voice – David's voice – but she couldn't concentrate enough to work out what he was saying. She found herself being lowered onto a soft surface. Unable to stand the pain, she slipped into oblivion.

19

T he first thing she noticed was a cool towel on her forehead. She was still in pain, but it was nowhere near as severe as it had been. There was a presence beside her, and for one absurd moment, she thought the wolf was near her, but the touch of a hand against her face quickly dismissed that thought.

Her eyes blinked open. Everything was blurry, the way it normally was when she wasn't wearing her glasses. She wondered briefly if she'd only imagined being able to see, but it had seemed too real to disregard, hadn't it? She looked around as much as she could, trying to avoid any sudden movements. It appeared she was back in her room at David's house. David was sitting beside her, gently rubbing a finger up and down along the side of her face. She could just make out the worry creasing his forehead.

"How are you feeling?" he asked, sounding relieved..

She looked up into his deep, blue-green eyes and thought again of the wolf. Why was she thinking about him so much all of a sudden? Maybe it was because she hadn't seen him in a couple of days. She focused her attention back on David, on the question he'd asked. "Okay, I guess. A bit drained, as if all my energy was sapped right out of me. Everything is sore."

"What happened in your apartment?"

"My apartment?" Nicole couldn't remember going to her apartment. The last thing she remembered was waking up after the explosion and being able to see without her glasses, or at least, thinking she could see. She still wasn't sure which one it was.

"You went into your apartment to get some of your things. You were in there for a while. When I came looking for you, you were standing in your bedroom in a daze. I tried to get through to you, but it seemed like everything I did caused you more pain. You passed out shortly afterward." David shook his head. He should never have let her go up there alone, but she'd needed time to herself Still, he should have pressed the issue and insisted he go up with her.

What David said sounded familiar, but she couldn't seem to remember. It was exactly like it had been the day the man in the sunglasses followed her.

Thinking about him struck a memory. She could see him standing in her room, but she couldn't remember what he'd said or done. She ran the image through her mind several times, trying to spark another memory.

She was concentrating so hard, she didn't notice when she started to be surrounded by light, or when her head started to clear and the pain faded. The memory started to piece together in her mind like a half-forgotten dream. "The man wearing the sunglasses was in my apartment," she started slowly. "He said he was there to help me, but I didn't buy it. I told him as much. Then he took off his sunglasses and watched me with those strange eyes, and my head started throbbing, and everything blurred. It felt as if every nerve ending was burning with pain. I couldn't think or move."

"He stole your energy before you had a chance to completely heal. That's why the pain hit you so hard. You didn't have enough energy to fight it," David said, more to himself than to Nicole.

She looked at him suspiciously. "How do you know all of that?"

He sighed. "Does it really matter right now?"

She stared at him and propped herself up on her elbows. "Yes, it matters! I— " It suddenly occurred to Nicole that she could see his face clearly. Everything in the room was clear again. "I can see again!"

The corner of David's lip curved up in amusement despite his efforts to stop it. She was so excited, but she had no idea about her healing abilities. The grin left his face. She was completely oblivious to what was happening to her. He should tell her what was going on, he'd let this situation go on for too long. The wolf was coming out, and she didn't know the first thing about it. He needed to find a way to explain all of this to Nicole. "Your energy has had a chance to build up again," he began, starting with what was easiest to explain.

"Years of myopia don't just clear up because someone gets a good night's sleep," she pointed out.

"I'm not talking about that kind of energy. You're beginning to tap into a different energy source." The ringing of the doorbell echoed through the house. "I'll be right back."

David sighed in relief. He needed a minute or two to gather his thoughts before he basically destroyed Nicole's entire concept of reality. Yeah, a minute would be nice.

Nicole watched in frustration when David left the

room. It wasn't long before curiosity got the better of her. She was feeling a lot better, so it wasn't as if she really needed to stay in bed. She might as well find out what was going on, she reasoned. Quietly, she slipped out of bed and tiptoed down the hall. Peeking around the corner, she discovered David talking to Officer Stevenson at the bottom of the stairs.

"How's she doing?" he asked.

This was getting stranger by the minute. Why would David be talking to the police officer? She vaguely recalled hearing David tell John he should only talk to Officer Stevenson, but that only confused her more.

The voices downstairs faded, and another voice filled her head. "Nicole," the voice repeated several times. She found herself inexplicably drawn to that voice. It sounded familiar, but she couldn't quite place it. She found she was compelled to follow the voice, needed to go to it.

Nicole walked back into her room, automatically opening the balcony door and stepping out. Following the voice, she walked quickly down the circular staircase, hardly aware of the cold metal. She padded across the dew damp grass, only coming to a stop when she reached a clearing in the woods.

A figure stepped from the shadows and Nicole snapped out of her daze. "What am I doing here?" She glanced around the clearing, noticing for the first time how cold she was in her thin clothing and bare feet.

The man who'd been in her apartment came walking toward her. "Now, perhaps we can talk without interruption."

When he stepped into the moonlight, Nicole noticed he wasn't wearing his sunglasses. Even in this dim light, she could see his eyes changing color. Her thoughts started to cloud, but Nicole shook it off. "Oh no, I'm not going to let you mess with my mind, again."

"You don't even know who, or what, you are."

He took another step closer, and she retreated another step. "Stay away from me." She tried to surreptitiously work out in which direction the house lay, but she couldn't figure it out. The trees blocked too much of her view, and she didn't recognize her surroundings.

"Now, is that any way to treat your uncle?"

Nicole stared at him for a second. "Uncle?"

"Yes, before his unfortunate death, your father was my brother. I've been looking for you for many years. I feared you might have died as well."

"How did he die?" Nicole found herself asking.

"A plane crash," he whispered softly.

Thoughts of the nightmare came to Nicole's mind: lighting, thunder, jolting movements, and surroundings which appeared to be the interior of a plane. What if he was telling the truth? Then something else he'd said came to the forefront of her mind. "What did you mean, when you said I don't know what I am?"

Time for the clincher. He came a few steps closer and leaned in. "You're a werewolf," he whispered.

"What?" Nicole backed up several steps. He was obviously insane, it was the only explanation that made sense. "Look, I don't know what you've been smoking, but I'm out of here." She turned around and started walking, hoping she was picking the right direction to reach the house.

"What I say is the truth." His words followed her. "You've felt different lately, as if all of your senses were heightened."

She froze mid step. How could he know about that?

"Strange things have been happening to you," he said in measured tones. "You heal faster... your eyesight has improved.". He knew he'd truly hit home when he saw her back stiffen. He smiled. Now he had her full attention.

Nicole turned around slowly and watched him guardedly. "It's not possible."

"Why not? You know it's true. You can *feel* it. You are a werewolf, just like your father, just like your mother, and just like me." He took another step toward her. "Don't be afraid." His voice was gentle, and he stared pointedly into her eyes. The colors swirled around his irises.

Nicole struggled to clear her thoughts. "How do I know you're telling the truth?"

He hid his frustration. This was proving to be much more difficult that it should be. He poured more energy into his efforts. "I could show you, if you'll come with me."

She almost agreed, her head starting to throb, but then, she heard David's voice inside her head, calling her name. "David. I have to get back to the house before he gets too worried."

"Forget about David!" he growled. He took a slow breath, and his voice became low and gentle again. "David has known what you are all along. He just hasn't told you the truth."

"What are you talking about?"

"David is a werewolf, too, but he wants to use you. That's why he hasn't said anything. Our family is very powerful, which in turn makes you very powerful. David wants to exploit that power."

Nicole narrowed her eyes. "What kind of power?"

"It's manifested itself in different ways throughout the years. The generations of our family have been filled with those whose strength was unparalleled; those so quick, their movements could not be seen, even by our own kind. There have been strong psychics, and healers also. The stories are endless. David Coverton is an evil man, not someone to be trusted. He killed his own family, set their house on fire while everyone was asleep."

Nicole shook her head. "David wouldn't do that. He's not like that." She pressed a hand against her temple, the pain was starting to affect her, making it difficult to think clearly.

"Why, because he saved you a few times? It was all part of his plan. You don't mean anything to him, Nicole. You're just a means to an end."

"No, no, I don't believe that." Nicole shook her head again and backed up. What he was saying couldn't be true. She knew it, felt it in her heart. Still, the words nagged at her insecurities.

He could feel her resistance weakening and hid a triumphant smile.

"Leave her alone, Artemis."

David stepped out of the darkness. Nicole's mind instantly began to clear. She looked from David to the strange man who claimed to be her uncle and noticed his eyes had stopped changing colors. Maybe it had only been her imagination.

She returned her attention to David. Nicole had never seen so much veiled anger in his eyes before. It emanated from his body and was clearly focused on the other man. David took a few steps closer to them. "So, you're the one who's been tormenting Nicole."

"I'm not the one who's been keeping things from her. I'm just concerned for the well being of my niece."

"I want you off of my property, Artemis."

"Your property?" Artemis' voice boomed. Anger filled him, his purpose here momentarily forgotten. How dare this upstart say such things to him? "You have no right to this land, and you know it."

"I have more right to it than you do. You hated Richard."

"He was my little brother! You were just a common thief who somehow wormed his way into Richard's good graces. Then again, Richard always did care too much for those damned servants, so I guess his bad judgment where you were concerned shouldn't be so surprising."

Nicole saw David stiffen. "My past is my past. Now, you can either leave on your own, or I can remove you."

Artemis was about to argue the point further when he noticed Nicole glancing back and forth between the two of them and remembered his reason for coming here. If he wanted to get on her good side, he needed to be more careful and not let his anger get out of hand. Better to go peacefully now and come back later, when Mr. Coverton wasn't around to get in the way. At least he'd already planted the seeds of mistrust in her, he could see it in her eyes. If only he could stay and watch that street slime trying to explain all his lies. Artemis almost grinned. It would be fun to watch. He dusted off his sleeves and tilted his head to each side, cracking his neck audibly. "Fine, I'll go." He walked toward Nicole and paused, looking into her eyes. *"Remember what I said."*

Nicole's eyes widened. His lips hadn't moved, but she'd clearly heard him speak.

The corners of Artemis' lips turned up in a smile. He continued past her, disappearing into the shadows.

David came across to her as the second Artemis was gone. "Are you alright?" He reached a hand out to her.

Nicole took a quick step backwards, and put her hands up, palms facing outward. "Who are you?"

David sighed. The time for secrets was over. He'd waited for too long. Now that he knew Artemis was the one who'd been approaching her, he knew he had to tell her everything, now more than ever. "Why don't we get out of the cold?"

Nicole shook her head adamantly. "I'm not moving until you tell me the truth."

He took a deep breath and began. "My name is David Coverton, or at least, that's the name I use now. David has always been my first name, but I've changed my surname a couple of times. I was born in 1814, not far from here actually. I met Richard, your father, when I was a kid. I was alone, living on the streets, and he took me in. What I told you before was true. He was the one who gave me a chance. He took care of me and gave me a home and a job. I'd never known that type of kindness before." His voice roughened with emotion. He hadn't talked about this in a while, but the memories were still very clear in his mind. It was almost as though it had only happened last week. "He taught me almost everything I know. When I was eighteen, he told me what he was."

"Which was?" She was nearly too afraid to ask, but she forced the question out.

"The best way to describe it... is a werewolf," he said, repeating what Artemis had told her.

She couldn't believe her ears, but she forced herself to stay still and listen to the rest of his words. She needed to hear what he had to say. "It's not the same as the ones you see in the movies. Richard explained he was more like a shape shifter than anything else. The wolf is a part of the person. It comes to their aid in times of trouble, or whenever it's called. It doesn't force the person to go out and kill during a full moon, or any of that crap. Richard was a natural born werewolf, and he told me he came from a long line of natural werewolves." David ran his hand across the back of his neck. "You see, there are two ways a person can become a werewolf. They can be born one if their parents are both werewolves, or they can be changed through a transfer of blood. Natural werewolves are usually stronger, and they're able to reach the wolf and the abilities it grants them at different times, depending on training and necessity."

"Necessity?" she questioned, despite the voice in her head saying this was crazy.

"In a dangerous situation, sometimes the wolf will reveal itself in order to protect the person. Sometimes the abilities reveal themselves over time, and sometimes it happens far more quickly. In your case, some of your abilities – heightened hearing and smell, as well as resistance to the cold – manifested early. It's only been recently, since you've had so many threats against your life, that the rest of your abilities have begun to reveal themselves. That's why your eyesight improved, and the injuries from the explosion healed so quickly."

Despite her doubt, Nicole found herself thinking that part made sense. It had seemed odd that she'd healed so quickly. The same thing had happened after her car brakes were sabotaged. She'd been sore and achy one minute, but when they'd reached the doctor's, nothing hurt. Still, she wasn't quite ready to believe all of this without thinking it over a little more. "That man said my family was very powerful."

"That's true," David conceded. "It's thought that yours could be the oldest werewolf family. No one knows how far back your lineage goes, but it's unquestionably up there as one of the oldest. There are stories of extremely powerful werewolves coming from your line. You heal quicker, run faster, have sharper intellects – everything you can possibly imagine has been said about them."

"Is it true?" She almost laughed. She wasn't even sure if she believed any of this. She should probably decide if were-wolves were real before she started debating the truth of individual details about their family line. But she kept her mouth shut. If this was a delusion, she might as well have her details straight so she could tell them all to the nice man with the white lab coat and the padded room later.

"Possibly. No one knows for sure, but your family is respected nonetheless. Except for Artemis, that is. He's pretty much the black sheep of the family."

"So, if my family is supposed to have these remarkable abilities, what about other werewolves?"

"They're quicker than most humans. Their senses are sharper. They can heal quicker than any human. You see, generally werewolves maintain good health. When they do get injured or sick, they heal swiftly, but they can die from injuries if they don't take care of them. Many have died in wars and other battles. I heard that some died during the plague, although their normally strong immune system kept most from getting sick. Basically, anything that can kill a normal person can kill a werewolf, it's just a little harder to do. Other than that, they don't really die of old age.

When I was twenty-one, I learned firsthand about the healing abilities of werewolves." David paused briefly, taking a deep breath before going on. "One day, when I walked into a mercantile to get something, I ran into some people I never thought I'd see again. At least, I'd hoped I wouldn't. It was obvious they were as thrilled to see me as I was to see them, so I got the hell out of there. Unfortunately, they caught up to me and shoved me between the buildings. There were three of them, and one had a knife. After the first two got tired of kicking and punching me, the other one used that knife, several times." His voice faltered. David could still see their faces, as if it had been yesterday, instead of close to two hundred years ago. He could remember the pain of the knife slicing into his skin. He rubbed over a couple of the spots where the knife had cut unconsciously, the memory of the pain almost real. "He buried it up to its hilt in my chest. As I lay there, I could feel the blood leaving my body but I didn't have the strength to do anything, and suddenly Richard appeared. He took out his own knife and sliced the palm of his hand, letting the blood drip down onto my injury. My energy gradually started returning. I was still very weak, but the bleeding stopped, and the pain began to subside. Richard took me back to his home and took care of me for the next week, giving me a little of his blood every day, until I was completely healed."

"Why did those men want to kill you?" The thought of how close David had come to death made a shiver run across her skin. Something that had happened that long ago could have kept her from ever getting the chance to know him. She sent up a silent prayer of thanks that he'd been allowed to remain in this world all those years ago.

"Remember how I told you I used to be a thief?" His attention focused on a point in the distance and he walked a few steps past her. "Before Richard found me, I was doing anything I could do to survive. Shortly before I met Richard, I'd managed to steal quite a large sum from those three men."

"But why didn't they just call the police, or sheriff, or constable, or whatever the law enforcement people were called back then, when they saw you?"

"They weren't exactly on the up and up themselves."

"What did you do with the money?"

"I saved it. Since Richard was taking care of me, I didn't have to worry about anything. Of course, I never thought it would last. I always figured Richard would get tired of having me around, but he didn't. The money remained hidden in a box in my room until about fifty years ago, when I started investing it." David smiled gently at Nicole. "What else would you like to know?"

Nicole thought for a second. Where to start? She had a million questions running through her head. "Is that man really my uncle?"

"Yes. His name is Vincent Artemis. Artemis is his middle name, but that's what everyone knows him by. He was Richard's older brother, but the two never got along. I heard Richard used to call him Artie, just to annoy him. He hated the nickname and thought it was disrespectful of Richard to use it. I never actually met him before tonight, but I've seen his picture a few times."

"When he left, I heard him speak, but his lips didn't move."

"He was using telepathy. All werewolves can communicate that way, with a little practice," he added ruefully.

"Does that mean you can read my thoughts?"

"Only if you want me to. New werewolves usually need to learn to construct a barrier around their thoughts, but you seem to already have one in place. You never let down your guard."

"That's not true." She revealed the first hint of emotion he'd seen since she started this conversation. "I opened up to you." As much as she could, anyway. Maybe she did push people away, always holding back. She pushed back her emotions now, reinforcing her control. She couldn't lose control. She had to change the subject to something she could handle better. "Do you have any pictures of my parents?"

"Yes, back at the house."

"Show them to me." Even though it sounded like a command, her eyes pleaded with him, and he could sense the vulnerability she was trying too hard to cover up.

They walked back to the house in silence and David led Nicole to the library and retrieved a dusty old photo album. He blew off the dust and opened it to a page near the back, handing the album to Nicole.

She noticed her hand was shaking as she took it. Maybe this hadn't been the best subject change to choose. She closed her eyes and took a steadying breath, before she finally let herself look at the picture.

Two smiling faces stared back at her. She unconsciously traced their faces. The woman, her mother, had long flowing hair which reached below her waist. It was very dark, probably black or dark brown. She couldn't tell. Her mother's dress flowed like her hair, reaching to her feet. In her face, Nicole saw a striking resemblance. "What was her name?"

"Caroline."

"Caroline," she repeated. She felt a tear run down her cheek and studied the other half of the picture. The man – her father – also had dark hair and he wore a turtleneck shirt and jeans. He looked strong and proud, his shoulders broad, his head held high. Around his neck was a pendant, exactly like the one she wore. She compared her necklace to the one in the picture and knew they were identical. "He's wearing the same necklace I do." She glanced up at David and noticed his eyes were filled with unshed tears as he stared at the photo.

"It's a family heirloom. Richard believed it carried all of the power of his ancestors with it. He gave it to you for your third birthday."

"He gave a family heirloom to a three-year-old?"

"It was a dangerous time. There had been several attempts on Richard's life. He was afraid something might happen to you, and he hoped the pendant would protect you."

"Artemis said they died in a plane crash."

"That's true, although, the plane was never found. A couple who lived in the mountains saw the place crash, but when they went to discover what had happened, they couldn't find the plane – only you. They took you to the police, who ended up putting you in the orphanage. When I found out about the crash, I had some friends ensure you were placed with a good family. They took care of the paperwork, so that basically, you disappeared. I figured it would be the best way to ensure your safety. If something had happened to Richard, with the kind of security he had, I didn't see how I could keep you safe unless no one could find you. After a few months, people forgot all about the crash. No one saw the plane, except for that couple who'd seen it come down, and since there was no evidence of the crash, everyone believed the couple had been wrong about what they saw. I never really found out what happened that night. I watched over you for a time, but I didn't want anyone to discover me watching you, or it would give your location away. There were plenty of others in the area who had known and liked Richard, so I moved out of town, , and left them to keep an eye on you. I wanted to be close enough in case anything ever happened, but far enough away to draw attention away from you."

"So, people have been watching out for me all these years?"

"Yeah."

"That explains a lot."

The grandfather clock began to chime. The sound filled

the house, echoing down the many halls. "It's late. You should get some rest."

"You're probably right." Nicole traced the picture again with her finger. She didn't want to put the album down.

"You can have the picture, if you'd like."

Nicole gazed up into David's eyes. "Thank you." She took the picture and handed the album back to David.

They walked upstairs to her room in silence. When they reached her door, Nicole turned to face him, a thought suddenly occurring to her. "You're the black wolf, aren't you?"

He had the decency to look self-conscious. "Yes."

She nodded silently and slipped into her room, closing the door quietly behind her.

20

The thunder was crashing down outside. Rain pounded on the metal ceiling, sounding like bullets. Everything was dark and eerie since the cabin lights had gone out. She heard a woman's voice for a couple of seconds, until thunder drowned it out along with everything else. She lifted her hands to cover her ears. It was so loud, it seemed as if a sledgehammer was hitting her skull. As the ringing lessened, she heard a new sound –laughter.

Lightning made it possible to see a shadowy image coming toward her father. She strained to see, catching glimpses every time the lightning flashed. It looked like her uncle and her father were fighting, but that couldn't be right, her uncle wasn't supposed to be here.

A loud shot rang out. Intense pressure slammed her body against the seat. She couldn't move. After a moment, the sounds of fighting erupted again. The pressure started to decrease.

Finally she could move again. Her seat shook violently. and the pressure returned briefly. The shaking worsened. Another shot rang out. There was a spark and then fire erupted. The flames cast an eerie light over everything. Her father was in the front of the plane, where the pilot should have been. Her uncle was on the floor. He looked dazed. She glanced at the seat beside her.

Her mom wasn't there. Panic filled her chest. She leaned forward and discovered her mother lying on the floor. Nicole called out to her but got no response.

The fire began to spread, and she stared into the flames, unable to look anywhere else. Her uncle's voice echoed in her head. "He killed his own family. Set their house on fire while everyone was asleep." Everything around her faded away except for the fire. It filled her vision. "He can't be trusted. He's just using you."

David's face appeared in the flames. He was laughing. "You actually thought I cared about you? Why would I care about you? Everyone you get close to dies. You've already gone through two sets of parents, and you're still just a child. I only want you because of how powerful you will be. You would be a great asset. No one would challenge me with you on my side." His laugh echoed around her, until it diminished completely.

David's face disappeared, Artemis' taking its place. "He's lied to you. He's using you. He can't be trusted."

There was a loud crash of thunder. A forest replaced the fire. Branches caught at her clothes as she ran. She was simultaneously old and young. Rain and tears soaked her body. She was alone, lost and afraid as she ran deeper and deeper into the darkness, trying desperately to escape whatever it was chasing her.

Something grabbed her. She struggled against it, but her arms were pinned to her sides. She grew increasingly desperate. She had to find a way to free herself. Her breaths grew shallow. Her skin crawled. She screamed to be released. A flash of lightning allowed her to see her tormentor briefly. Color changing eyes stared back at her for just a moment before darkness engulfed her again.

"Nicole!" David's voice called. Lightning flashed again, only this time, it was David's face she saw in the burst of illumination.

"Let me go," she shrieked repeatedly, until it became more of a tearful plea than a demand.

"Nicole." Her room replaced the image of the dark forest she'd been trapped in. David was leaning over her with his hands resting on her arms. The sheets, her clothes, even his hands made her feel claustrophobic. She bolted out of bed, shaking her arms and straightening her clothes. She hurried out onto the balcony, hoping the cold outside would cool her down. After a couple of minutes, she started to feel a little calmer. She leaned on the railing and took a deep breath. She could still feel some of the desperation from her nightmare. Cool tears slipped down her cheeks.

David placed a reassuring hand on her shoulder and her control snapped, her body racked with sobs. She slid down onto the balcony floor, unable to stand anymore. David gently pulled her into his arms, not saying a word, letting her cry.

After some time, Nicole's thoughts began to clear a little. They were still a jumbled mess, but she could pick out the occasional coherent thought. The nightmare remained hazy, but she could remember parts of it. It had been so real. She could still see the fire, still hear her uncle's words. What he'd said about David couldn't be true. She didn't believe David killed his family, but what if he didn't really care about her? Even if he wasn't as sinister as Artemis said, he could still be taking care of her out of some obligation to her father. Besides, she lost everyone she ever got close to. How could she risk letting someone get close to her again? She sat up and wiped the tears from her face, sniffling.

David brushed away a couple of tears she'd missed. "That must have been some nightmare."

Nicole nodded, still sniffling.

He waited a moment to see if she would say anything about it, but she stayed quiet. "I have some good news for you. Rodney Steagel has been arrested for arranging the explosion at the meeting hall. It seems the police have plenty of evidence to connect him to it. So, that's one less thing for you to worry about."

The weight on her shoulders seemed to lessen slightly. There was still a lot left to deal with, though. She had to find out more about the night of the plane crash, the night her parents died. "Where did the plane go down?" she questioned.

David studied her closely. He wasn't sure they should be talking about this subject right now. She was already upset, and it could only serve to upset her more to talk about that night. Then again, she'd spent her entire life not knowing what happened. In the end, he couldn't refuse her questions, not any more. "Near Bear Mountain. I went up there myself and never found any evidence. Was that what your nightmare was about?"

She shook her head. "It doesn't matter, I'm okay, now. I'm starved." She hurried out through the bedroom and headed downstairs to the kitchen.

David decided to let the subject drop for the time being and followed her. He wouldn't push. There would be time enough to talk later, when she was ready.

* * *

BILLY SIFTED through a stack of papers on his desk, pausing briefly to rub a hand over his tired eyes. His hand brushed fleetingly across his unshaven face. There had to be at least three days growth there. No time to worry about that now.

Wearily, he continued the search. "Now where is that... oh, there it is." He held the paper up to the light. "Ah, there's the author. I knew it started with a 'J'," he muttered.

A knock sounded at the door. Billy ignored it at first, but it came again, the sound more urgent. "Yes, what is it?" he called absentmindedly, already sifting through more papers and taking notes.

The door creaked when it opened. A skinny, blond-haired boy of no more than twenty tentatively entered. "Dr. Cam—Cameron?" he stuttered. "May I—uh— speak with you for a moment?"

Billy glanced up from the paper he was reading and smiled at the boy. "Sure Al, come right in." He put the papers down and leaned back in his chair, recalling that he'd sent Al to get something. He really must be working too hard. Whatever it was, it had completely slipped his mind. He desperately needed a vacation. Inspiration finally hit. "Where's the package?"

"Well, um, I went down to the main office like you requested, but they said they don't have the book you told me to bring back."

"What?" Billy's eyebrows came together. "That doesn't make any sense." He picked up the phone and dialed the office number. "Hey, Barbara, it's Bill Cameron. Could you get that package which came in for me the other day? Yeah... how... you only called me about it yesterday. No, I'm sure. Your message is still on my answering machine." He glanced over at the machine and noticed the red light wasn't blinking anymore. That was odd. He didn't remember erasing the message. "I need you to look again. It's a very valuable manuscript. Okay. Let me know." He set down the phone and sighed. "Thanks for letting me know about this, Al."

"No problem. Do you know what happened to it?"

"No. Hopefully they've just misplaced it."

Al shrugged, tugging at his shirt sleeve. "You know how organized things are around here. I'm surprised they don't lose the paychecks."

"Yeah, but that manuscript is the only one of its kind at the university," Billy said, more to himself than to Al. "I had to pull some strings to even get the opportunity to look at it."

"I'm sure they'll find it. They probably just mixed it up with some other stuff. I've seen stranger things happen. But, um, I have to go now. I hope everything works out Dr. Cameron. Bye."

"Bye." The door squeaked when it closed, the only sound in the otherwise silent room. Billy reached over and pushed the play button, on his answering machine, just to be sure, but there was no message. He checked his other mailboxes, but it was nowhere on the machine. It was confusing, he'd made a point of saving that message, and now it wasn't there. Either way, there was nothing he could do about it right now. He'd just have to hope they found the manuscript in the front office. Billy pushed thoughts of the incident aside for the moment and returned to work.

NICOLE TOOK a circuitous route around the garden for the tenth time. She couldn't see David, but she knew he was nearby. He'd been keeping a close eye on her all day. Raised voices reached her through her thoughts. She surveyed the garden in surprise before she realized the voices were coming from the front of the house. She shouldn't be able to hear them from this distance, but apparently, she could. Things like this had been happening to her all day. She'd always possessed excellent hearing, but this was ridiculous. And it wasn't only her hearing. She could still see perfectly without her glasses, and she was beginning to notice more intensive smells, too. Thinking about it too much only gave her a headache, so she tried to concentrate on the voices instead. It sounded like Artemis and David were arguing. She walked closer to the garden gates, so she could hear what they were saying better.

"I'm not letting you anywhere near her," David said firmly.

"You have no right to keep me from her. You've kept the truth from her for too long. I will see her, with or without your permission."

"So you can try that mind trick again? I don't think so."

"I have only her best interests at heart, unlike you. This is a difficult time for Nicole I have every right to be with her now, to assist her in handling the transition. I should be the one who helps her unlock her abilities. I'm a blood relative. I should have been guiding her all along, after Richard and Caroline's deaths. I would have been, if you hadn't interfered where you had no place. She belongs with family."

"Don't go spouting that bullshit with me. You never tried to be a part of her life before they died, but now you're all gung ho to do the family thing? I don't know what you're trying to achieve, but I'm not going to let you manipulate her."

"Why don't you ask Nicole what she wants? Are you so sure she doesn't want contact with her closest remaining connection to her family?"

David was silent for a moment, and she felt his mind

momentarily touch hers, discovering she was listening to them. He backed off, but she was aware that he remained partially connected. "If she really wants to speak with you, I won't stop her. But I won't leave her alone, unguarded around you, not as long as I think you're still a threat to her."

David spoke to Artemis, but she knew he was also leaving the invitation to her, letting her choose whether to speak to her uncle or not. Quietly, she backed away from the gate and walked deeper into the garden, silently telling David know she'd heard his offer, but she didn't want to talk to Artemis right now.

She couldn't believe how easily she'd accepted David touching her mind, how easy it had become to send thoughts and impressions back to him. Just last night, everything had seemed so impossible, and today she was accepting these strange abilities as if they made perfect sense. It was still hard to believe any of what she'd been told, but she had discovered that she wanted to believe it, at the same time. It made so many things make more sense; the way she'd been feeling lately, the reason why this house seemed so familiar. If it was true, it proved that the paranormal abilities and creatures she'd always researched perhaps did exist. It was an appealing thought and would justify her obsessive searching.

It also meant her parents truly had died in a plane crash when she was a child. There was no hope of ever finding them, getting to know them. She would never know if they were proud of their daughter. It wasn't until the possibility had been completely removed that she'd realized how much she'd secretly hoped for it.

She wanted to get out of the house, drive up to Bear Mountain. She needed to see for herself where the plane crash happened. But first, she needed to get away from

David. Part of her wanted him to come along with her, but another part was already pulling away from him, putting her mental barriers back in place. Nicole knew she was using the events of the previous day as an excuse to shore up her defenses. She was running away from her emotions, just the way she always did. It might not be the right thing to do, but it was familiar, and there was something comforting about familiar.

Consequently, if she got a chance to sneak out of the house and travel to Bear Mountain... she was going to take it..

21

M eg crumpled the note in her fist and held it there for a moment before straightening it back out. Without bothering to read it again, she folded it neatly several times and tucked it away in her pocket.

Catching a glimpse of herself in the mirror, she sighed. She was a wreck, placed completely on edge by this simple note. She needed to talk to someone about it, but she loathed the prospect of doing so. All she wanted to do was put the entire event out of her mind and get on with her life, exactly the way she had before. Whoever had sent this note probably didn't know anything anyway. It was probably some sick joke. Even if they did know anything, it wasn't as if it mattered. It was in the past. She was letting a few words on a piece of paper have way too much power over her. After all, she'd survived and moved on. The worst part was over. What damage could a few memories do?

Even so, she needed to get out, experience a change of surroundings for a few hours. Grabbing her address book, she flipped back to the last entry she'd made. *David Cover-*

ton. From what Nicole had told her, his house shouldn't be too difficult to find. The drive would give her a chance to clear her head, and she could check out how Nicole was doing. Grabbing her keys and jacket, she headed out the door.

Meg drove on automatic pilot most of the way, only paying more attention as the trees grew thicker. Checking the address she had against every mailbox, she finally found a match and drove hesitantly down the driveway. The large house appeared, more magnificent than anything she'd imagined. She almost went back down the drive to check the address again, but in the same moment, she saw David standing outside, talking to another man. Even from this distance, the conversation seemed tense. When she parked the car she sat and watched the two men for a minute or two, noting the obvious hostility between them. She didn't recognize the second man, but even looking at him gave her the creeps. When she got out of the car and approached the house, the man put on a pair of sunglasses and walked back to his own vehicle, which was parked nowhere near hers, thankfully.

David smiled, but it was obviously strained. "Hello Meghan. How are you today?"

"Oh, I've been better. I've been worse. You?"

His smile brightened. "I'd say that about covers it. I'll get Nicole for you."

Before he could finished the sentence, Meg was engulfed in a hug, Nicole's arms wrapped tightly around her neck.

"Hey you! It's so good to see you. Let me show you around."

Before Meg managed to get a word out, Nicole ushered her into the house and started giving her a tour. Meghan noted with some confusion that David had remained outside. She didn't hear the front door open and close again until they had made their way upstairs.

"And this is my room for now. Pretty enormous, huh?" Nicole absentmindedly noticed that she could hear classical music running through Meg's mind. Trying to ignore it, she rubbed at some dust on the dresser, distractedly, trying to get her mind under control.

"What's wrong?" Meg asked, closing the bedroom door behind them.

Nicole's eyes widened. "That transparent?"

"Yep. Spill." Meg plopped down onto the end of the bed and waited for Nicole to talk.

Nicole leaned against the dresser and sighed. "To be honest, I don't think I can explain right now. Things have been kind of crazy the last couple of days, and I've honestly been feeling like I'm losing my mind. There are a million things I want to tell you, but I've still got a lot that I need to figure out for myself. All I know is I'm *really* glad you're here." Nicole shook her head, attempting to clear the music from her mind.

"Is this something to do with David? 'Cause I can take you back to your apartment, or even back to my place if you want to get out of here. You know you can always stay with me if you don't feel safe alone."

"I appreciate it, but I'm afraid it's more complicated than that. You remember how I told you this house made me feel that first time I came here?" Meg nodded. "Okay, amplify that about a thousand times and you have how I'm feeling right now. Do you understand?"

"Not really," Meg looked at Nicole apologetically. She really wished she knew what was going on with Nicole, but Nicole herself couldn't seem to wrap her mind around it. It made Meg feel helpless, almost as if she and Nicole were strangers, instead

241

of best friends. Grabbing the side of the sheets, she pulled them off the bed. She laid the quilt out on the floor. Nicole watched quizzically as Meg meticulously tied one corner of the top sheet to the bedpost before hooking the other side over a chair. She dragged over other random pieces of furniture to hold the other two corners. Standing with hands on her hips, she nodded with pride at her makeshift fort.

"Okay," Nicole giggled, "what's next?"

"S'mores," she answered, matter-of -factly. Turning on her heel, she went back the way they came and raided the pantry until she came up with the necessary ingredients. "Plates?" she asked. Nicole looked around and began checking the cabinets until she found one. Layering out graham crackers, chocolate bars, and mini marshmallows, Meg popped the plate into the microwave and hit the timer. Nicole grabbed soft drinks from the fridge, and the two of them carried their treats back to the bedroom.

Taking Nicole by the hand, Meg pulled her down to the floor. Together they crawled into the blanket fort. Meg poked her head out long enough grab the pillows from the bed, and the two of them began to eat. "Can I see that phone John gave you?"

Nicole nodded and stuck her head out the blanket to retrieve it from her dresser. "What do you want it for?" she asked while handing it over.

"I want to play 'Breakout," Meg answered, settling in against the pillows and tapping buttons on the phone.

Nicole laughed. "Why don't you just play a game on your phone?"

Meg shrugged. "My phone needs the minutes reloaded, so I left it at home."

The beeps and dings of the game joined the sound of

music in Nicole's head. She plopped down on the quilt and pillows and stared up at the blanket. Absentmindedly braiding the end of her hair, she looked over at Meg, hunched over the game. "Do you think I could pull off red hair?"

Meg raised an eyebrow and looked over. "Hmmm, maybe." Meg pulled a compact mirror from her purse and handed it to Nicole. "Here, sit up." Me positioned herself behind Nicole and held her hair over Nicole's while she held up the compact to see how it looked. "Not bad. Hey, I think I saw a can of beets in the pantry. We could try coloring your hair with that."

"Beets? What if it looks terrible?"

"Then, we'll go to the store tomorrow and get you a new hair dye."

"I don't know. What if it goes terribly wrong and all my hair falls out?"

"Don't worry," Meg patted her shoulder. "I bet you'll be beautiful bald." Nicole groaned as Meg pulled her out the fort. Two hours and a few ruined bath towels later and they were done. "Voila!"

Nicole looked in the mirror at her new hair color. It was darker than before, with red and purple highlights in the sunlight from the bathroom window. "Not bad."

Nicole rubbed her temples to ease her ever increasing headache. Not sure if it was the smell of the beets and vinegar or the constant stream of music playing in her head, she tossed her towel into the hamper and went back to her bedroom with Meg following. Nicole clamped her hand down on the edge of the dresser to avoid screaming in frustration as the music continued. "Meg, since when do you think so much about classical music? What is that, anyway?

I think I've heard it before, but I can't remember where, and it's driving me crazy."

"It's just some sonata, I think. I heard it at a concert I went to last week for one of my classes." Meg searched Nicole's eyes. "Since when do you hear so much of what I'm thinking, anyway? You've always picked up on a song or two, maybe a phrase or a few words – but this is downright eerie."

Nicole stared back at her in surprise. "I thought it was only because you were just thinking about music more than normal."

"Are you kidding? I've always got one song or another going through my head. Doesn't matter if I'm watching TV or taking a test. Sometimes I think I'm living in some kind of deranged musical."

"Oh." Nicole rubbed her temples, unable to speak as the music progressed into a loud crescendo.

"She doesn't look so good," she heard Meg's voice announce softly in her head. "You don't look so good," Meg echoed aloud.

"I'm fine." Out of the corner of her eye, she caught Meg worrying at her lower lip.

"She doesn't look fine. She looks like she's in pain and she seems confused. Maybe I should go, let her get some rest . but I don't want to just leave. I should stay and try to help her feel better. I should do something. What could I do? We could watch a movie, but I have a class... never mind, I'll ditch. Nicole is more important.

"Go to your class. I'll be fine."

Meg's eyes held a hint of surprise and she raised a skeptical eyebrow.

"I'm not fine right now, but I will be," Nicole added. "I promise. I just need a little time to collect my thoughts and rest... a little time alone. I promise to call you the second I need anything – day or night," she added before Meg had a chance to voice that last thought."

Meg stood up, still a little off balance from their conversation, and walked to the bedroom door. "If you say you'll be all right and you want to stay here then that's good enough for me. But the second you change your mind call me, and I'll be here as soon as I can."

"Thanks." Nicole hugged Meg tightly, then opened the door. "Do you want me to walk you out?"

"Nah, that's okay. I can find my way. It's straight past the penguins and a right at the swan ice sculpture, right?"

Nicole smiled at the sarcasm and led Meg down the hall. "In that case, I'll walk you to your car."

She watched Meg's car until it disappeared down the driveway, hidden from view by trees. The music faded away with her departure. When she could no longer hear the car in the distance, Nicole turned and walked back around to the garden. She still needed to decide what to do. It was getting late, but she wasn't too worried about that the time. She'd always had excellent night vision, and she wasn't planning to drive too quickly.

She listened until she was certain David was busy and snuck in to the house to get his keys. Quietly heading back outside, she slipped behind the wheel of his car. A quick glance at a map, and she was on her way.

David watched the car peel out of the driveway and shook his head. He'd been expecting this was going to happen all day. Other than their brief connection while he was talking to Artemis, he'd felt Nicole pulling away from him ever since last night. Luckily, he had a second car and a fairly good idea of where she was heading, so he waited a few minutes to avoid her seeing his car, then he started to follow.

It didn't take Nicole long to arrive at Bear Mountain. It was almost as though she'd known exactly where she needed to go. She stepped out of the car and a shiver ran down her spine. Thunder rumbled low in the distance. "Great," she muttered. A storm was the last thing she needed right now.

She followed a dirt path for several minutes, before a strange sensation drew her away from it. She pushed branches out of her way as she walked through dense foliage and made her way through what seemed to be miles of trees, until she came upon a large clearing. Most of the clearing was filled with wild flowers and weeds, except for one large spot in which very little grew. The dirt and what little foliage was present had been pressed down as if by a large, heavy weight. It reminded Nicole of the crop circles she'd sometimes seen investigated as part of a UFO sighting.

Walking towards the area, a tremendous surge of anxiety swept over Nicole.

A drop of water hit the top of her head, then a second, and a third. She held out her hand and several drops of cool rainwater hit her palm. Maybe this hadn't been such a good idea.

She turned to head back to the cover of the trees, and stumbled over something. She hit the ground hard, on her knees, sending a jolt of pain up one leg. Getting up to her feet and dusting off her jeans, Nicole glanced back at what had tripped her up.

Light reflected from a shiny surface.

Nicole dropped to her knees and started to dig with her fingers, but she froze when she became aware of a presence behind her. She glanced over her shoulder and saw David standing in front of the line of trees. He was soaked, his shirt sticking to him like a second skin.

And so was she, she realized. Her hair was pasted down over her forehead, and her clothes were heavy against her limbs, soaked from the rain. She shivered when the rain started to come down harder, the wind blowing it in different directions. It was growing unusually dark for this time of day, as heavy black storm clouds filled the sky.

David walked toward her, taking off his jacket and wrapping it around her shivering shoulders. "I know it's soaked, but maybe it'll help a little."

"Why are you here?" she demanded.

"I couldn't let you come up here alone."

"But why? Why do you care so much? Is it because of my father? Is that why you're doing this?"

"I won't lie. My friendship with your father was initially my main motivation for looking out for you and watching over you, but that's not why I'm here now." He gazed down into her eyes, his hair plastered down against his skin. "I'm here because I care about you, Nicole. I haven't been able to get you out of my mind ever since that night when you bandaged my arm. Just being around you, thinking about you, makes my heart beat faster. You make me feel as if I've found a missing part of myself." He pulled her close, until every inch of them was touching. "I want you more than I've ever wanted anyone. Do you know how hard it is, for me not to rip your clothes off right now?" He almost growled the last few words.

She could see and feel how much he wanted her, from the wild desire visible in his eyes to the hardness which was made apparent by their bodies being pressed so closely together.

He lowered his head, running his nose along her neck,

then planting soft, slow kisses all the way up from her shoulder to her ear. "Do you still wonder why I'm here?"

"No," she whispered. She shook her head. "But we can't do this. I can't—"

"Why?" he demanded as his teeth nibbled at the skin on her neck. "Because you can't let yourself get close to anyone? I know where you're coming from." He gazed down at her lustfully, rubbing his nose along the side of her face, his tongue darting out to lick the tender skin on her neck. "None of that matters here and now. Forget about all of that and just tell me the truth. Do you want me?"

"Yes," she answered truthfully. A shiver erupted and ran from her neck down to her toes. A soft moan escaped her lips just before David captured them with his own. The kiss was frantic and powerful, and she gave herself up to the moment, shoving all her worries and uncertainties to one side. She slipped her hands under the edge of his shirt, clutching his back, and he pressed against her even more firmly. She couldn't get enough of him. She needed to touch every inch of him with both her fingers and her lips.

"We... should get... out of the rain," he muttered between kisses.

"Who cares about the rain?" she asked in a husky voice, fueled by passion and the growing presence of the wolf within her. She wanted this. She wanted David to be her mate. She recognized now, that their spirits belonged to each other. She knew it as truth, to the core of her soul.

She kissed his lips, his face, and his neck, devouring him.

A moan escaped David's lips. Nicole was driving him crazy. He secured her lips with his own and lifted her up in his arms. She released a surprised sound against his lips before she wrapped her legs around his waist.

One after the other she shook of his jacket... then her own... then her shirt, desperate to feel his lips against her bare skin.

One look at Nicole's lacy black bra and David knew he was losing control. He ran kisses across her neck and arms, stopping to suckle against a few interesting spots along the way. Nicole threw her head back and moaned. David moved on to her breasts, kissing, nibbling, and licking every available inch.

Nicole unhooked her bra and tossed it onto the pile of clothing gathering on the ground. David buried his face between her breasts for a moment before taking one nipple into his mouth. He sucked and teased at it with both his tongue and teeth eliciting a long moan from Nicole. Then he moved to the other breast, giving it the same treatment.

"I want to feel your skin against mine," Nicole demanded, her voice breathless.

David looked up at her with passion glazed eyes. "As you wish."

He carefully set her down on her feet and once he was certain she was steady he took off his shirt, spreading it and the other discarded clothing out on the ground.

He pulled Nicole into his arms again, reveling in the sensation of her naked breasts against his bare chest. They kissed each other wildly, intensely, both experiencing a depth of passion they'd never had before. Nicole's legs weakened several times, but David kept her from falling, holding her securely. He kissed her neck again, sending waves of pleasure coursing through her body. Flicking his tongue over her skin, he took one breast in his hand, slowly plucking at the sensitive nipple. His hips ground back and forth, pressing his hardness against her, and she trembled with desire. With exquisite tenderness, he lowered her down onto the clothes he'd laid out on the ground, dropping down on top of her. Nicole wrapped her legs around him, pulling him even closer.

"I want you so bad," she moaned. David moved down along her body with his lips, until she was squirming uncontrollably. Peeking up at her mischievously, he removed her pants, kissing her legs as he pulled the sopping material down. Then he licked and kissed at the skin above her panties, removing them painfully slowly. His mouth moved lower, and lower again, until he buried his face in her. Nicole gasped as he licked and sucked, pushing his tongue inside her. Her body twisted and shook, incapable of remaining still under his sensuous assault. She tangled her fingers in his hair sitting on the edge of ecstasy.

After he'd driven her insane with pleasure, David moved back up her body, kissing and investigating all the way. As soon as he was close enough she rose up and captured his mouth with her own, aware of the taste of herself on his skin. Like a crazed animal, she kissed his face, his neck, his chest. She circled one nipple with her tongue before nibbling at it and sucking it into her mouth. Then she moved across to the other nipple, giving it the same treatment. She explored his entire chest with her lips and tongue before moving downward.

Her hands shook as she removed his pants and underwear. She held his hardness in one hand and experimentally flicked her tongue over the tip. David moaned, and her lips curved into a smile. She lowered her head and took him into her mouth, sucking, licking and teasing, as his hips moved beneath her.

After several minutes of Nicole's sweet torture, David could take no more. He pulled her up and rolled back over the top of her. Kissing her powerfully, he slipped a hand between her legs, teasing her with his fingers as he'd done with his lips and tongue earlier. Slowly, he pressed one finger inside her. Nicole's arms tightened around him and he began to move his finger in and out, feeling her grow wetter with every sweet. He slipped a second finger inside her and she kissed his mouth and face, growing more frantic by the second.

David pushed deeper, increasing his tempo and Nicole moaned. She didn't know how much more pleasure she could stand, but she also knew she didn't want this sensation to stop.

David removed his fingers and positioned his legs between hers, teasing her and himself by just barely touching her. She used her arms to pull him closer and he started to enter her. Every movement sent explosive shocks through them both and David captured her mouth with his, entering her fully in one quick, sharp thrust. He caught her gasp against his lips.

He remained still for a moment or two, letting them both get used to him being inside her body. When he did begin to move, Nicole found every movement sent her spiraling to another level of ecstasy. He filled her so completely, body and soul. She'd never had anything feel more right.

They reached the zenith together, and David held her tightly until the tremors stopped, neither one of them in a hurry to get out of the rain.

Nicole was completely at peace. They rested in one another's arms before they finally decided to get up and put on their rain drenched, muddy clothes.

When they kissed again, it was much more gentle, their passion spent. Nicole breathed in his scent and smiled. She felt giddy. David pushed back a strand of her hair and smiled back. "Your hair looks nice."

Nicole blinked, then smiled. "Oh, yeah, I completely forgot. Meg helped me color it."

"Do you want to go back to the house?"

"In a minute. That's what I was doing when you arrived – I tripped over something." She went back to the spot where she'd begun digging and finished excavating the item.

It was a dagger. The handle had been carved into the shape of a snake and created from some type of metal, and red gems created the eyes.

David knelt beside her and studied the dagger. "That's remarkable."

"Yeah, but what's it doing up here?"

"I don't know. Come on, we should get going."

She glanced around the clearing and the hairs on the back of her neck stood on end. "Maybe you're right. This place gives me the creeps."

Wrapping his arm around her, David led them both back to the waiting vehicles. "Meet you back at the house." He lifted her hand and brushed a light kiss against it.

She smiled. "See you there." Kissing one last time, they got into their respective vehicles and left.

* * *

"WHERE DID YOU GET THAT?" Mark crossed the room and picked up the snake handled dagger.

"Nicole found it up at Bear Mountain."

Mark looked up at David with a frown. "Do you know what this is?"

"What?"

"This is Artemis' dagger."

"Are you sure?" Nicole's voice voiced the question from the doorway.

David and Mark looked at her in surprise. Neither of them had heard her approach.

"I can walk quietly, too." She smiled at Mark. "Hello, Officer Stevenson."

"Um, hello, Miss Cameron."

"I hadn't realized the two of you knew each other so well."

"We've known each other a long time," Mark admitted.

"What are you doing up?" David asked.

"I was too restless to sleep, and then I heard voices down here, so I thought I'd come and see what was happening." She turned back to Mark. "You said that dagger belongs to my uncle."

Mark nodded. "Yeah, I saw him with it many times. He had it specially made for him. If you look at the bottom here, you can see his initials."

She came closer to look at the dagger and Mark pointed out the initials. "But why would it have been up there at the mountain?" She recalled her nightmare, the images of her father and uncle fighting. "Could he have been in the plane, too?"

David shook his head. "I wouldn't think so. Artemis and your father weren't exactly on speaking terms. I can't think of a single reason why he would have been there. Besides, no one ever suggested it as a possibility."

"Maybe nobody knew." She surveyed the room, momentarily drawn into the past. She could almost see her father, sitting in a chair across the room. That sort of vision had been happening more and more lately. Ever since she'd found out the truth, she was finding it increasingly difficult to be anywhere in the house. It was beginning to seem like a ghost house, where every room brought back images and sensations. She closed her eyes against the vision, goose bumps erupting on her flesh.

"I have to be going." Mark retrieved his jacket from the arm of the couch and put it on. "Oh, and Miss Cameron, I talked to the university. Considering everything that's happened to you lately, they've offered you a leave of absence. You can go back whenever you feel up to it."

She smiled appreciatively. "Thank you, that was very kind."

"No problem. I hope everything works out for you."

She remained in the living room while David walked Mark out. If her dream was true, Artemis *had* been on the plane. That meant the remains of the crash were probably near where she found the dagger. She needed to go back to that clearing.

22

Sunlight gleamed off the dagger as Nicole turned it in her hand, examining it. It seemed almost as if she was expecting it to provide her with the answers she was seeking. "I don't see anything," David called, appearing from out of the trees. "There's no sign of anything around this clearing that would hint at a plane crash."

Nicole slipped the dagger into her pocket. "It's got to be somewhere near here."

David came up to her. "Maybe not. Maybe Artemis just came up here to search for the crash, like we are, and lost the dagger then. Admittedly, that doesn't really sound like him, but maybe he wanted proof that Richard was dead, so he could celebrate."

"He hated him that much?"

"From what I've heard, it certainly seemed like it."

Nicole surveyed the clearing again, as always, drawn to the area where the grass had been flattened down. She absentmindedly rubbed at her necklace, staring at the spot. A dark forest and color-changing eyes flashed into her mind. She heard loud crashes of thunder overhead, despite it being a storm free day. A brief vision of the plane appeared before her eyes, made visible by a flash of lightning. She could feel herself running through thick mud, suction making every movement difficult.

The sun-lit clearing disappeared, replaced by a darkened, ominous forest. She found herself running in complete desperation.

Suddenly, an arm shot out and grabbed her. "Your mind is mine," a voice said. Eyes, colors swirling in them hypnotically, stared into hers. "You will forget this night and all that came before." She struggled, even as her mind grew hazy. Her energy was disappearing. Her eyelids got heavier by the second.

Light abruptly flashed over her face, briefly shocking her out of the daze. She kicked her uncle's leg, slipping out of his grasp and running toward the light. The sudden rush of adrenaline left her just as she reached the source of the light – a flashlight held by an old man. Beside him was a woman, who appeared to be about the same age as he was. They were the last things she saw before the rest of her energy drained, leaving her in darkness.

The darkness morphed into light, a brilliant light. She felt a hand on her shoulder and jumped. The light dimmed enough for Nicole to see her surroundings. She realized the light had been emitting from her necklace, the same necklace which had once belonged to her ancestors and was said to possess their incredible powers. She was certainly beginning to believe that could be true. She peered up into David's worried face.

Nicole offered him a reassuring smile as her breathing returned to normal. "I'm okay. You said that a couple found me. What did they look like?"

David considered the question. "They were both elderly,

with gray hair and wrinkles. They seemed nice enough. I don't know much more, I'm afraid. I only saw them once, years ago, and it wasn't for long."

Nicole nodded. They had to be the couple in her vision. "I'm positive that Artemis was in the plane the night it crashed," she said with certainty. "He followed me off the plane, and I think he did something to my memory." Her head gave the impression that years of cobwebs were beginning to clear away. Vague memories were starting to take shape in her mind.

A faint light caught her attention. She searched for its source, but it was gone as quickly as it had appeared.

There it was again. It seemed to be appearing from out of thin air. The light from her necklace must be reflecting off something, but what? She moved her necklace around and saw the light reflect in different places. "Do you see that?"

David turned around. "What?"

"The light. It's reflecting off something."

David stared closely, seeing faint reflections of light. "Yeah, I see it."

She walked forward a few steps, ignoring the apprehension which built in her chest this time. She started to see light reflecting wherever her necklace wasn't shining. A thought occurred to her. "How powerful is Artemis?"

David shrugged. "Quite powerful, I think. I don't really know for sure. Wait, you don't think..."

"Could he do it? Could he hide a plane?"

"I don't know. I don't even know if it's possible. I mean, that would be a powerful illusion to maintain for any amount of time, and it's been over a decade."

"There's only one way to find out." Nicole walked swiftly toward the area where the grass had been flattened.

Just before she reached it, dizziness brought her to her

knees. David ran to her side, fought his own dizziness, and helped them both to stand. Together, they walked the last couple of steps, each one taking tremendous effort.

Nicole reached forward, touching a smooth surface. Beginning at her fingertips and moving out swiftly in every direction, the surface of the plane became visible. They both stepped back and watched in awe, their dizziness gone.

David looked at the designs on the outside of the plane. It was Richard's all right. "My God, he did it. He actually did it."

Nicole walked to the open door of the plane, stepping cautiously inside. Part of the interior looked as if it had been scorched by fire. She remembered the fire she saw in her nightmare. Everywhere she looked, it seemed as if she was seeing ghosts, as images from the present and past over-lapped. Her feet brought her to a seat near the middle of the plane. She sat down, feeling like she'd just entered someone else's body.

The interior of the plane darkened. The rain was coming down hard. She jumped when another crash of thunder sounded outside. Her father appeared from the front of the plane and wrenched her uncle up from the floor. "What the hell do you think you're doing? You just killed a man!" Her father motioned to the pilot's body, crumpled on the floor. "You could have killed us all!"

Nicole stared at her mom's still form. She hadn't moved in a long time. Nicole slipped out of her seat and went across to her mother. There was a trail of blood coming from the body. She peeked out from behind the seat in front of her. Her father and uncle were fighting again. Suddenly, she heard a shot.

At first, she thought it was thunder, but then she saw her

father slump to the floor, clutching his stomach. Artemis was holding a gun.

Nicole began to tiptoe quietly towards the door, but her uncle saw her, so she ran. She stopped in the doorway, temporarily blinded by bright sunlight. There was no storm and no one chasing her.

She turned back to the inside of the plane. David was standing beside her. The plane looked different, now and memories flooded her mind. The first three years of her life began to fall into place. She could remember some small things about her parents and her home. She could almost hear the way her mother's voice had sounded.

Nicole looked across to where she'd seen her parents, but all she saw now was dried blood. "That's their blood." Her voice shook a little. "He must have moved the bodies."

"All but one."

Nicole looked at him questioningly, then she remembered the pilot. David blocked her from seeing the front of the plane's interior. "It's better if you don't look. It appears he was shot in the head."

She nodded. "Artemis had a gun. I think it was an accident, thought. He was fighting with my father."

"I know." She could hear amazement in his voice. "I could see everything you saw."

"You did? Is that normal?"

"No," He shook his head. "It's never happened to me before, but we have a very strong connection, and the vision had a lot of raw emotion behind it."

"What's going to happen to Artemis?"

"He'll have to answer to the Council."

"The Council?"

"It's made up by many of the ancients. They handle issues of werewolf crime, along with anything which might impact werewolves. They're extremely powerful and highly respected. The Council was founded by your grandfather. After he died, your father was offered his father's position, but he declined."

"What about Artemis?"

"No, he had a lot of enemies. He wasn't well liked, and no one really respected him, or his judgment. There's no way the Council would ever ask him to join."

She surveyed the plane again and a chill ran down her spine. "Let's get out of here."

She'd spent enough of her life in this plane.

* * *

David lowered a sleeping Nicole onto the bed and tucked her in. She moaned softly and turned toward him. "We're back?" she mumbled, opening her eyes slightly.

"Yes. I have to go out, but I'll be back soon, okay?"

She nodded, her eyes already closed again. He quietly left the room and shook his head. The fatigue had come over her so suddenly. She'd slept the entire ride back. Seeing that vision had really drained her energy. He wasn't all that surprised. It must have taken a lot of energy to break the powerful hold Artemis had kept on her mind all these years.

He drove swiftly to Mara's, needing to talk to her. He didn't really want to leave Nicole alone, but she was exhausted, and Mara didn't have a phone. He could have tried telepathy, but he still wasn't used to using that again. He still preferred talking to people face-to-face. He ran up the steps at Mara's, barely noticing that the door opened before he could knock. "I need to talk to you about Artemis."

"Artemis?" Mara closed the door and turned her confused gaze toward him.

"He's the one who's been bothering Nicole, and I have reason to believe he killed Richard and Caroline."

"What?" Mara sounded shocked. "I haven't sensed him nearby. He must be the one I initially sensed, but why couldn't I tell it was him?" Something wasn't right. There was no way Artemis was powerful enough to hide himself from her so completely. "What proof do you have that he killed them?"

"Nicole. She's been experiencing memories from the crash, and we found the plane, with Artemis' dagger nearby. Nicole had a vision at the crash site, and I could see it too. It was as though I was seeing it through her eyes." David couldn't hide the wonder in his voice.

"That's not all that surprising. Once one has physically and emotionally joined with another, there is a very strong connection. Added to that, is the fact that Nicole is a very strong sender. I've experienced her sending out her emotions many times. As for Artemis, I'll tell the Council immediately. You should get back to Nicole, but keep your eyes open for anything untoward. This situation is not what it seems."

David let her words sink in as he drove back to the house. He was still a little unnerved that Mara knew about his relationship with Nicole. It had only just happened – how could she know about it so quickly?

He was also more than a little unnerved regarding the other things Mara had said. What was it about the situation that wasn't what it seemed? It seemed as though there was something Mara wasn't telling him. Of course, knowing Mara, that was probably the case.

He turned the key in the doorknob and simultaneously

heard Nicole scream. The sound was more mental than physical, and David rushed up to her room. Images of the plane crash came to him as he took the steps, two at a time.

Nicole was thrashing restlessly in bed, moaning softly, when he settled on the bed beside her. He placed a hand on her shoulder, and the images instantly grew stronger. It was as if David had been transported into her nightmare, seeing it through Nicole's eyes, experiencing what she felt. He had felt the same phenomena in the forest, at the plane.

Richard and Artemis were fighting. A shot rang out. Richard crumpled to the floor, clutching his stomach. Suddenly, Nicole's vision was filled with flames. "He killed his own family," Artemis' mocking voice said. "He killed them in a fire... killed them in a fire." The words echoed. "He's using you. He doesn't care about you." The flames were suddenly extinguished in a bright flash of light. The plane reappeared. Nicole ran past the bodies of her parents, attempting to escape her uncle. Images of Artemis surrounded her. He was everywhere, laughing, scoffing. David's heart raced – or was it hers? He wasn't sure. He attempted to calm Nicole, by calming himself. Slowly, it started to work. Artemis disappeared, as did the plane and dark forest, to be replaced by a forest dappled with soft sunlight.

David experienced a shift in awareness. He was no longer looking through Nicole's eyes. He was looking at Nicole. She was watching him quizzically, apparently surprised to see him. He placed a hand on her shoulder. "It's just a nightmare. It can only hurt you if you let it."

The forest slowly faded, the bedroom taking its place. Nicole looked up at David through sleep filled eyes. "Where am I?"

"You're in your room at my house. You were having a nightmare."

"You were there, in the nightmare."

"Yeah, I know."

"How could you know?"

"I don't know. It's similar to what happened at the crash site. Somehow, I get pulled into your nightmares. I don't pretend to understand it, but I don't care. I only wish there was something I could do to help."

"You've been helping me get through my nightmares ever since I met you again, even when I didn't know it was you."

He ran his fingers through her hair. He loved her so much. He would take her nightmare on to himself every time if he could.

Nicole gazed up at him and smiled. "I love you, too."

"What? But — you do?" He smiled uncertainly.

She laughed. "Yeah, I do." She quickly batted away a tiny twinge of uncertainty. She might not be sure she was good for him, but she did know she loved him. The feelings were too strong to ignore anymore.

David couldn't believe it. Nicole felt the same way about him. He hadn't thought it was possible. His smile broadened, and he leaned down for a kiss, a kiss which seemed to go on forever. It was deep and sensual, carrying them both away. When it finally ended, they were both smiling.

"So, tell me Coverton," she whispered in his ear. "Do you know what I'm thinking, now?"

"Hum, let me think." He put a hand to his head and pretended to be in deep concentration. "You're thinking... we should both get undressed as quickly as possible."

Nicole put a hand to her chest. "You're a mind reader," she announced in mock surprise.

He laughed, lowering his mouth to her neck, nuzzling and nibbling, as he slipped his hand under her shirt. Her back arched when he captured her breast in his hand.

David's other hand slipped between her legs, rubbing against her thin panties. He brought her to a couple of orgasms that way, before he undressed them both and buried himself inside her. Nicole screamed in ecstasy a few minutes later, when he came deep inside her.

They held each other close while their breathing settled, and their bodies slowly stopped shaking. David was still semi-hard inside her. "I just can't get enough of you," he growled against her neck.

His breath on her skin sent shock waves rippling down her body to where they remained joined. He grew hard again and their bodies moved together. Nicole kissed him deeply, their tongues dueling.

as they climaxed together a second time.

They lay quietly for a long time, until their heart rate slowed back to normal. "I could stay like this forever," Nicole breathed.

David ran his fingers through Nicole's hair, gently brushing his palm across her face. "So could I."

Nicole sighed deeply and drifted back to sleep, not worried in the least about the nightmares.

23

Meghan pushed her hair back from her face and finished her last set of shoulder presses. She sat back, breathing out a grateful sigh. After catching her breath and grabbing a drink of water, she started working the weights. Her muscles burned, but she pushed through until the last set was done. Wiping sweat from her brow, she grabbed her things and left the workout area. "See you tomorrow, Meg," the guy at the front desk called. Meg lifted a weary arm in farewell and smiled at him before pushing open the front door.

Bright sunlight hit her as she walked outside. She let her eyes adjust for a minute before continuing. It was a beautiful day, the perfect day for a run. Pulling her purse strap over her neck, she started running in the direction of her apartment.

She ran without giving much thought to her surroundings. She didn't think about much of anything, only the way the wind felt as it hit her face and the sensation of her feet hitting the concrete. As she got closer to home, she checked her watch. She was making good time.

The even fall of her feet on the ground took her focus again. She almost passed her apartment building before she realized where she was. "That didn't take long." She inhaled a few deep breaths and ran up the steps to her apartment.

Meg walked into the bedroom and tossed her belongings on the bed, before heading to the bathroom, kicking her shoes off on the way. Her legs were killing her, but it felt great. She was exhausted and exhilarated simultaneously.

She grabbed a towel from the cabinet and turned on the water in the tub. A nice warm bath sounded brilliant right now.

A flash of movement in the mirror caught her eye. She glanced into the bedroom but couldn't see anything. She decided to check the apartment anyway, otherwise she's be paranoid the entire time she was in the bath and wouldn't enjoy it.

Unclipping her hair, she took a step forward, but she was brought up short by a hand on her arm and the touch of cold metal against her neck. Her breath caught in her throat.

A voice whispered near her ear. "Are you Meghan Freeman?" She nodded hesitantly, afraid of making any sudden movements. "Good, I have a little job for you."

* * *

NICOLE WOKE UP AND GRINNED. She breathed in David's scent, loving the feel of him in her arms. When she opened her eyes, she discovered he was grinning, too. He rubbed against her neck with his nose, and she giggled, squirming. "Good dreams?" he asked, thought it didn't really sound like a question.

"Only the most erotic dreams of my life." She studied

him suspiciously. "You wouldn't have had anything to do with that, would you?"

David gave her his most innocent look. "Who, me? What could I possibly have done?"

"Um, hmmm. You know, you're a terrible liar."

He chuckled. "All right, I admit it. I sent you a few ideas. I was curious to see if I could." He was a little shocked to discover it actually worked.

"You seem to be having a lot of influence over my dreams lately."

David thought back on the nightmare she'd been having when he returned from seeing Mara, the one he'd somehow become a part of. He was still amazed he had been able to influence her nightmare the way he did. Of course, he'd already been a part of it before he tried to calm her down. He thought about what Artemis had been saying about him in her dream. Could she really believe any of that? She probably. Why else would she be dreaming about it? But she hadn't said anything about it. If she had questions, she would ask, wouldn't she?

Nicole gazed deeply into his eyes, sensing the thoughts churning in his brain. "What do you want to ask?"

He took a minute before he answered, watching her and smiling. "I guess I should know by now, I can't hide anything from you anymore, especially not when we're touching. I was curious about why you haven't asked me about my family – about how they died."

Nicole thought back to what Artemis had. Then recalled the nightmare, realizing David would have heard the same echoed words she'd heard.

"Why haven't you asked me if it was true?" The words were hard to say aloud, but he needed to know.

"Because I didn't believe him."

"Really?" he asked, hopefully.

She thought carefully. "If I did have any doubts, they were gone quickly. I know you're not capable of cold-blooded murder."

"Some part of you must believe it though, to be having nightmares regarding what he said."

Nicole shrugged. "I don't know. I haven't known what to think about anything these past few days. Sometimes, nothing seems real. All I know is that I trust you, and I love you with all my heart. Nothing else matters. You and me is all I have right now. When I'm with you, I can shut out everything else, even my own insecurities." What had made her add that part? It seemed she couldn't keep any thoughts to herself these days.

David picked up on it instantly. "What kind of insecurities?"

"I—." She shifted uncomfortably. "It doesn't matter. I can forget about them all when I'm in your arms."

"Are you sure that's necessarily a good thing?"

"Why not? You make me happy. What could be wrong with that? Things are crazy right now. Everything is turned upside down, with something new coming up every few minutes it seems. But this connection between us, it's real. It's more than I ever thought I would find. That's the only thing I'm sure about right now, amid all these other problems. So, I'm going to hold on to that. I'm going to let that get me through everything else, because I have no other choice but insanity."

He nodded, accepting her response. "Do you want to know what really happened?" He'd never talked to anyone about it, but he knew he could talk to her.

"If you want to tell me. I'm not going to press."

That settled it. Just her offering the choice was enough

for him. He smiled gratefully, then prepared himself to tell the story. "I was told the house burned down."

"You were told?"

"Like I said before, I ran away from home when I was young. I'd been gone about a year when I started to wonder if I should go back. I was alone, I had no money, and I missed my home. So, I decided to at least return for a visit. Even if I didn't stay, I thought I could regroup." His expression darkened. "There was nothing left when I got there. The house had burned down a week earlier, with every member of my family in it."

His pain throbbed through her as if it was her own, her heart breaking with it. "I'm so sorry."

"It was a long time ago. I don't know how Artemis found out about it. I guess since Richard left this place to me, instead of to Artemis, he investigated my past."

Nicole suspected she was closer to David now than she'd ever been before. They had something in common – they'd both suffered the loss of family. They'd both been left to face the world alone. Maybe it could work for them. They were perfectly matched for each other, both understanding one another's loss. Maybe she wasn't destined to be alone after all. In some cosmic way, it all made sense. She laid a comforting hand on David's arm, feeling for the first time that everything was going to turn out all right. "We both know what it's like to be alone, but we don't have to be alone anymore."

He smiled and kissed her gently. The ringing of Nicole's cell phone interrupted their kiss. David reluctantly pulled away from Nicole and leaned over to answer it. "Hello. Yeah, she's right here." He handed the phone to Nicole. "It's Meg."

"Hello?" Nicole answered.

"Nicole, listen, I need your help. Could you come to my apartment, right away?"

Nicole frowned. "Are you okay? You sound like a wreck. What's wrong?"

"Nothing. I'm fine. I just need you to come over." Meg didn't sound fine at all. Her voice was shaking, and her words were spoken far more slowly than Meg's usual speed.

"Okay, I'll be right over."

"Thanks. You're a lifesaver." The phone clicked off before Nicole could say anything else.

"That was strange," she muttered. "Mind if I borrow a car? I need to go check on Meg."

David looked concerned. "Do you want me to go with you?"

"Nah, I've got it covered. Besides, she sounds really upset about something. I don't know if she'll want you around, not when she doesn't know you very well." Nicole leaned over and kissed him. "I'll be back as soon as I can."

David followed her to the door and watched her leave before he headed to the kitchen to grab something to eat. He needed to recharge after all the exercise he'd been getting with Nicole. A smile crossed his lips. For the first time in his life, he believed things would actually turn out all right. The phone started ringing as the microwave finished, the two sounds overlapping, so at first, he wasn't sure if the phone was ringing. But the ringing continued after the microwave stopped beeping, so he grabbed his food and went to answer it. "Hello," he muttered around a mouthful.

"David," Mark said, "is Nicole with you?"

"No, why?" he responded distractedly. Maybe he should order dinner in tonight. He'd have to ask Nicole when she got back.

"Steagel has escaped."

"What?" David's stomach twisted in a knot. The remainder of his snack fell from his hand. "When?"

"About an hour ago. Where's Nicole?"

"She went to Meghan's place. She's a friend of hers." He thought back over how upset Meghan had been. He didn't like this at all. "Mark, do you think you could send someone by Meghan Freeman's house to check on her?"

"Sure thing."

David barely remembered to say goodbye before he hung up the phone and rushed out to the car.

* * *

NICOLE PULLED to a stop in front of Meg's building and got out. A chill ran over her skin as she hurried up the stairs to Meghan's apartment. She pulled her jacket closer around her body and knocked on the door, but there was no answer.

Ominously, the door swung open as she knocked.

"Meg!" She called out but got no response. Nicole stepped into the apartment cautiously. There was a light shining in the bedroom, so she headed in that direction, listening for sounds.

When she looked into the bedroom, she saw Meghan lying on the floor, unconscious. Nicole took a step forward to check on her friend and an arm clamped around her chest, holding her arms down to her side, and prohibiting any other movement. Another hand held a cloth to her face. Nicole struggled for as long as she could, but the room quickly faded into darkness.

* * *

Nicole jerked awake. Her hair was dripping wet, and her face was freezing. Rodney Steagel stood in front of her, smiling wickedly. He held a bucket in his hands. "Sorry about the cold water, but I wanted you to be awake for this. You see, I'm going to burn down the company building, and you're going to have a front row seat. I've disconnected the sprinkler system and added a few stacks of newspaper and other flammable materials in various strategic places, and I've poured gasoline all around, so the fire should spread nicely."

"You'll never get away with this." Nicole cringed even as she repeated the clichéd line. Now she understood why people in the movies always said it. "The police know you caused the explosion. They'll tie you to this too, and you'll spend the rest of your life in prison."

His eyes were wide, crazed. "Don't you see? Burning down this place will provide the distraction I need to get out of town. Besides, they never figured out that it was me who got rid of those two scientists. You remember them, don't you? I believe they were your parents." He barked out a hysterical laugh. "You know, it's somehow fitting that you should all die for the same cause, don't you think?"

"What?" The color drained from Nicole's face, and she thought she was going to be sick.

"Yeah, it was a shame you kept coming after me. I thought taking care of the two of them would get the rest of you off my back. Guess I was wrong."

"You killed my parents?" She couldn't believe it. First, she found out her real parents had been murdered by her uncle, and now this. She didn't know how many more shocks she could handle.

"All I did was arranged a little distraction on the road. They were good enough to have the wreck." He laughed again, the sound maniacal. "No more time for talk. I've got to get to work."

Rodney picked up a container of gasoline and emptied its contents around the room. Nicole would have known, even without his earlier words, that this wasn't the first time Rodney had done this. The place reeked of gasoline and the fumes were giving her quite a headache, super-healing abilities or not. When he'd finished, he retrieved a packet of matches from his pocket and lit one, holding it in front of him. His eyes focused on the flame as if he'd become momentarily entranced. Abruptly, his attention snapped over to Nicole again, and the grin reappeared. "Later... or not." He started laughing as he dropped the match and hurried out the door.

The match hit the floor, instantly lighting the gasoline with an audible whoosh. Nicole stared into the flames as they began to spread. The colors danced around the room, creating a truly sublime scene. This was nature at its most beautiful and its most deadly. She desperately tried to free her hands, but they were tied too tightly. The rope was cutting into her wrists as she struggled. She coughed, smoke filling the room and her lungs. It was already difficult to see through the thick haze.

"Help!" she screamed at the top of her lungs, praying someone would hear her. The plea ended in a hacking cough, the lack of oxygen bringing black spots to her vision.

The only response to her screams was crashing sounds as parts of the ceiling began to collapse and dropped to the floor. Burning ashes and smoke were displaced into the air, swirling around above where the ceiling struck the ground. The smoke thickened, making breathing more difficult. Remembering the cell phone in her pocket, she fumbled blindly to open and dial the phone, hoping she was pressing the correct buttons. Her fingers were mostly numb, now. She heard the phone dialing, but it slipped from her blood and sweat covered fingers and fell to the floor. Struggling in vain against the ropes, she was losing consciousness and losing hope.

* * *

DAVID STARED at the burning building in horror. He dialed Nicole's number and listened for the ring. She was close, now. Turning in the direction of the sound, he ran faster. He gave the door one good, solid kick, leaving it in splintered pieces. The smoke instantly surrounded him, but he covered his face and went inside without delay. Flames were everywhere, so he needed to watch his step but move as quickly as he could. He choked down a rush of negative emotions. Fear of losing another person he loved to fire filled him with horror. He'd often imagined what his family must have gone through that night, and he wasn't about to let that happen to Nicole. He couldn't lose her, not now, not when they'd just found each other. He called out to Nicole but got no response. The room was large, with burning crates and office supplies blocking the way. He raised his phone to call again, but an awareness blossomed in his chest, pulling him in one direction. He followed the feeling through the maze of obstacles and easily found her at the far side of the room.

Nicole's limp form was tied to a chair, surrounded by flames. He called out to her, but her head was flopped forward, and she wasn't moving. He gathered his remaining strength and called out to her again, louder this time.

He saw her move just a little, giving him a surge of hope. The floor between them was blocked by several pieces of burning rafter and chunks of debris from the ceiling. They didn't have much time before the entire place was going to collapse. "Nicole!" he shouted again, forcing the word out mentally as well as aloud. Her head jerked up and she started coughing.

David breathed a sigh of relief. She was alive, at least, but she seemed dazed. He had to find a way across to her. Judging the distance, he took a few steps back and started to run, jumping over the burning wood. He landed hard, pain shooting up through his legs, but it was summarily forgotten as he gave his attention to Nicole. He hurriedly set about untying her. Her wrists were raw and bleeding, her blood soaking his hands as he worked.

"David, is that you?" Her voice was hoarse, the attempt at talking bringing on another coughing fit.

"Yeah, it's me. Don't worry. I'll get you out of here soon." Once the ropes were undone, her arms fell limply by her sides and she slumped against him. The flames flared up when another large portion of the ceiling fell down, joining the growing pile of debris on the floor, and further blocking their way to the door.

David turned back to Nicole. She was already out of it again. He shook her a few times, staining her shirt with blood. "Nicole, you have to help me out here. I can't do this alone."

Her eyes fluttered open. "Huh?"

"Nicole, we have to get out of here, but that burning wood is blocking our way." He shook her again trying to keep her awake. "Stay with me here. I barely made it when I jumped, and now the fire is bigger. The only way to get across is to jump as wolves. Do you understand?"

"Yeah, yes, I think so," she slurred. "I have to change into a wolf."

"That's right, and we haven't got much time. I want you to concentrate. I know that's hard—" he choked on the smoke. "I know that's hard, but you have to. I want you to imagine yourself as a wolf."

She closed her eyes and tried to do as he said. After a moment, she shook her head. "It's not working."

David turned around to face her. "Look into my eyes." He stared deeply into her eyes, sending as much of his energy to her as he could.

Nicole's necklace began to glow and her head began to clear. Even the air momentarily seemed cleaner. This time, when she tried to imagine herself as a wolf, the light from the necklace grew brighter and brighter, until it outshone the fire around them. Her senses were heightened and she she was aware of movement and weightlessness. The light began to dim, until it had subdued enough for her to again see her surroundings.

She was on the other side of the fire. She caught sight of the black wolf, who was jumping over the burning debris. He landed beside her and collapsed, changing into David in a flash of light. She hurried over to him, helping him get to his feet. Together, they left the building, mere seconds before before the entire ceiling caved in.

24

Nicole allowed the paramedic to bandage her wrists while she watched the many people hurrying about. The firefighters had managed to keep the fire from spreading to the rest of the buildings, but the area she'd been in was almost completely destroyed.

David watched the men fighting the fire. Another few minutes and he would have lost Nicole forever. "So, I drove over the Meghan's place as soon as I got Mark's call. She was just starting to wake up when I got there."

"Is Meghan okay?" Nicole asked when the paramedic finished up.

"Her apartment was the first place I went, after Mark warned me Steagel had escaped. She seemed okay physically, but she was quite distressed. Apparently Steagel threatened her with a knife to force her to call you. After she did what he wanted, he knocked her out with chloroform. Meghan was with the paramedics when I came searching for you."

"How did you know where to find me?"

"Your phone called me. I just kept dialing it back, so I

could hear the ringing, until I got close. Then, I could sense where you were, through our connection."

"It's a good thing you did." Nicole flashed him a grateful smile. "It seems as if you've saved me again. I'll have to think of a way to repay you."

David grinned. "Oh, really? And what have you got in mind?"

The sound of a throat clearing behind them caught their attention. Officer Stevenson stood there, and he was smiling at them. David smiled back. "Hey Mark." The two men clasped arms before David spoke again. "You know, I never have properly introduced you two. Nicole, this is Mark Stevenson, one of my closest friends, and Mark, this is Nicole Cameron, the woman I love."

Nicole's cheeks got warmer. She held out her hand to Mark. "It's a pleasure to finally meet you properly."

Mark nodded. "I'm glad you two are okay. Just wanted to let you know, we caught Steagel trying to board a bus and he's back in jail. You won't have to worry about him anymore."

"That's great news." A weight lifted from Nicole's shoulders. "Oh, you should know Rodney confessed to causing my adoptive parent's deaths. He said he created some kind of distraction so that they would wreck their car."

Mark frowned. "I was afraid of that. I'll add that information to the report."

"Nicole!" Meghan shrieked as she ran up to Nicole and wrapped her in a fierce hug. "Are you okay? I'm so sorry I called you. I didn't want to do it, but..." A sob burst from her throat.

"Don't worry about that. Are you okay?" Nicole placed a comforting hand on Meg's shoulder. She'd rarely seen Meg this upset before. She knew the incident would be traumatic for her friend, but Nicole hadn't realized it would be this bad.

"Yeah, I'm fine. I'm only relieved he didn't hurt you." Meg hugged her again, tears streaming down her face. "I don't know what I'd do without you."

"It's okay. I'm not going anywhere." Meghan wiped the tears from her eyes and sniffled. "Are you okay?" Nicole asked again, meaningfully.

Meg met her gaze, knowing Nicole understood exactly what she was going through. Nicole was the only one in the world who could possibly understand. Anyone else would blame Meg, chastise her for putting Nicole's life at risk, but not Nicole. She knew. "Yeah, I'm okay now." She realized people were looking at her and pulled herself together. She couldn't let everyone see her like this. Once she'd established some semblance of control over herself, she glanced across at David and Mark. Her eyes focused on Mark. "I don't believe we've met. My name's Meghan Freeman."

"I'm Mark... Mark Stevenson." His breath caught when she looked up into his eyes.

Nicole watched the interaction between Meg and Mark for a minute, before she turned back to David. "I'm really tired. Could you take me home?"

"Sure. You don't need anything else, do you Mark?"

"Huh? Uh, no, you can go." He turned back to Meg. "How about you Miss Freeman? Do you need a ride anywhere?"

Meg smiled warmly. "Yeah, that would be great."

Nicole and David watched Mark and Meghan walk off together before they walked to David's car.

"Looks like those two have taken to each other." David smiled and turned the key in the ignition.

Nicole grinned, glad someone was taking Meg's mind off

recent events. "Yeah, sure does. Is Mark…he's like us, isn't he?"

"Yes. He's actually considerably older than I am."

"How did you two meet?"

"I met him at the same time I met your father." David felt a little weird discussing this with Nicole, but she wanted to know, so he'd tell her. He wasn't intending to keep any more secrets from her. "He was with Richard, the night I tried to break in. They had been friends for some time before I met them, and Mark has taught me a great deal over the years. He was one of the people I left to watch over you, in case anything happened."

Nicole arched one eyebrow. "How many more people have been watching me?"

"Quite a few. Richard was well liked and his death hurt many people. Since there had been threats made against him, everyone knew they needed to protect you. They didn't watch your every move. Mostly, they remained nearby in case you ever needed help. There's hardly a werewolf alive who wouldn't have given their life for Richard, Caroline, or you."

Nicole pursed her lips. "Except for my dear uncle."

He nodded. "Artemis will be brought before a werewolf tribunal as soon as he's found. He'll have to answer to them."

They lapsed into silence for the rest of the journey home David stopped the car by the front door.

Nicole pushed open her door and immediately became aware of the difference, as the smoke-filled air in the car was replaced by fresh night air. Their clothes stank of smoke, but she'd gotten so used to the smell she hardly noticed it. Now though, she felt filthy, grimy, and disgusting. She waited for David to unlock the front door, completely lost in the delightful prospect of a long warm bath, but before she could step inside David pulled her into his arms. Her mouth gaped open in surprise but was quickly covered by his own. Her knees weakened, the thought of a bath completely forgotten.

"I love you," he spoke in her mind, not yet ready to let go of her lips. He needed this kiss. He needed to be near Nicole right now, to reassure himself she was really here, next to him. He didn't want to miss a single moment with her.

"I'm not going anywhere," she said aloud, ending the kiss.

"I don't ever want to lose you." He struggled to keep from getting choked up.

Nicole squeezed him gently. "You won't. Look what we've already survived! Just finding each other was a miracle. We're the same, two halves of the same whole. I'm never going to leave you." She cleared her throat, the smoke starting to affect her again. "I need to freshen up a little bit and change out of these revolting clothes."

"Sounds like a good idea. How about we meet back down here, and I'll cook something to eat?"

Nicole nodded. "Okay. We can talk more then."

He pulled her close for another quick kiss before they headed upstairs, and he reluctantly released her at the door to her room. "I love you."

"I love you, too."

Nicole went into the bathroom, splashing some cold water on her face. She left the water running and stared at her reflection in the mirror. Her eyes widened. She hadn't realized how much blood she was covered with. Two red hand prints were visible on her shoulders. Between the blood, the dirt, and the soot, she couldn't tell what color the shirt had been originally. She looked about as bad as she felt. Her hair was a tangled mess, there were smeared streaks of soot and blood on her face, and her eyes were bloodshot. She suspected she seriously needed a vacation, away from murder attempts and bad memories.

Nicole sighed and splashed some more water on her face before she turned off the faucet and watched the water disappear down the drain. She glanced back at her reflection and started, her breath catching in her throat.

Artemis' face stared back at her from over her blood-stained shoulder. She turned to face him, noticing he wasn't wearing his sunglasses, and surprised that his eyes weren't changing color. She suspected the color changing thing was what caused her to have difficulty remembering their encounters. It stood to reason that it had to be something he could control. If that was true, this was a good sign, because he apparently didn't feel the need to use it on her now. If she was lucky, it would stay that way. "What are you doing here?" She struggled to keep her voice calm.

"I just wanted to see how you're doing. I heard you had a rough day."

Nicole moved past him as casually as she could, walking into the bedroom. She peeked over at the door and saw the lock had been turned. Okay, so there wouldn't be any quick exits in that direction. She needed to think of another way to get away from him. "As you can see, I'm fine. Thank you for your concern though."

"What's an uncle for? I do admit I'm a bit surprised to find you still staying here. I would have thought you'd have left before now."

Nicole crossed her arms. "And why is that? It's my house."

"Why? Because of Mr. Coverton, of course. He's danger-ous. He wouldn't even let me see you. You surely understand

I'm only looking out for your well being." Artemis took a step toward her and she fought to keep from stepping back. "You don't know the man. He can't be trusted."

Nicole chewed at her lip. "He hasn't done anything to give me reason to mistrust him." She need to stall Artemis long enough for David to come searching for her. She didn't dare try mentally summoning him. There was no telling if Artemis would be able to pick up on it. "Oh, Uncle Artie, I just don't know what to believe."

Artemis looked at her sharply. "Did you just call me 'Uncle Artie'?"

"Yes. Why?" she asked cautiously. What had she done? Would it help her, or hurt her? And where was David when she needed him?

Artemis considered the implications of her use of that name. Richard always used it to annoy him, but no one else had called him Artie. The few times he'd visited Nicole before the plane crash, without anyone's knowledge of course, she had called him that name. She'd gotten it from her father back then, but how did she know about it now? "That's the name you used to call me." He watched her suspiciously, his eyes beginning to change color. He took another step towards her. "What else have you remembered?"

"I don't understand." Nicole took a step back. She tried her best to avoid eye contact, without seeming obvious. "I haven't remembered anything. What would I remember?" She took another cautious step backward.

"Don't play games with me. Why did you call me Artie?"

He continued stepping towards her, and Nicole continued to back up. "I don't know. It just came out. I didn't mean to upset you, you're the only family I have." She tried to sound as honest as she could.

He paused, seeming unsure what to think. His eyes stopped changing color, and Nicole let herself breathe again. She needed to make the most of his uncertainty.

Artemis placed a hand on a statue which sat on the end table beside him. He traced the lines on its smooth surface, while he considered what to do. "All right then, if you don't want to leave the house, allow me to get rid of Mr. Coverton. He has no business being in this house."

Nicole shook her head. "I don't want to make any hasty decisions. This house has been his for many years."

"It doesn't belong to him!" His voice filled with anger again and Nicole flinched. Artemis noticed her discomfort and took a calming breath, walking the remaining distance and putting a hand against her face. His voice was gentle when he spoke again. "I don't want him to hurt you. He's evil. You're too young to understand true evil."

She forced herself to stay still. "Maybe you're right. I don't understand how anyone could kill their own family, or anyone else for that matter. It's beyond my comprehension."

Artemis stared at her for a few moments, and a grin almost appeared. If she believed Coverton killed his family, she'd be easy to turn to his advantage. He angled his head, and light glinted off something behind her. He narrowed his eyes, trying to distinguish what it was. Streaks of red flashed across his eyes and his hand tightened painfully on a chunk of Nicole's hair, drawing an involuntary whimper of pain from her. "How did you get that?" he hissed.

"Get what?"

"That." Still holding her hair, he wrenched her around and pointed to the snake-shaped dagger lying on the nightstand.

She swallowed nervously. This was getting quickly out of

hand. "I found it and I thought it looked neat, so I thought I'd keep it."

"Where did you find it?" he demanded.

"In the mountains. David took me to the place where I was found. Why does it upset you so much?" she asked, trying to sound innocent. "Do you know who it belongs to?"

Before she could gauge if he was buying it, Artemis twisted her around and focused on her eyes. The colors in his eyes began to swirl in their hypnotic rhythm, and pressure built in Nicole's head.

In her mind's eye, she could see a hallway filled with locked doors. The door handles on each one were shaking, but none would open. The pressure in her head increased, tears brimming in her eyes.

The doors flew open simultaneously and a flood of images hit her. It seemed as if her entire life was flashing before her eyes. Every thought. Every memory. *This must be what it's like to die,* she mused. She was pushed up against the wall. The pressure in her head went away, and her mind started to clear but something else was wrong. She fought for breath and realized something was preventing it. Blinking her eyes open, she discovered Artemis standing in front of her with his hands wrapped around her neck. She tried to shout, to scream, but no sound came out. The room began to blur.

She tried to fight him, but she was too weak. Too much had happened today, she'd inhaled too much smoke, she'd dealt with too much stress.

A loud crash of someone hitting the door drew Artemis' attention, and he loosened his grip. Nicole gathered all her remaining energy and raised her knee, slamming it into Artemis' groin.

Artemis howled in pain, further loosening his grip on

her neck. Nicole slipped out of his grip and stumbled away, dizziness bringing her to her knees.

Artemis grabbed her arm. Nicole pulled free, dragging herself up onto her feet, but he grabbed at her again. She batted away at his arms and continued to back away. A cool breeze and the touch of cold metal against her skin briefly caught her attention. She wondered momentarily how they'd gotten out onto the balcony, but Artemis soon commanded her full attention again, pushing the question from her mind.

He finally managed to rope his hands around her neck again. Nicole knew she didn't have a chance of prying his fingers loose, so she reached for his neck instead, tightening her fingers around his throat.

Artemis slammed her body against the railing several times in a row, trying to force her to let go. She started losing consciousness again. Artemis slammed her into the railing once more, only this time, the railing didn't stop her.

Nicole started falling, and the pressure left her neck. The falling sensation abruptly stopped, but she experienced a painful yank on her arm, which was stretched above her head.

Nicole looked above her to discover Artemis was gripping onto her arm. Beyond him far below was the ground. She looked in the opposite direction, with great effort, to her feet. The broken railing was visible and her pants leg was caught up on the metal, but the material was already starting to rip. It wouldn't hold her for long.

Nicole hear the sound of ripping fabric and she dropped down by another inch.

Artemis' hand around her wrist started to slip. He frantically fought to hold on, his fingers closing around her jacket sleeve, but his struggling only made her pants leg rip more. She risked another look upwards.

She was hanging on, almost literally by a thread. Her jacket slipped from her shoulder, creeping down her arm until it was all Artemis was holding onto.

She heard the material of her pants rip again, and knew they'd torn free from the railing. Almost simultaneously, Artemis screamed as her jacket slipped off, sending him falling toward the ground.

Nicole braced herself, but she didn't follow him in the downward spiral to the ground. She looked up to discover David holding her leg. He braced against what was left of the railing and reached for her other leg. Very carefully, he pulled her back up onto the balcony and wrapped his arms around her.

Nicole held him tightly and let herself relax into his comforting embrace.

25

"Thanks for bringing me home." Meg unbuckled her seat belt and opened the car door. Cold air outside hit her, making her even more reluctant to leave the warm car and friendly company.

Mark leaned back in his seat. "No problem. Are you sure you're all right?"

Meg glanced over at him and smiled. It was the first time she'd really looked at him since they first got in the car. For some reason, she felt uncharacteristically shy around him. It was probably only because of everything which had happened "I'm fine. Hey, I've been through worse." She shrugged and gave a shaky laugh.

"Really?" Mark asked, turning to her. He studied her face and opened his senses to her, but she was too closed off. He couldn't read anything. How could she have been through much worse than tonight? She was threatened into tricking her best friend and then knocked out with chloroform. Most people never experienced so much drama in their entire lives, and she couldn't be more than twenty years old.

The smile left her face and she shifted uncomfortably. If she wasn't already on edge, she'd be able to keep up the mask she'd perfected over the years, but she couldn't. Too many of her real emotions were slipping through, too close to the surface. Why did he have to use a knife? "Yeah, you know how it is."

Mark lifted his chin. "And how is it?"

Meg shrugged. "It's rough. It's life. It makes you want to be someone else for a few minutes, just to escape from yourself. Anyway, I really must be going. Thanks again." She tried to stand, but her purse dragged her back down. She glanced down and discovered the strap was caught on the gearshift. A small sigh of relief escaped her when she heard a cell phone start to ring. With Mark on the phone, he wouldn't be able to question her anymore.

She stood up, ready to make a hasty retreat but Mark's conversation made her pause. It sounded as though he was talking to David, but why would David be calling him now? It wasn't that long since they'd seen each other. She pretended to tie her shoelace and listened closely to the conversation.

"Tonight? Just now? Wow, how's that for timing? Is she okay? All right, I'll be right over." Mark snapped the phone shut, and put it back in his pocket.

"What happened? Is Nicole okay?" Meg leaned back into the car and looked over at Mark.

Mark studied her closely. Should he tell her anything? He couldn't get into her head, but her concern seemed genuine, and Nicole obviously trusted her. "Nicole was attacked, but she's okay. I don't know any more details yet."

Meghan leaped back into the car and closed the door. She took one look at the expression on Mark's face and shook her head. "Don't even think about telling me to get out. I have to make sure Nicole's okay.

Mark admired her loyalty. With everything that happened to her, she'd still pushed it all away the second Nicole was in trouble. "Okay, but buckle up, or I'll have to give you a ticket."

She smiled at the unexpected joke and put her seat belt back on. "Okay."

Mark put the gearshift back into drive and turned the car around.

* * *

"How are you feeling?" David lowered Nicole onto the couch and settled down beside her.

"I—" Pain shot through her throat with the attempt to speak. She could still feel Artemis' hands around her neck, strangling the life out of her. She trembled. If David hadn't shown up when he did...

"Let me get you some water."

She put out a hand to stop him. "*Wait.*"

He smiled and raised one hand to her face. "I see you're getting the telepathy thing down."

She smiled faintly. "*Artemis?*"

"I tied him up in the study, and I called Mark. He should be here soon. Then we can decide what to do from there."

"*Thank you.*"

"I'm just glad I got there in time." He shook his head. "I don't know what I would have done if I hadn't."

She ran a hand along the side of his face. "*It's over now.*"

The doorbell rang and Nicole jumped. She glanced over at David with a shaky smile. "*I guess my nerves are a little shot.*"

"That's okay. You're entitled." David stood and kissed Nicole's hand. "It's probably Mark. I'll get the door and bring you some water for that throat of yours."

Nicole watched him leave the room and leaned back against the couch, all the energy leaving her body. She closed her eyes and listened to the sound of her own breath. She didn't ever want to move again.

Well, maybe she could be compelled to move for a couple of things. A grin came to her lips, but even the thought of making love with David wasn't enough to make her move currently.

She didn't even realize she'd dropped off to sleep until the sound of Meghan's voice made her jerk awake. "Nicole, are you okay?"

Nicole stared up at her friend in confusion. She didn't remember calling Meg. "What are you doing here?" she asked in a raspy voice.

"I was with Mark when David called. What happened?" Meg settled in a nearby chair and placed a protective hand on Nicole's shoulder.

"It's a long story," Nicole croaked. She coughed a couple of times, holding her hand against her throat. Every word she spoke made her throat seem as if it was rubbing against sandpaper.

David reentered the room and handed her a glass of water, helping her to sit up a little and lift the glass to her mouth. "Mark is checking on Artemis."

"Who is Artemis?" Meghan asked, sounding completely confused.

"My uncle." Nicole cringed. The water had helped her throat a little, but it still hurt to speak.

"The ropes seem to be holding him for now," Mark announced, walking into the room. "But I added a pair of 'special' reinforced handcuffs to be sure." He looked meaningfully at David.

The doorbell rang again, and Nicole looked up at David questioningly. He shrugged. "I didn't call anyone else. I'll go see who it is." David leaned over and kissed Nicole briefly on the cheek. "I'll be right back."

A few minutes later, David came into the room, followed by an elegant woman. She had long black hair with a streak of white, and she wore a long, flowing, dark purple dress.

Nicole recognized her at once as the woman who owned Cleo's. Nicole realized she wasn't in fact, all that surprised to see her tonight, considering the way she'd always felt around the woman.

"What's going on here?" Meg asked, sounding exasperated.

Nicole offered Meg a comforting smile. She suspected Meg must have recognized the woman, too. "Why don't you come with me to the kitchen, and I'll fill you in." She stood up wearily and motioned in the direction of the kitchen, following behind Meg. She paused when she reached David and gave him a quick kiss. "I'll be back in a little bit."

"Are you sure you're up to this?"

"No," she smiled. "But I thought I could make some tea or something to help my throat."

"I love you."

"I love you, too."

Nicole continued towards the kitchen, but when she past Mark she felt him brush his hand lightly against her shoulder. She glanced up into his eyes and noticed some of the pain in her throat subsided. Her shoulder felt warmer where Mark's hand had touched it. She wasn't sure what had happened, but she smiled, accepting the small favor quietly before she continued towards the kitchen.

Meg backed up from the kitchen doorway. She wasn't certain what had just happened between Mark and Nicole. Maybe he was just trying to comfort her after the horrible night she'd experienced. That had to be it. After all, Nicole was obviously crazy about David. So why was Meg feeling so jealous? It wasn't as if she had a thing for Mark, that would be crazy. They'd only just met. She almost jumped when she felt Nicole's hand on her back. Pushing back her confusing emotions, she followed Nicole into the kitchen.

"Do you want some tea?" Nicole noticed her voice sounded a lot better, and it didn't hurt to talk anymore.

"I guess. What's going on here?" Meghan let her curiosity come to the forefront again, taking the place of her other, troubling emotions.

Nicole put two cups of water in the microwave and got out the tea bags. "It's a long story." She considered how much she should tell Meg and decided to tell her everything. If anyone would understand, it would be Meg, and she needed to tell someone. First things first, though. "How are you doing?"

"Me? I'm fine."

"Are you sure? You were fairly shaken up earlier. I haven't seen you even close to being that upset since we were kids." Meg usually never let anything get to her. She always put forth a cheerful face, even when she was upset. To cry like that in public, Meg must have been really freaked out.

"I'm fine," Meg insisted, the tone of her voice discouraging further discussion. "I'm more worried about you right now. What happened here tonight?"

Nicole sighed. This was more like the Meg she knew. Maybe she hadn't been affected as much as Nicole thought. No, it had definitely gotten to her – she was just ignoring it for now. Maybe she could get Meg to talk about it later.

She might as well tell Meg what she wanted to know right now. "The man who tried to hurt me tonight had something to do with my biological parents. I've found out a lot of stuff lately about my birth family, where I come from, and the nightmares. I even found proof that I wasn't crazy for believing in all that paranormal stuff." She took the cups out of the microwave and put the tea bags in them. "You know all those legends about psychics, vampires, and the Lock Ness monster that I used to tell you about?"

"Yeah." Meg was almost afraid to let Nicole go on. Where could she be going with this?

Nicole took a deep breath. "Well, it turns out that some people in my family can shape shift. Specifically, some have been able to change into wolves."

"What? Where did you hear all this?" Things were getting stranger by the minute. Meg was almost certain she would wake up soon and realize this had all been a dream.

"From that man in the other room, the one who attacked me. You see, he's my uncle."

"If he tried to kill you, I don't know if he's the most reliable source."

"True, but I've seen some things. Meg, haven't you noticed that I'm not wearing my glasses?"

"Yeah, now that you mention it." Meg must have been more distracted than she realized to miss picking up on that earlier.

"The truth is, I can see without them now. When the meeting hall exploded, I was badly hurt, but I healed amazingly quickly. And you remember how that black wolf saved my life? You saw the wolf. I'm not going crazy here. It's really happening." Nicole rested her hands on the table, thinking a second too late that she should watch out for her wrists, but the expected pain didn't come. They weren't hurting anymore. She pulled up the edges of the bandage on one wrist and noticed the many scratches which had been there were gone. Other than some dried blood, her wrists were completely back to normal. "Look, this is just what I was talking about." She pulled off the bandages and held her arms out for Meg to inspect. "They were all scratched up and bleeding from the ropes Steagel used to tie me up. You can see all the blood which has been left on the bandages, but there isn't any injuries left on my arms." Nicole pulled back her hands and sat back in a chair, tossing the bloody bandages into the nearby trash can and rubbing off a little of the dried blood with her fingers.

Meg thought over Nicole's words, trying to get everything straight in her head. She didn't know what to say about how quickly Nicole's wrists had healed. Instead, she grasped at the other things Nicole said before she took off the bandages. She'd talked about the black wolf saving her, but who was he, if he was some kind of shape shifter like Nicole said? Why had he been hanging around her? "So, was that wolf supposed to be a member of your family, or something?"

Nicole grinned. "Not exactly. He's more like a friend of the family."

"Wait, so there's other people who can do this?"

"Yeah. Meg, this is something big. It's not only my family."

If Meg believed this, it could change the way she thought about everything. It could change her whole perception of reality. She might have been around people like that for years, without even knowing it. She could have passed them on the street or seen them in the stores. "What about you? Can you do it?"

Nicole stirred in a spoonful of sugar and handed one cup to Meg. "Apparently. That's how I escaped the fire." She watched Meg's face closely. She couldn't tell if Meg believed her or not. "*Please, please let her believe me,*" she prayed silently.

Meg took a sip of her tea and let everything Nicole had said sink in. It sounded crazy, but Nicole had made some good points. After all, she never went anywhere without her glasses, and she didn't have contacts. She'd been through a lot lately, and it hardly showed. There was the miraculous healing of her wrists. Even her throat seemed better, and she'd hardly been able to talk a few minutes ago. All these things added credence to Nicole's story. Something was going on here and Meg couldn't dismiss what she was hearing outright without thinking it over a little more. "If he's your uncle, why did he try to kill you?" It was the one point she could think of that didn't directly involve all this werewolf, shape shifting stuff.

It was a good question. Artemis could have just disappeared, denied the truth. Nicole still didn't know exactly what the truth was. "I'm not sure on the details, but I think it has something to do with some kind of jealousy he held for my father."

Meg nearly snorted. "Figures. Families are such a waste of time, they never get along. There's always some jealousy or another, or something hidden under the surface, or else they just don't care about one another. If you're lucky, everyone pretends to like everyone else a couple of times a year for the holidays."

"Meg," Nicole pleaded. Why did she always have to be so

down on families? Then again, considering her history, maybe she was entitled.

Meg ignored the plea and continued. "Just look at you. In your adoptive family, Billy had so many problems with your parents, he left as soon as he could and didn't even come back for the funeral. Your adoptive parents always made you feel as if you couldn't believe in anything which wasn't based in science. You always doubted yourself because of them. Then, in your real family, your uncle tried to kill you because of some jealousy he had over you father. It's ridiculous." And Meg wasn't even bringing up her own family troubles. That would be enough evidence to close the case for good.

"Does that mean everyone should just give up on families?" It had been so long since either one of them brought up this topic, Nicole had forgotten how cynical Meg could be on the issue.

"Why not? At least then you don't feel some senseless guilty obligation to people you can't stand. Why should you have to think good things about someone, just because you're related to them? That doesn't make them a good person. That's all families are good for, guilt. Everyone would be better off without them."

Nicole ran a hand through her hair in exasperation. "Look, I don't feel like getting into this tonight. Maybe later, but not tonight. I've had a rough day, in case you hadn't noticed. Hell, I've had a rough month. All I want to do is take a long hot shower, get something to eat, and go to sleep, not necessarily in that order."

Meg snapped back to the present. "I'm so sorry. I didn't mean to get carried away like that." Even if she only believed half of what happened to Nicole, her friend had still been through more than enough to constitute a long break from everything. "Here, let me take care of these." Meg took their cups and started washing them.

"Thanks," Nicole said, sounding relieved.

"No problem." Meg set the glasses and spoons in the dish drainer and took Nicole's hands, trying not to think about how they'd healed so quickly. "Come one. Let's go back into the living room with the others."

"Okay. Um... Meg?"

"Yeah?"

Nicole looked anxious. "Do you believe any of what I've told you?"

"I don't know. I think I do, but I'm not quite sure yet." It was the most honest response she could give right now.

"I guess that's fair enough." At least Meg hadn't said she disbelieved her.

"Could you answer me one more question?"

"Sure."

"Do David and Mark know about this?"

"I'll put it to you this way." Nicole leaned in close, a grin lifting the corner of her lips. "David's the black wolf who saved my life." She laughed at Meghan's stunned expression before she headed back into the other room.

26

Mara studied the figure tied to the chair. She walked around to the front of the chair and stared silently at his face.

Artemis lifted his head and looked at her in surprise, but he didn't say a word. He looked a lot different to the last time she'd seen him. He seemed older somehow, even though she couldn't quite pinpoint why. There were none of the normal signs of aging. He didn't have wrinkles, or gray hair. To the regular eye, he appeared to be a normal twenty or thirty-year-old. But for some reason, he seemed old. She concentrated on seeing his aura, noticing many dark spots. His aura was corrupted, in horrible shape, and she could sense the dark presence that permeated the air around him more than ever It wasn't as strong as what she'd been sensing, but it had some connection to it. It seemed to be a weaker version of the same thing. Somehow, he was connected to the dark presence. She'd thought that was the case, but now she was certain of it. It was probably what was corrupting Artemis' aura so badly. It would kill him in time. He obviously had no idea what he'd gotten himself into this time. "He will kill you, you know? One way or another, whoever this person you have allied yourself with is, he will be the end of you."

The hairs on the back of Artemis' neck stood on end. Advice from Mara should never be taken lightly. He'd known her for some time, and he'd never known her to be wrong. Still, she could be bluffing this time.

"Oh, I don't bluff." She smiled and walked back through to the other room without another word.

"It was the strangest thing. I had to kick and run at that door a dozen times before it finally gave in." David glanced over Mark's shoulder and watched Mara as she reentered the room.

Mara nodded. "It makes sense. What I've been sensing, the powerful presence I've felt – he would be able to prevent you from breaking down the door." She pushed out with her senses and found the dark presence, even stronger than before. It was nearby. She pulled back just before it's darkness could hit her again.

"You talk as if this power is something completely different from Artemis. Does that have anything to do with what you said, about his powers somehow being false?"

"Yes," Mara said, thinking carefully. "This is an extremely perplexing situation. I'm afraid I can't give you the answers you seek at this time." She cocked her head to the side. "They're here."

Her words were followed by the ringing of the doorbell. "I'll get it," Mark said, getting to his feet. He exchanged a pointed glance with David and walked to the door. Neither one of them had heard anyone coming to the door, yet Mara had known they were there.

He passed Nicole and Meghan in the doorway, his gaze resting briefly on Meg before he continued. Meg caught herself watching him and quickly turned back to the others. David and the woman from the store were still in the living room, but the woman seemed slightly distracted. Studying her, Meg suspected she was almost enough to convince Meg that everything Nicole had said was true. The woman's eyes shifted to Meg, catching her before she could pretend she hadn't been staring. Meg quickly turned her attention to Nicole and David.

Nicole looked up at David with a question in her eyes. "Who's here?"

Mara answered the question. "They're couriers, go-betweens for the Council. They are going to take Artemis to face judgment."

Mark led two solemn-faced men wearing long dark cloaks into the room. Without saying a word, they continued through the room, heading for the study where Artemis was tied up. Meghan watched the two men disappear into the other room. "Wow, I bet those two are loads of fun at a party."

Nicole laughed. She'd been thinking something similar but leave it to Meg to vocalize the thought. She noticed Mark bark out a short laugh before he could stop himself. He cleared his throat and regained his composure, pretending he hadn't reacted to what Meg said.

Tension settled over the room and Nicole turned. Artemis was there, standing between the two men on the other side of the room. They weren't touching him, but they had a presence about them. The air around the three men seemed charged with energy. As they passed silently through the room, Nicole shivered. "Wait!" She stared at Artemis. This could be the last time she ever saw her uncle. He was her last tie to family, her last connection to what happened that night, and she still wasn't sure what happened to them. Where had he put the bodies? Maybe she could find their graves. If she let him leave now, without asking, she might never know. *"What did you do with the bodies?"* she asked him silently.

Artemis stared at her quizzically, then a smirk replaced the confusion. *"What bodies?"* he replied. He started walking again, obviously pleased with the reaction he'd caused.

Her widened eyes met his when he passed. "What?" she asked, but he didn't say another word. The three men kept walking until they were out of sight. Nicole listened to the soft click of the front door closing and stood there for a minute longer before releasing a deep breath and focusing back on the others in the room. "I don't know about the rest of you guys, but I'm starved." She smiled. "Who wants pizza?"

* * *

"YOU KNOW, you're making a mistake taking me to the Council like this. I haven't done anything wrong." Artemis glanced back and forth between the two men, but neither of them said a word or acknowledged he'd said anything. He tried again to move, but the psychic hold they had on him was too powerful. The only thing he could move was his legs, and even then, he could only move them enough to walk.

They walked through the shadows, heading deeper into the woods. Soon, the moon had become their only source of light. Artemis suffered a stinging sensation when a branch scraped against his hand. He studied his hand, his excellent night vision revealing more to him than most would be able to see. The skin was broken in a rough line, slightly deeper at one end than the other. A drop of blood trickled down over his fingers, falling soundlessly to the ground. He angled his wrist to get a better look.

Shock almost made him stumble, but he managed to avoid making any sudden movements. He'd moved his hand! He'd moved his head to study his hand! He tested his other muscles cautiously, careful to avoid any large movements that might be noticed by the two Council couriers. Painstakingly, he reassured himself that control of his movements was back. Somehow, he was no longer imprisoned by the psychic hold. He rolled his eyes from the left to the right, surreptitiously glancing at the two men, but they hadn't seemed to notice anything.

The bushes to the right of the path started to rustle, and a biting chill ran across the back of Artemis' neck.

The two Council couriers stopped, motioning for Artemis to do the same. They listened carefully for a minute, eyes searching in every direction, but the night remained eerily silent. No animals moved through the undergrowth. Even the wind was still.

Another rustling sound erupted in the bushes to their left. The two men twisted in that direction, training every sense on whatever was out there, but once again, silence dropped over the woods.

A moment later, a rush of cold air flashed past Artemis on his right-hand side. It was followed by a heavy thud and a grunt of pain. Forgetting his need to hide his movement, Artemis turned his head and his eyes widened. The man who'd been on his right was on the ground, trying, with great effort, to stand. There was no one else around and no sign of what had caused him to fall.

The man managed to get up onto his hands and knees before he tumbled back onto the ground, landing on his back. His head rolled to the side, revealing his lifeless face to them both. Artemis stared in horror at the man's throat. It had literally been ripped open. He was covered in his own blood, and his eyes stared at them blankly.

Artemis twisted his head around to look at the second man. He was staring at his companion in shock, unadulterated terror visible in his eyes.

Without a word, the man abruptly turned and ran into the woods. Artemis heard his frantic footsteps, the sounds he made as he pushed past the trees and bushes. Another rustling sound to Artemis' right began to travel in the direction the man had taken. In the distance, he heard an abrupt scream followed by silence.

Artemis remained standing there for a moment or two, unable to believe what had just happened. Shaking his head, he pulled his wits about him and turned to run in the opposite direction. Before he'd gone too far, he was brought up short by a large form blocking his path.

Backing up, he saw a dark figure, dressed all in black, wearing a hat pulled low, which covered all but an unnaturally red mouth. The mouth was curved into a menacing smile, revealing a couple of sharp, vicious-looking teeth. "And just where do you think you're going?" an ominous voice asked.

"I was— I was going to come and find you." The wind blew the scent of blood to Artemis' nose and he could have sworn the smell was coming from the covered figure.

"He will be the end of you." Mara's voice whispered in his head. Artemis swallowed against a large lump in his throat.

"Good. Let's go, shall we?" The figure turned and walked off the path, becoming one with the shadows, a misty shape without form.

Artemis' skin erupted in goosebumps. If this was the creature responsible for what happened to the two Council couriers, he was far more dangerous than Artemis had ever realized. Those men had been well trained by the Council, and they died as if they were completely helpless. They'd never known what was coming. Artemis glanced back at the dead man on the ground, before he followed the shadowy figure into the darkness.

* * *

Nicole swallowed the last bite of pizza and wiped her hands on a napkin. David walked back into the room with Mark and smiled at her. She suddenly realized how incredibly comforting that simple smile could be. "Will Mara be okay going home by herself so late?" she asked. "She seemed so preoccupied before she left."

"Yeah, uh…" David settled beside her on the couch and eyed the single slice of pizza left in the open pizza box. He'd already eaten a lot of pizza, but his stomach was still growling a little. "You want this?" He motioned to the slice of pizza.

"No, that's okay. You can have it." She and David had gone through those pizzas fast. She must have eaten eight or nine slices already, but admittedly, it had been a while since either of them had eaten. She stifled a yawn and slumped back against the couch. Now that her stomach was full, sleepiness was beginning to settle over her.

"Thanks." He took a large bite of the pizza slice and sat back. "Mara will be fine. She can take care of herself."

Nicole nodded in response and turned her attention to Meg. She was passed out on the other couch, covered by Mark's jacket. Nicole grinned. Meg looked so adorable with only her face and hands poking out from underneath the jacket.

Nicole leaned in to David's side and sighed, and David put his arm around her shoulders, holding her close. "It's a good thing we ordered three pizzas."

"Yeah, especially since you and I practically ate two of them." They smiled at each other and enjoyed being able to sit together in silence.

Mark watched the two of them and suffered a twinge of loneliness. David and Nicole looked so happy together. And it was great that David was finally opening up to someone.

Meghan shifted on the couch and a small sound erupted from her lips, bringing a smile to his face. He was starting to understand why Nicole liked her so much. Meg was funny, strong spirited, and from what he'd seen, she had a fascinating personality.

All things considered, Meghan hadn't had an easy day either, yet she seemed to be in remarkably good shape. She'd only let it get to her that once when she'd first met up with Nicole outside the burning building.

Mark frowned. He had to wonder what Meg had been through in the past, something that she believed out shadowed this. It must have been bad. "I should get Meghan back to her apartment and let you get some rest... or whatever." He smiled knowingly at David.

David returned the smile and rubbed his cheek against Nicole's. She giggled softly and hugged him tighter. "Okay. Thanks for coming out tonight," David said, returning his attention to Mark.

"Hey, no problem." Mark leaned over and picked up Meghan, careful not to wake her. His blood warmed when she shifted in her sleep, settling her body closer to his. Her hand flattened up against his chest, and a tiny moan escaped her lips.

David got up reluctantly from the couch and headed

towards the front door. "I'll get the door for you and walk you out."

"Thanks." Mark glanced over at Nicole on his way to the door. "I'm glad you're all right, Nicole."

She smiled warmly and followed them. David saw them to Mark's car and then returned to the front door. Standing with Nicole, he watched as Mark drove off.

David put an arm around her and pulled her close, planting a possessive kiss on her lips. She returned the kiss, leaning into David, wrapping her arms around his neck.

David ended the kiss and lifted his head enough to look at her. He was smiling broadly. "So, are you ready to go get some rest... or whatever?"

She laughed. "Hey, I'm up for whatever."

NICOLE CROUCHED DOWN and picked up a broken piece of brick and mortar. Part of it crumbled in her hand when she turned it around, examining it. Just a few days earlier it had been part of the dilapidated SES meeting hall. She couldn't even remember how long ago it had been. Was it yesterday, the day before? So much had happened, her days had begun to run together.

"Hey, John," she called, without looking up to confirm the identity of the approaching steps. She continued to be amazed by how much her hearing had improved since the wolf began to grow within her.

John crouched beside her and shook his head. "How did you—. never mind. You look different. New hairstyle?"

Nicole thought about her now-redundant glasses and smiled. "Something like that."

John surveyed the site and sighed. "It's going to be a lot of work to rebuild. Are you sure you're up to it?"

"Are you saying you want to move on and forget about reestablishing the SES?"

"Nah. It's just that all of our stuff was in there. We'd have to start up from scratch again. I wasn't sure if you'd be up for that type of responsibility right now, or if you'd think it was too much trouble."

Nicole got to her feet and dusted off her hands. "Actually, I've recently come in to some resources which might be of help for that."

From what David had told her, she was rich. For once in her life, money wasn't going to be an issue. "I'm not certain what I want to do in the long term, and you're right. I do have a lot going on right now. But if you want to keep it running, I'll do what I can to help. That is, of course, unless you want to cut your losses while you can and move on to something else."

John straightened up and smiled. "I wouldn't dream of leaving. I'll be more than happy to run things."

Nicole smiled. "Thanks, because I really don't think I could do it alone. I need to get going now, but I'll be in touch."

After one final glance, Nicole got into David's car and drove to her new home – or her old home – depending on how you looked at things.

Opening the front door she called out, "David, I'm back!" both verbally and psychically.

David came down the stairs and brushed a quick kiss across her lips before he picked her up and carried her up the stairs and into his bedroom. After another, longer kiss, he gently lowered her onto the bed. "I've missed you."

Nicole brushed the hair out of David's face and kissed

his cheek. His skin was warm and soft beneath her lips. "I never get tired of you being beside me, touching you, kissing you." Her lips touched his as she spoke, kissing him deeply. She ran her hand across his chest, tracing a path down to his hip. She flicked her tongue along the side of his face and scraped her fingernails lightly over his skin.

A low growl erupted in David's throat and desire rippled through her body. "I love it when you growl." Her voice was rough with passion.

He offered her a knowing grin and growled again, this time pinning her down with his body. He ran his own nose along the sensitive skin of her neck, lightly biting , then burying his face in her hair.

Nicole giggled and arched against him. Her hands roamed across his body, rubbing against his bare back and pressing against his skin. She vaguely wondered when he'd taken off his shirt, but her thoughts quickly scattered. She moved one hand lower, down over his butt and she massaged his skin, kneading and stroking.

David's lips created a path from her neck to her chin and onwards up to her mouth. He kissed her deeply, thoroughly, as he pulled off her clothing.

He covered one breast with his hand, his fingers plucking at her sensitive nipple. David took it between two fingers and pinched lightly.

Nicole moaned against his mouth and pressed her nails into his back and butt,. as David's fingers tickled and teased her.

He ended the kiss and moved his attention to the other side of Nicole's neck, licking, swirling his tongue. His tongue flicked over her ear, licking all around the delicate shell. He captured her tiny earlobe between his teeth, tugging gently and then sucking the lobe into his mouth. His hand drifted down her body, brushing across her stomach, exciting her with every touch. His attention slipped lower, to the apex of her thighs. His fingers played lightly over her skin, teasing her, stroking, exploring. Using his knee, he nudged her legs apart and rubbed his erection against her.

Nicole's entire body shuddered with desire. She wanted to be filled by him completely.

As if reading her thoughts, and perhaps he was, David recaptured her mouth and simultaneously thrust deeply into her. His tongue forced its way between her lips, exploring every corner of her mouth, while his rock-hard shaft slid smoothly in and out of her body.

They moved together, Nicole meeting every thrust with equal fervor. The pressure built inside her until she suspected it would destroy her. She dug her nails into David's skin when her release spiraled through her limbs. For long, blissful moments, she felt as if she was falling, utterly weightless. The room was gone. Everything was gone. All that existed was herself and David. She clung to David, her only anchor in the torrent of sensations. Slowly, her muscles relaxed. Her heart rate slowed, her breathing became less frantic. She didn't think she could move, even if she wanted to. Her limbs were heavy, sluggish, completely drained of energy.

She became aware of David's weight on her. He let his head fall with an exhausted sigh to rest against her shoulder. His breath hit her neck when he exhaled, and it sent a small shiver down her spine, but she was too exhausted to do anything other than acknowledge it.

After some time, David rolled over, taking his weight off her, and he raised his hand to her face, turning her to face to him. They stared at each other, smiling warmly. Nicole rolled onto her side and draped an arm over David's chest, snuggling closer. David ran his fingers through her hair, and they both enjoyed the moment in each other's arms.

David inhaled deeply, noticing that Nicole's breathing matched the same time and pace as his. They were completely in sync. For the first time in his life, he was at peace. This was what had been missing all these years. They hadn't talked about the future, but he thought about it a lot. He couldn't imagine his life without her. Every time Nicole's life was threatened, he died a little inside. No one had ever affected him the way she had. No one else had been able to get past his defenses. No one had ever cared enough about him to try.

They had a connection which was beyond anything he'd ever experienced before, and he knew beyond a shadow of a doubt that he loved her and wanted to be with her for all time. Now, he just had to figure out how to ask her. It needed to be perfect, but how should he go about it? *"Nicole, you mean so much to me."* No. *"Nicole, you're the most beautiful woman I've ever met."* No, that wasn't it. *"I know I'm old, and stubborn, and can be really difficult to deal with, but do you think you'd like to— What do you think about a winter wedding?... Hey, if you're not doing anything next month, what do you think about getting hitched?"* Should he go for comedy and catch her off guard, or should he be serious and sentimental? *"From the night we met outside your apartment building, you've been in my thoughts constantly. I'm happier when I'm around you. I feel alive. You do that to me. You fill a void that's been in my life for as long as I can remember. I know I could never live without you with me. Life would just be unbearable. I want to spend the rest of my life with you by my side."* Maybe he should do it down on one knee. *"Nicole, will you marry me and make me the happiest man alive?"*

"Yes." Nicole spoke softly, a tear in her eye. Those were

the most beautiful words she'd ever heard. She raised herself on her arms and looked down into David's eyes. He had such a surprised expression on his face, she started to giggle.

"You heard..."

She nodded. "Everything. If you really mean it, then my answer is yes."

"If I really mean it? Of course I mean it. I—" He smiled broadly and hugged her close. "I love you so much."

"I love you, too," she said, brushing a kiss against his lips. When she lifted her head, David was staring at her as if he couldn't quite believe what he was seeing, and she noticed his beautiful blue-green eyes were glimmering with unshed tears. She gently kissed his eyes, tasting the salty liquid on her tongue and lips, and smiled lovingly at him.

He gazed up at her, seeing the love shining in her eyes. How had he gotten so lucky?

"We're both lucky."Nicole replied.

"You're getting a little too good at that."

Nicole giggled. "Hey, I can't help it. I'm not even trying. You sure you want to spend the rest of your life with someone who knows what you're thinking?"

She smiled, but he could see her unconsciously nibbling her lip, and he could sense her uncertainty. "Yes, I want to spend the rest of my life with you. I want to be with you forever. And I want to make love to you each and every night.

"Sound like fun for me." He grinned mischievously, raising an eyebrow. Suddenly he flipped her onto her back and lowered himself on top of her, seizing her right nipple in his mouth.

Nicole yelped in surprise and started giggling, but only seconds later her back arched as he sucked and nibbled her sensitive breast. After some minutes of this sweet torture, David raised himself up on his elbows and brought his face closer to hers. Teasingly, he rubbed the tip of his nose against hers and pressed against her. "Do you know what I'm thinking now?"

His warm breath on her face made her neck tingle. "Nope. I guess you're just going to have to show me," she said innocently.

He grinned and proceeded to show her every single thought, in great detail.

"Get in there." Rodney Steagel stumbled into the cell and stared back over his shoulder in disgust at the police officer who'd pushed him. He straightened his shirt indignantly and grunted his disapproval. How dare they treat him like this? He had rights.

The police officer dismissed him with an unimpressed look and let the door slam shut. The loud clanging sound reverberated through the cell. It was a hollow sound, the death toll on a wretched existence.

Rodney trembled at the power of his own imagery. He might as well be dead. What good had come out of his life? He'd stumbled through every moment, trying to carve out something for himself, and he'd been thwarted at every turn. His parents had abandoned him first, leaving him in a juvenile detention center when he was fourteen. They hadn't even tried to help him avoid his fate. They'd said it would do him some good, teach him a lesson. If it wasn't for his uncle, he wouldn't have had anything at all. His uncle had always stood up for him, until now.

After his parents died – of a heart attack and a bad case

of pneumonia respectively – his uncle had helped him with a job and a place to stay, but now he'd abandoned Rodney, just like his parents had. If there was any justice in the world, his uncle would get dragged down off his high horse by sickness, just the way his parents had. Who were they to criticize him for the way he lived his life? They weren't so perfect. In fact, they were hypocrites. That's what they were.

The same could go for that other guy, the dark one whose identity he still didn't know. *He'd* approached Rodney. *He'd* said he could help. Now, he'd abandoned Rodney, just like everyone else.

Who needed them, anyway? He sure didn't. He would get out of this and show them all. He would get back on top, and when he did, he would make everyone suffer for what they'd done to him. They would learn what a mistake it had been, to cross Rodney Steagel.

As bold as those words were, he couldn't do anything until he got out of this current situation, and he didn't have a clue how he was going to do that. He was in deep this time. He was locked away on numerous charges and there was a lot of evidence against him. It didn't look good. He could be spending years in this cell, or another one like it, if he couldn't figure out a plan.

Rodney surveyed the small, dark cell. The only piece of furniture was a simple bed on a metal frame, bolted to the ground.. There weren't any windows, so the only light came from a dim light bulb which looked as if it was about to blow. the globe flickered, as if it had heard his assessment.

The floor was the only thing which seemed to be in relatively good shape. It had been swept, maybe even mopped, recently. A cold breeze blew over his, making him shiver and his teeth chattered.

Well, this was just perfect. Not only was he in prison, in a dreary, dark, little cell, but he couldn't even get decent heating. He needed to find a way out of this. He couldn't stay in this place, he just couldn't. He needed his big screen television, lush carpet, king sized bed, and central air conditioning and heating. Another breeze blew across him, and he turned his head quickly, eyes moving before his brain could register what it had seen. Rodney could have sworn the shadows had moved, but the movement had been at his periphery, so he couldn't be certain. It had probably been a trick of the light. He inspected the cell to make sure, but didn't see anything.

Just as he was about to dismiss the phenomenon and go back to cursing the world, he saw it again. He squinted, trying to figure out what it was, but he still didn't know what had caused it. Absentmindedly, he lifted his hand to rub the back his neck. A strange stinging sensation caught his attention, and he felt something wet, something wet and slimy. He lifted his hand to his face, saw red liquid dripping off his fingers.

His hand was covered in blood.

Rodney's shirt seemed to be sticking to his chest all of a sudden and he lowered his gaze from his hand to his chest. Blood was running down his shirt and pants, collecting in a rapidly spreading puddle on the floor.

The last thing Rodney heard as his body fell and darkness consumed him, was the sound of evil laughter.

Nicole stretched, moaning softly when she did.

"Did you sleep well?" David walked across to the bed and sat beside her.

"Yes. I slept wonderfully." She threw her arms around

his neck and kissed him. "How about you? How did you sleep?"

"Pretty good."

"Good. Um... I wanted to talk to you about something. I was wondering about some things, about the transformation."

David smiled and nuzzled her neck to put her at ease. "Shoot."

"I was wondering about that light which was all around me. I couldn't see anything, and I didn't really know what I was doing. It was so quick."

"There's always a flash of light when you change. You were basically just stuck in the transformation stage. It takes a lot of concentration to hold the shape. Once you get the hang of it, you'll be able to hold it for longer, and then you'll be able to see things as an actual wolf would."

"If it takes so much concentration, how come you could stay as a wolf when you were sleeping with me at my apartment?"

He smiled. "Lots of practice. Once you've gotten good at it, it isn't as hard to maintain the shape. It becomes more natural, like breathing."

"Could you... teach me?"

His smile broadened. "Of course. Do you want to work on it now?"

She gave a hesitant nod, and he kissed her reassuringly. "There's nothing to be afraid of. I'm here with you. Now, do you remember what I told you before?"

"Yes."

"All right. Start with that."

Nicole took a deep breath and closed her eyes, trying to visualize herself as a wolf. Even through her closed eyelids, she could see the light gathering around her. Warmth filled her chest, and her senses all tingled.

Nicole blinked her eyes open, and she briefly saw a paw before the energy rushed out of her body, and the light disappeared, leaving her as she'd been. She collapsed back on the bed. "I can't do it."

"Yes, you can. You almost had it that time. Do you want me to help until you get used to it?"

She rose up on her elbows and shook her head. "No. I want to do this on my own."

She didn't close her eyes this time. Instead, she let the light fill her vision, let herself be consumed by the sensations, and immersed herself in the process. Instead of fighting against the weightless, the falling sensation which threatened to overwhelm her, she gave herself over to it. As the light faded, her senses heightened. Smells became stronger. Sounds were louder. She peered down and saw paws and legs, covered in white hair. She jumped up in excitement, clumsily running across the bed and jumping to the floor, testing her legs. Something pressed against her side and she turned to see the black wolf beside her. He rubbed against her and nuzzled her neck. Nicole returned the affection, loving the sensation of her fur against his. She rubbed her nose with his and he licked the side of her face.

David motioned toward the balcony and she heard his voice in her head.

"Want to go for a run before breakfast?"

"Sure." Nicole followed the black wolf out onto the balcony and down the steps. It took her a moment to get her balance as she tried to maneuver the stairs on four feet. The black wolf paused and waited for her, as she moved tentatively. Waves of reassurance flowed over her, giving her the confidence she needed to trust in her wolf's instincts. With

certain steps, she quickly made it the rest of the way down to the ground.

Nicole stretched out her legs, discovering how fast she could run. The black wolf was ahead of her, but she quickly closed the gap. They ran side by side for quite a while. Then, she pushed a little harder and pulled in front of him. She leaped over bushes, her paws barely touching the ground.

"Show off."

She laughed in her mind and slowed down a little, allowing David to catch up.

He pulled close to her and rubbed his head against her neck. They slowed again, tumbled together on the ground, rolling, rubbing their noses against each other, occasionally licking. Nicole released a playful whimper.

The wind blew over them, and Nicole noticed something on the wind she hadn't smelled before. The black wolf sat up and turned his head in the direction of the smell. *"What is it?"* she asked.

"I don't know. I'm going to go check it out. You stay here."

David's wolf form disappeared into the trees. Nicole stayed in the clearing for a few minutes, before curiosity got the better of her. Quietly, she made her way in the direction of the smell.

"I thought I told you to stay there," she heard David say aloud.

She let the light surround her, standing up in her human form. "You know I never listen to anything I'm told." She pushed a tree branch to one side and ran straight into David. He blocked her view, turning her around and leading her back the way they'd come. "What is it?" She struggled against him, but he had a firm grip on her arms.

"It's just some dead animal. Nothing you want to see."

David turned back to Nicole without mentioning the piece of torn material he'd noticed caught on a nearby limb.

Nicole gagged as the smell was blown in their direction again. "I'll take your word for it."

"Come on. Let's get back to the house. We've got a lot of plans to make if you want that winter wedding you were thinking about earlier."

She smiled. "I thought I was the one who did the mind reading in this relationship."

"Hey, what can I say?" David rubbed his knuckles against his chest. "I'm good."

"Um, hummm. You just wait 'til I get you back to the house." Nicole pulled away a little, turning to face David. Her eyes gleamed with mirth. "Race you back." In a flash, the white wolf replaced Nicole's human form and started running toward the house.

Another flash of light, and the black wolf followed.

EPILOGUE

David knelt silently before the tombstones. Sunlight hit the names, and he could feel tears in his eyes. "I miss you all. I wish you could be here today, could see how happy I am. For the first time in my life, I'm truly happy. I wish I could share that with you." A breeze blew, blowing his hair and clothes.

"I think they're here with you, my friend."

David glanced back at Mark in confusion, but when he did, he realized the wind wasn't affecting anything else. The trees, the bushes – even Mark's hair and clothes remained still. The wind was only whirling around him. He turned back to the tombstones, the sun still shining on the names, and offered up a silent prayer. If they were watching over him, he could only hope they were proud.

"Come on. You've got a wedding to go to."

David smiled. "That I do."

* * *

"Ow!" Nicole rubbed her head where the hair pin had poked her skin and peeked at Meghan out of the corner of her eye. "I thought the bride was supposed to be the nervous one."

"I'm sorry." Meg smoothed Nicole's hair back and carefully put the last pin in place. "I'm just so excited. I've never been to a wedding before."

Nicole smiled. "It's okay. Just don't eat any more of those cookies Mara brought, or I'll need to peel you off the ceiling, and I don't feel like doing that in these shoes."

"Okay." Meg reached for the choker and tied it in place. "You sure are calm."

"I'm a little nervous, but mainly I'm just happy."

"I can tell. At least, that's what I figured it was. You know, I don't think I've ever seen you really happy before." Meghan dodged Nicole's elbow and finished straightening her veil. "There. You look beautiful."

"Thanks for all your help."

"No problem."

Nicole turned toward the door when she heard a soft knock. "Come in."

Mara opened the door and closed it quietly behind her. "My, you do look magnificent."

"Thank you."

"Your brother is here. He wanted to know if he could come in."

Nicole smiled brightly. "Oh, sure, I'd love to see him."

"I'll get him." Meg dropped the last of the hairpins on the counter and left the room quickly, her shoes clicking against the tile floor.

"She seems enthusiastic," Mara observed.

"Billy used to hang out with us when we were kids, and

he and Meg always got along really well. It's been a few years since she's seen him."

"It's always good when old friends are able to see each other." Mara frowned slightly at the forlorn tone she could just make out in her voice. At least Nicole hadn't seemed to notice.

Nicole examined herself in the mirror and brushed back a few stray hairs, looking, as she did, at Mara's reflection. "Did you know my parents?"

"Yes, I did."

Nicole swallowed heavily and glanced away from the reflection of Mara's eyes. "Do you think they would have been proud of me?"

Mara smiled and placed a hand on Nicole's shoulder. "Yes, I do believe they would be. You are a very kind and brave soul. After all, you got through to David. That was no easy task."

"Really? I hadn't realized things were so bad for him."

"He had been closed off for a very long time."

"Like you— Oh! I'm sorry." Nicole's hand came up to cover her mouth, and she nibbled her lower lip uncertainly. "I shouldn't have said that."

"No, it's quite alright. As I've told you before, you have excellent instincts. I should go and let you finish getting ready. Oh, but first I wanted to give you this." Mara pulled a small blue butterfly hairpin from her purse. "I thought you might be needing something blue."

Nicole watched the pin sparkle in the sunlight. "Oh, it's beautiful. Thank you." Careful not to catch her heels on her skirt, Nicole stood and wrapped her arms around Mara in a warm hug.

"Would you like me to put it in your hair for you?"

"Yes, please."

Mara carefully placed the pin in Nicole's hair and stepped back. Nicole smiled gratefully and checked her reflection in the mirror, turning her head to see the butterfly pin better.

The door creaked softly, opening a crack. "Hello?"

"Billy!" Nicole ran across to hug her brother. "It's so good to see you again!"

Billy hugged her back, careful not to crumple her dress or hair. "I leave you for a month and you're getting married." He held Nicole's face between his hands and smiled down at her. "What am I going to do with you?"

"I was kind of hoping you would give me away."

"You want me to give you away?" His eyes widened with surprise.

"Will you?" Nicole asked hopefully.

"Well, uh… yeah." He pulled his shoulders back, standing a little taller. "Yes, I'd be honored to give you away."

Mara was struck by the presence Billy had about him. The way he behaved with Nicole was something to watch. She could easily see how much he cared about her, and for some inexplicable reason, she experienced a little jealousy of Nicole. Mara abruptly found herself imagining Billy was holding her that the way he did his adopted sister.

She shoved that thought away and brought herself back to the present. Suddenly she felt like an intruder. She didn't belong here. Silently, she headed toward the door.

Billy caught movement out of the corner of his eye and turned to see the woman he'd spoken to earlier. He was struck by how beautiful she was. She had long dark hair and sparkling, ethereal eyes, and the way she moved was incredibly graceful.

Nicole followed his eyes and spotted Mara trying to leave. "Oh, Mara, you don't have to go."

"I really should get out of your way." It took all her control to keep from staring at Billy.

"Oh, okay then. Thanks again for the beautiful hair pin."

Mara nodded and walked across to the door, unable to avoid brushing past Billy on her way. "Excuse me." Forcing herself to keep walking, she hastily left the room.

Billy heard Nicole talking to him, but he had to concentrate hard to understand what she was saying. Luckily, he caught enough of her words to pretend he'd heard her. "Yeah, you look great. How 'bout you tell me what I have to do, to give you away?"

DAVID STRAIGHTENED his tie for the fourth time and shuffled from foot to foot. Mark laid a comforting hand on his shoulder. "Nervous?" he whispered. David glanced over at him and nodded briefly, but a hush fell over the room before he could respond.

Meghan entered the church in her bridesmaid gown and walked up the aisle to take her place at the front, casting a glance toward Mark before she turned to face the back of the church.

The bride's music started to play and everyone stood and faced the church doors.

Nicole stood, illuminated in the doorway, gripping Billy's bent arm. David's heart beat rapidly, his breathing stopped for a moment.

Nicole looked absolutely radiant. Her gown had long sleeves and dipped down at the neck, revealing her cleavage. A magnificent lace train trailed behind her as she walked, making her appear even more elegant, and her long hair hung loose, with a v-shaped headpiece connected to the veil. A glittering blue hair pin rested just above the headpiece, adding a little touch of color.

But all the outside embellishments paled in comparison to the person wearing them. Nicole seemed more elegant, more exquisite than he'd ever seen her before. She seemed to glide up the aisle toward him, her smile lighting up the entire room. Taking her place at his side, David knew he had never been so happy, lucky or blessed in his entire life.

Taking her hands in his, he repeated the words the preacher said. "With this ring, I thee wed." He held her hand tenderly and slipped the ring on her slender finger. Nicole did the same, her hand shaking slightly.

David couldn't take his eyes off her. They stared into one another's eyes as they spoke their vows, and everyone else in the room disappeared. "I do," David said, kissing her fingers.

"Do you take this man to be you're lawfully wedded husband, to have and to hold, in sickness and in health, in good times as well as bad, as long as you both shall live, so help you God?"

"I do." Nicole repeated.

"I now pronounce you man and wife. You may kiss the bride." David gathered her up in his arms and kissed her deeply. Stepping back, he looked at his bride and smiled broadly. "*I love you.*"

"*I love you, too. You'll never be alone again.*"

"*Neither will you.*"

Dear reader,

We hope you enjoyed reading *Wolf Of The Past*. If you have a moment, please leave us a review - even if it's a short one. We want to hear from you.

The story continues in *Wolf Of The Present*.

Want to get notified when one of Creativia's books is free to download? Join our spam-free newsletter at http://www.creativia.org.

Best regards,

A.D. McLain and the Creativia Team

ABOUT THE AUTHOR

"What do you want to be?"

When I was little, I answered that question with actor, writer, artist, astronaut, singer, fashion designer, and a few other things. Adults would grin at my answer and say I hadn't made up my mind, yet. I told them, "No, I want to be all of them."

I never understood the idea of limiting yourself to one thing. Life is so big. There is room for many adventures.

As I grew, I continued to draw. I wrote and performed songs at talent shows. I drew out designs for clothing and even sewed some outfits. I made my own wedding dress by hand. I studied digital design and learned to do some basic work in photo programs. Friends will tell you, I'm always jumping from one crazy project to another.

Again and again I've been told what I was doing was too difficult, I didn't know enough, I could never do it. And every time I've plunged head first into whatever my passion was driving me towards with a near unwavering faith that I could do anything I put my mind to. People always want to tell you what you can't do. We are all capable of incredible things when we have faith and believe in ourselves. You may not succeed at everything you do, but you will never succeed at something you do not try.

Despite my vast array of different interests, writing has long held a special place in my soul. When I was twelve years old, I spent an entire summer writing a story. Now, I often started projects without finishing them, before. This was different. I wrote every day. I wrote in the car, my room, and the laundromat. I wrote until, just as vacation was coming to an end, my story was done. I finished it. I knew in that moment, this was my calling in life. This was what I was meant to do.

From that moment on, I studied and wrote. Teachers and siblings told me to pursue a more practical career. I ignored them and followed my instincts.

When I needed a break, I still had all my other creative projects to help me recharge and have time to think. But I always returned to writing.

Through college, meeting and marrying my soulmate, working through jobs I hated, becoming mother to three wonderful boys, and homeschooling those same rambunctious boys, there have been challenges. There were times I've had to take a break from regular writing to care for newborns and sick children. Though, even when I wasn't actively putting pen to paper, (yes, I still use good old fashioned notebooks and handwriting much of the time) my books are always somewhere in my mind. I've spent many nights crouched over paper, using the dim light from my phone or a night light to see enough to put down my thoughts, while my children sleep a few feet away. Writing is who I am.

My passion is in paranormal romances and fantasy books. I love writing about werewolves, and other shapeshifters. I've also written about psychics.

I began writing fantasy after I was married. My husband and I used to get together with friends to play dungeons and dragons every Saturday. My husband wanted to create his own world with his own campaigns, so he enlisted my help in writing the background stories. He told me what his world was like and some of the key players and asked me to write backgrounds on other characters I told him what I had, and he added content or made changes to fit his vision. It was a lot of fun to work on this with him.

Later, I was looking for a quick project to write for nanowrimo (national novel writing month) and decided to put some of our notes into a full story of it's own. That was the birth of our first collaborative fantasy book project. It is great to be able to share something that is such a big part of my soul with my husband. He has always supported my writing. Even when it hasn't paid off financially, he has never once asked me to stop.

I don't know what the future holds, but I know this is what I'm called to do.

Lightning Source UK Ltd.
Milton Keynes UK
UKHW021848301120
374378UK00006B/1170